The Sweet Spot

A novel by
Joan Livingston

Casa Rosa Books

ISBN-10: 0-9985854-0-8
ISBN-13: 978-0-9985854-0-6

Cover and book design by Michelle M. Gutierrez

For my mother, Algerina

Acknowledgments

I am blessed to have the encouragement of my family, Hank, Sarah, Ezra, Emily, Nate, Zack, Julia, John, and Chris. Then there are my longtime friends Fred Fullerton, Teresa Dovalpage, and Amy Peck Murphy.

And thanks to the folks living in the hilltowns of Western Massachusetts who made our family feel welcome for so many years. Certainly the hilltowns inspired this novel although I attest the town, characters, and story come strictly from my imagination. But I'd like to think I could plunk the fictional Conwell in the middle of Worthington, Cummington, and Chesterfield, and it'd fit just fine.

Memorial Day 1978

The rap on the bedroom door was light and quick. Edie St. Claire sat up in bed.

"Crap, it's after nine," she said.

Her daughter's voice came through the door in a thin, worried wail.

"Ma, you up yet? We gotta go."

"Yeah, yeah, Amber, I'm getting ready."

Edie reached over Lonny for the black bra on his side of the bed. He groaned in his sleep when she touched him, and then she was on her feet, running to use the bathroom, grabbing whatever clean clothes she could find. She was a pretty woman, the type who made men smile and want to be with her. Short, she favored her father's side, the Sweets, with her slight build and light blue eyes. She combed her fingers through her brassy brown hair, cut straight at the jaw.

Lonny opened one eye and watched her hasty dress. He mumbled something low and creaky in the back of his throat.

"I gotta go. I told you last night," she said.

Lonny propped himself on one elbow.

1

"When you comin' back?"

"I dunno."

Edie slipped out the door with her purse and a bottle of mouth-wash. Amber was on the other side, her blue eyes blinking fast, brows arched high. Edie shut the bedroom door behind her.

"Amber, I gotta teach you how to use the coffee machine."

"But I'm only seven and a half."

"Seven and a half? You're old enough."

They raced out the kitchen door to the car. Pop's pickup blocked their way. Edie studied her father's half of the house. Nothing stirred, except two gray cats jumping off a couch to the porch's floorboards.

"How we getting out, Ma?"

"Don't you worry about that, Amber. Just get in the car."

The wheels of Edie's white sedan spun into the high grass when she drove across the front yard, steering hard to the right to avoid the drainage ditch. Her mouth was full of wash, and she worked at the sharp liquid until she spat out the open window.

"See?" she said.

Her daughter's head moved in several small bounces.

"Yeah, Ma."

They were nearly at Aunt Leona's house, one of three on this dead-end dirt road. Amber spent the night there and walked back this morning. Leona's dog, a mix of golden retriever, collie, and some other breed, trotted slowly like the old mutt he was along the road's shoulder. The dog halted briefly and raised his head when he recognized the sound of her car.

"Uh-oh, old Bob's following you." Edie slowed the car when it tires chattered and slid sideways over the road's hard ridges. "We'll just have to bring him back later. I don't have time for it now."

"Are we gonna be late?"

"No, no, we're fine. Honey, fish in my purse for my sunglasses. Any aspirin? No? Shit. Oh, yeah? Open the bottle and give me two. Thanks."

Edie pushed the car forward to the main road, past the edges of dense forest toward the town's center, where she found a parking space behind her in-laws' Thunderbird.

Amber knelt to reach the car's back seat.

"See. I remembered," she said.

Amber clutched a framed photograph, the one taken of her father weeks before his helicopter was shot down in Vietnam. It happened one month before Amber was born, and the sun glinted off Gil's long, thin face in a way that broke Edie's heart all over again. His hand was on his hip. His khaki shirt was unbuttoned as he leaned against the chopper. He and his crew, who died together, called it the Angel of Darkness. Gil's dark eyes went through Edie as if he was cool and tough, but she knew better. Those were boys who died that day in Vietnam, and sweet boys if they were like her Gil.

"I'm glad you brought Daddy's picture. Come on. It hasn't started yet."

Edie and Amber slipped through the small crowd clustered on the town commons. People nodded or spoke her name. Edie knew every one of them because people had a way of sticking close to the hill-town of Conwell in Western Massachusetts.

"Marie, Fred," she greeted her in-laws, but her attention was on her mother-in-law. "How are you?" Edie asked although she didn't expect an answer.

Marie smiled instead at Amber. Edie's father-in-law, Fred, his bald head shining as if it had a pink shell, hugged a wreath of red and white carnations. A blue ribbon said, "OUR BELOVED SON GIL."

Marie's head chopped toward her husband.

"Where's Walker?" She worked the corners of her mouth. "It'd be just like him to forget his brother."

Fred raised his chin.

"He's over there. See him?"

Walker, wearing a black cowboy hat and boots, marched across the mowed grass. His face, thin, with a straight nose, was tanned from

3

working outdoors. One of the builders in town, he greeted people he knew, firm handshakes all around. He leaned in to speak with someone in the crowd.

Marie hummed.

"It's about time he showed up." She sniffed. "I don't see Sharon or the boys. Do you?"

Fred shook his head.

"No, I don't."

Marie pursed her lips.

"She never comes. Never. He could've at least brought the boys. Gil was their uncle after all."

Fred clutched his wife's arm.

"Marie, take it easy."

Edie closed her eyes behind her sunglasses. Her head throbbed.

"Honey, what do you have there?" Marie asked Amber.

Amber showed her the photograph.

"It's Daddy."

Marie held her hand to her chest.

"Oh," she said in a broken way.

Amber glanced large-eyed from her grandmother to her mother. Only a head shorter than Edie, she was going to be tall and skinny-boned like Gil. Her hair, somewhere between black and brown, just like his, fell over the left side of her face. Edie tucked it behind her daughter's ear.

"That's better." Edie swallowed. "You have Daddy's picture. Wasn't he so handsome?"

Amber held the photo face out, so everyone could see her father. Edie used a knuckle to smear the tears that spilled down her cheeks. Thirty, maybe thirty-five people were here today. When Gil died, the church was so full people had to stand outside in rain mixed with snow, and she let the baby she carried keep her upright throughout the ordeal. Now Edie rested her hand on her daughter's shoulder to calm herself again.

Walker pecked his mother's cheek.

"Mom?"

"Shh, Walker. It's going to start. Take off that damn hat, will you?" Marie hissed.

Walker swiped the hat from his head and smoothed his long, dark hair in place. His eyes shifted toward Edie.

"I came. Didn't I?"

Edie tried to smile.

"You did, Walker," she told him. "Thank you."

He nodded.

Schoolchildren and scouts in droopy uniforms clutched flags or lilac sprigs. A color guard of men who fought in World War II or Korea hauled flags from the back of a station wagon. One of Gil's great-uncles watched from the passenger seat of a car parked on the edge of the commons. The ceremony was so brief it wasn't worth getting his wheelchair from the trunk. He gave Edie a ghostly wave from the open door. She waved back.

The veterans in the crowd saluted as the color guard marched toward the town's memorial stone and flagpole. Lots of boys from Conwell fought in Vietnam, but only her Gil died. His full name, Gilbert James St. Claire, was painted in black on a white wooden cross beside the ones for the two boys killed in World War II. Edie knew their last names because their families still lived in town. But like the children here today who never met Gil, she didn't know either of them.

People stared sadly at Edie and Amber while one of the color guard read President Lincoln's "Gettysburg Address." Some years, a group of children recited a poem or sang a song, but not today. The pastor of the Conwell Congregational Church spoke, his voice a drone as he praised the three brave soldiers, who grew up in Conwell and died so far from home.

Edie saw past the row of scouts to a man standing near the edge of the road. His head tilted to the right. He was tall, but he held his

5

body in a twist as if a part of him were incomplete. Deep scars cut the flesh of his face below his aviator sunglasses. She hadn't seen him before. Maybe he was visiting someone in Conwell or driving through, and he stopped when he saw what was going on at the memorial. Maybe he fought in Vietnam. Maybe it's how he got hurt.

The pastor was silent. He gestured.

"Marie? Fred?"

It was their signal. Fred set the wreath in front of the large stone, and then he and Marie stood at Gil's cross. Fred put his arm around Marie when she began to weep. After several minutes, they were back.

Marie reached into her purse for a handkerchief. She studied Amber's upright face.

"Sweetie, did anyone ever say you look just like your Daddy?"

"You do, Grandma, all the time."

Marie smiled.

"That's right."

Two high school boys played taps, one hidden behind the church, so it sounded as if there was an echo although one boy's horn was better than the other's. Afterward, men in the color guard raised their rifles and fired blanks into the air. The ceremony was over, and the crowd broke apart. Edie searched for the stranger, but he was gone.

Her mother-in-law tapped her arm.

"Edie, you're coming to the house?"

That, too, was the same. Her in-laws held a Memorial Day barbecue, and they invited about a quarter of the town. People ate and drank their fill, and after the crowd thinned, those who stayed swapped stories about Gil. Marie stuck with it until she got teary. Fred shot stony stares at his wife, but eventually the memories touched him, too, and he went away quietly. Gil and Walker were Fred and Marie's only children. It was a hard scene to get through.

"Uh-huh, Marie, I'll be there, but I have to go home first to get the potato salad. Could you take Amber with you?" Edie turned toward her daughter. "Let me bring Daddy's picture home for you."

Amber handed her the photograph. Edie stared longingly at the image. Her daughter's fingerprints on the glass formed a thick halo around Gil's head.

The diamond rings on Marie's fingers glittered when she took the girl's hand. Raising a brow at Walker, she asked, "The boys are coming, aren't they? And Sharon?"

Walker replaced his cowboy hat.

"Yes, ma'am, they'll all be there."

That Old Sadness

When Edie returned home, her aunt's dog, Bob, lay in the sun on the right side of the porch. A family of cats living in one of Pop's rundown shacks watched from a distance. This was supposed to be their spot during the day.

The duplex, built long before the Sweets came to Conwell, was painted white on three sides, a project that took her and Pop a month of weekends last summer. The house never owned a coat of paint on the back as long as Edie remembered. Pop swore the town had to charge him fewer taxes because one side was unpainted, but it just meant anyone who might drive by would be fooled into thinking theirs was a well-kept house.

Edie insisted Pop keep all the junk he brought home from the dump in the back yard if it couldn't fit in the barn or one of his shacks. Pop worked as the town's dump attendant for about thirty-five years, and the barn was crammed with stuff he stored there: doors, farm tools, rolls of screening, furniture, anything someone was throwing away that Pop thought useful. Washers, stoves, and metal cabinets lined the barn's walls in foot-high grass near two junked cars.

Edie moved here from the apartment above her in-laws' store when Amber was still a baby. She spent a week, with Pop's help, cleaning the side of the house he rented to a series of drinking buddies, all impossible slobs, and another to get the junk from the front yard. "Take it all back to the dump," Edie pleaded with her father, but he found places out of sight for all of it. She was not as fussy as her two older sisters, too embarrassed to be the dump attendant's daughters they high-tailed it out of town as soon as they could marry.

Edie remembered when Marie came for an inspection. She went from room to room.

"See here. Amber has her own room. And we have a yard," she told her mother-in-law. "Those stairs to the apartment were awfully dangerous for a baby."

"I suppose," Marie said.

Now Leona's dog raised his head and flailed his tail against the porch's floor. Edie bent to pat him as she glanced at Pop's windows. Nothing moved behind the glass. He must have gotten home late from that dive bar he liked in Tyler.

Lonny was still in bed although awake. He looked like a kid the way his curly, brown hair was messed. He wasn't a kid although he was probably at least five years younger. Edie normally didn't go for younger men, but she was a bit drunk last night at the Do-Si-Do Bar in town when she and Lonny got extra friendly. One thing led to something else, and then he followed her home in his pickup truck.

Edie nodded as she placed Gil's photo upright on her bureau. She threw her purse onto a chair.

Lonny folded his hands behind his head.

"I made coffee. Left some in the maker. I'm afraid it tastes like shit. But I was hoping you was coming back." His eyes stopped at the hem of her skirt. "That's some getup for a memorial service. You must've given those old vets a thrill."

Edie tugged at her skirt. It was too short. She shrugged.

"Tell you what." She kicked off her shoes. "I'll take it off."

She pushed the skirt down her hips and pulled the top over her torso. She gave a shake. Lonny's mouth twisted into a grin as he threw the sheet aside.

She tossed a rubber from the top of her bureau.

"Here," she said.

She slipped next to Lonny. Her fingers slid across his logger's arms and chest.

"Lonny," she cooed. "Come on, baby. You know how."

He moaned.

Later, while Lonny used the shower, Edie rolled toward the bedroom window. He sang a country tune about being in love. She hoped she wasn't making this guy too happy because she wasn't interested.

Edie thought about Gil. They were in his pickup going for a ride along the back roads in town. They hadn't been together long, maybe six months. Both were still in high school, and Gil smiled as if he kept a big secret from her. He didn't say a word, but at that moment she knew Gil loved her more than anyone in the world, and she couldn't ask for anything else.

They were married a month after their graduation. Everyone figured she was pregnant although she wasn't. She and Gil couldn't wait to be husband and wife, and considering what happened, she was glad they didn't listen to his parents. Pop and Aunt Leona were pleased for her. Both declared Gil was the nicest of all the St. Claires.

She and Gil couldn't have been happier. Gil worked on getting his electrician's license although he talked about becoming an engineer because he was so smart with math. They lived in the apartment above the store, but her in-laws were going to help them buy a house.

Then there was the lottery draft in 1969. It was December. She and Gil watched it on TV. Edie cried when Gil got 124. He definitely would go to Vietnam although not right away. They tried to stay as happy as they could until it happened, and they knew they were going have a baby before he left.

The day she learned Gil was dead, she was lying on her couch, feeling out of sorts. She heard a woman scream in the store below, and she sat up immediately, her heart running hard when she heard heavy feet on the stairs. She saw her father-in-law's pale face through the door's window. Walker and a uniformed man were behind him.

She knew at that moment her life would never be as good again.

Lonny sang in the shower still. Edie glanced out the bedroom window. The sun played on the tops of the swaying bushes, and she felt that old sadness all over again.

A Way About Her

Edie tried to lure her aunt's dog into the car with a piece of bread, but she ended up asking Lonny to lift him onto the back seat. Lonny did it easily, and after she shut the car's door, he stood there, wrapping his arms around her waist. He kissed her twice.

"How about doin' this again?" he said low in her ear.

Her head cocked to one side.

"I'm usually at the Do on Friday and Saturday nights, sometimes Sunday," Edie said. "You can catch me there."

She could tell he expected more, but he was trying to be cool about it.

"Okay."

She checked over her shoulder at the bowl of potato salad in the car's front seat. The dog raised his nose.

"I gotta go," she said. "It was a lotta fun."

Lonny drove by when she was at Aunt Leona's. He tooted the horn and shouted her name as she dragged the dog from the car.

Edie opened the front door to her aunt's house and called. Leona sat on the couch, watching TV. She grunted when she realized her niece was inside.

"Edie, it's only you," her aunt said.

"Yup, it's only me."

"Hell, you know I don't mean it that way."

"I know."

Her aunt brushed dog hair from her housecoat. She lifted her head, her hair a ridiculous shade of red for a woman her age. She had powder on her face. Her eyebrows were plucked thin as wires.

"Got my roots covered, and my face made up. Not too bad for an old broad, eh? Maybe I should go down to the American Legion bar and try my luck. Maybe some of those old soldiers can still salute. What do you think?"

Her aunt joked, but Edie knew what she wanted to hear. She looked better than she felt. She still had a way about her.

Edie kissed her aunt's cheek.

"Very nice."

"I see you brought Bob home. What can I tell you? Bob's dumb as dirt." Leona took a quick peek at the television screen. "Who's the guy?"

"What guy?"

"The guy just hollering your name out the truck window. Sounded like a mating call to me."

Edie grinned.

"He's just a guy from the Do."

"I hope he showed you an extra special time if you know what I mean."

Her aunt cackled. She was always this direct, but Edie was used to her ways. She lived next to Leona, her father's only sister, most of her life, and after Ma died, she took over those womanly things Edie needed. Leona was good to Amber, too, never minding she came over when Edie wanted to go out. Truthfully, she enjoyed the girl's company since she never had children, or as Leona put it, "Something's wrong with my plumbing."

When Edie came to visit, she and her aunt played cards. Leona kept a tumbler of something dark and sweet beside her as she gabbed through games of cribbage and gin. Edie stuck to beer.

Her aunt was alone, and she was not the type to be a part of what went on in town, the granny groups, she called them. She liked going to the Do-Si-Do, especially when it had a band, and to bingo at the American Legion in Tyler. She spent the worst months of winter at a trailer park in Florida.

"I've got some news," Edie said. "My first game's Friday. It's in Tyler."

"Hell, it's about time."

Edie shrugged.

"It's not gonna be the same without Birdie coaching."

"Too bad about his ticker. Clean living can kill you."

"Aunt Leona."

Leona pawed the air.

"I didn't mean anything by it. He was a good man."

"Still is. His doctor says he just can't coach anymore."

"Then they might as well stick Birdie in the ground."

Edie played on the Conwell Women's Softball Team since high school, except for a couple of years when she was pregnant and right after Gil died. The team was in a slow-pitch league, and Birdie, who coached for over two decades, had the right attitude. He never got worked up about a lousy call, and everyone got a chance to play. His wife kept score, and their daughter, a good bat, played right. His son coached third and helped with the field.

Leona's eyes squeezed nearly closed.

"And now we have Vera," she said.

Edie sighed. Vera, who worked part-time at her in-laws' general store, was the older sister of Sharon St. Claire, Walker's wife.

"I hope it's still fun with her," Edie said.

"Guess we'll find out soon enough. I'm betting it won't. The woman's a real pill. You should know. You work with her."

The other week, Vera came up to Edie in the store and said, "Birdie had you down for third. You still with us?"

It was a fair question. Between September and May, a lot can happen to a group of women who live in the same town. Someone could get pregnant or divorced, or sign up with another team, usually over some slight, or in the case of one player last year, kicked out for making off with another player's husband. But Edie got the feeling Vera hoped she wasn't coming back.

"It'll be nice seeing the girls all together," Edie told her aunt.

"Yes, it will."

Leona's interest waned. She watched the TV again. She frowned when Edie said her name.

"Wanna come to my in-laws' with me?" Edie asked.

"I forgot." Leona swiveled to face her. "How was it today?"

Edie smiled sadly.

"The same, but I'm glad people remember Gil."

Her aunt's head rocked slightly.

"They should. Gil was a great guy. The best. I should know. I was married to three bums who weren't."

"He was the best all right," Edie said, her head tucked down.

Her aunt's face softened. Edie hadn't felt this low in a long time, and it was hard shaking it.

"Aw, honey, it can be real tough," Leona said, and she kept repeating, "Now, now, Edie, now, now."

Prove Himself

Edie headed to the beer cooler in her in-laws' back yard after she brought the potato salad into the kitchen, where Marie made it clear she was not needed. She plunged a hand through the cooler's watery ice for a beer. The headache was long gone, but the cold helped revive her.

She popped the top and looked around. Her in-laws had a nice house that's been in Fred's family forever. They could afford to take care of a large place like this since they owned the town's only store. Edie worked for them. Her in-laws were generous, and that helped along with the check she got from the government because of Gil dying in Vietnam.

Most of the town, it seemed, was gathered in Fred and Marie's yard for the barbecue. Besides family, old friends from town, loyal customers, and even newcomers came. Leona was invited, but she always begged off. Too much family, she said, and they weren't her family. Pop wasn't welcome. He blew it a few years ago after he got stinking drunk and insulted one of Marie's sisters. Edie had to drive him home.

Walker and his wife, Sharon, stood on the house's stone patio a few feet apart as if they were strangers. Their twin boys, Shane and Randy, charged past them into the crowd. Sharon was a large woman although she wasn't when Walker married her. She was one of those women who got fat being pregnant and didn't go back to the body she had before. Edie was surprised when she heard Walker and Sharon were going out, and then when they got married, but she didn't see much of him during those days. Amber took all of her time.

Walker left Sharon and crossed the lawn to a group of men standing near the barbecue grill. His wife stayed back, a sour expression on her face. Walker didn't say a thing when he left her behind, and it wasn't long before he was the center of the group's attention, the men laughing at something he said. Walker told the kind of jokes men liked, dirty and with a good punch line. Their heads tipped back as they barked.

Edie knew some in Conwell didn't like Walker because they thought he was too cocky, that he had too much, but he worked harder than most. He was at the job site before the first man showed and usually was the last to leave. He built his construction business from nothing. Fred and Marie didn't lift a finger or offer him money. Then again, he didn't ask for their help. Walker wanted to prove himself. Edie knew because he said it many times in bed.

Fred stood on the edge of the patio. He rang a cowbell to announce the food was ready. People began lining up.

Amber was on the far end of the yard. She hung to the edge, watching the other kids joke and tag each other. She raised a hand when Amber spotted her, and before Edie knew the beer was done, so she got another. She tossed the empty in a pail.

Amber came beside her mother.

"Hey, there, who're your friends?" Edie asked.

Amber chewed her lip.

"They're not my friends."

"I could tell. I see your cousins are here."

Amber made a face.

"Shane and Randy are brats," she said.

"Brats."

"They fight over the stupidest things."

Marie waved from the patio. She tried to get Amber's attention. Edie sighed.

"I believe you're wanted over there," she said.

Her daughter nodded.

"Where's Aunt Leona?"

"She wasn't up for it," Edie said. "Tell me. What did you two do last night?"

"We watched shows and played cards." Amber screwed up her nose. "She cheats."

Edie laughed.

"She does it to me, too. You must be getting better. Aunt Leona doesn't like to lose."

From the patio, Marie called Amber's name and waved again.

"I better see what Grandma wants. You coming?"

"In a while. Go ahead. Make her happy."

Later, Edie gnawed on a chicken bone while Gil's great-uncle napped beside her in his wheelchair. He had a smile on his sleeping face. Gil loved the man, and she was content watching him while she tried to build a buzz from the weak beer her in-laws bought.

Marie took the chair next to hers. Her face was flushed.

"Edie, I don't know why I do this every year," she spoke loudly. "It's getting to be too much."

Edie closed her eyes briefly. She smiled at her mother-in-law. Women who didn't drink for fun got so sloppy when they do to forget. She didn't blame Marie. This was tough day for her. So was Gil's birthday, Christmas, or any day that reminded her she was a mother to a good son who died young.

"You don't have to, Marie," Edie told her. "People would understand."

Edie knew her mother-in-law wanted to talk about Gil. It wasn't always this way between them. She remembered how much Fred and Marie disliked her when she and Gil went out in high school. Their Gil loved Benny Sweet's daughter, the girl who used to go with her father when he worked at the town dump. They were too polite to say it directly to her, but Edie knew by their stiff comments and the way they checked the clothes she wore. Both wanted another girl to marry their son, someone who went to church and whose father had a respectable job. But it was behind them now.

She only had to glance at Marie, and the woman began blubbering about Gil.

"I was so scared when he went." Marie's brown eyes, like Gil's, dug into her. "I knew something terrible was going to happen to my Gil. I just knew it."

She could finish her mother-in-law's sentences. Gil didn't deserve to die. He would have been a wonderful father to Amber. She was grateful Edie made him so happy.

Marie grasped Edie's hand.

"Edie, Edie, what am I going to do?"

"Marie, you're gonna be okay."

"No, I'm not. Sometimes when I see men Gil's age come into the store, I wish they were dead instead of him." Marie's hand wound around Edie's as if it grew there. She whispered, "I feel wicked saying it, but I can't help it."

Edie sniffled.

"Marie, it's not gonna change a thing. Gil's never coming back. Never." She slipped her hand from Marie's and stood. "And you're sure not making me feel any better."

Edie went through the door of her in-laws' garage and between their cars to the workbench, where the cases of beer were stacked. The cooler was getting low. Through the walls she heard the voices of people still at the barbecue. It sounded as if they were having a good time.

She jumped when the garage's side door shut, and Walker, wearing a sly grin, came toward her.

"Walker, you scared the shit outta me."

"You should've seen your face. I think I'll go back out and do it again."

"Go ahead. I'll lock it this time."

He laughed.

"I already did."

She gestured toward the corner.

"I'm just getting more beer."

"Let me help you."

Edie glanced out the dusty window.

"Walker, you sure no one saw you follow me?"

"Stop worrying, sweetheart."

"I can't help it," she said.

For the past two years, they did a good job hiding what they were doing from everyone, except Aunt Leona, who was too nosy not to know, and Pop, who said she could do a lot better. What did he say the last time? "You get found out, and who's the one who'll catch hell? It'll be Edie Sweet, the dump guy's daughter."

Walker pulled her to him, calling her his pet names, kissing her.

"Were you a good girl last night?"

His words were warm and low, but Edie knew better.

"I'm always good, Walker."

She smiled, keeping her voice light.

"You know what I mean," he said.

She pressed herself against Walker, distracting him with a kiss and another as she leaned back against the hood of her mother-in-law's Thunderbird. Walker's hand was up her blouse, touching her breasts. He moaned.

"Edie."

She froze when a group of kids ran by the door. Their feet thudded against the ground. There was a shout, and someone pulled at the knob, but Walker smiled as if he were drunk. The doorknob rattled again. Edie pushed at Walker's chest until he let her go.

"This isn't a good idea." She fixed her clothes. "It's too dangerous. We could get caught."

Walker chuckled.

"That's what makes it fun, baby."

"Walker, I gotta go."

"Hey, hey, don't leave."

Edie hurried past to grab a case of beer. She shifted the box's edge onto her right hip and unlocked the door. She let it close behind her.

Walker's wife, Sharon, came toward the garage. She scowled and pumped her arms. Edie's heart ticked harder.

"Edie, you see Walker anywhere?"

The bottles clinked inside the case.

"Did you check the house, Sharon?"

"He wasn't there. Somebody said they saw him heading this way."

Edie shook her head.

"I dunno."

Sharon squinted at Edie. Then she was at the garage door, peeking through the dusty glass of its window. She twisted the knob, but it didn't budge.

She glanced over her shoulder.

"If you see Walker, tell him I'm lookin' for him. Will ya?"

Edie adjusted her hands on the case before she began moving. All she said was, "Yeah."

A Great Find

Edie, with Amber in tow, carried a plate covered with foil into Pop's place. Pop sat in his recliner in front of the TV. The picture was so poor that if it weren't for the sound, she wouldn't know he was watching a baseball game. The antenna came loose during a storm this spring, and Pop had yet to go on the roof to fix it although he mentioned it every time he turned on the set.

"We brought you dinner," Edie said.

She set the plate on the end table.

"Such good girls," he said.

Pop squeezed his blue eyes closed and rubbed his days-old whiskers. His white t-shirt had an oil stain down the front. He grinned at Amber.

"Hey, there, sweetie pie."

"Hey, there, Poppy."

"What'd you bring me?" He peeked beneath the foil. "Uh-huh. Appears Marie went whole-hog again. Funny, didn't see an invitation with the name Alban Sweet in our mailbox. Did ya? Must've got lost in the mail again."

Her father chuckled. Edie ignored him as she sank into the upholstered chair next to his. Pop's legal name was Alban Sweet, but
everyone called him Benny, except her late mother, his sister, Leona,
and a few of the old-timers. Besides being the town's dump attendant, he worked as a handyman, two jobs that gave him a bum back.
When he wasn't sitting in his recliner, Pop lay flat on the floor trying
to soothe his muscles.

Edie poked at the beige cotton batting sticking through a cigarette
burn in the arm of the chair.

"Pop, you know why," she said.

He made sucking noises in the back of his teeth.

"Guess I'm too much fun for that crowd."

Pop pulled the plate onto his lap. He picked at the greasy skin
of the chicken and wiped his hand across his shirt. His head rested
against the tape patching a hole made when a guy killed himself with
a shotgun. It happened when Edie was a little older than Amber, and
Pop hauled the chair home after the dead man's family brought it to
the dump. Pop asked the tenant next door, one of his drinking buddies, to help him bring the chair into the living room.

"What do ya think? Real leather," he told Edie's mother when she
came from the kitchen.

Ma stuck her finger in the bullet hole.

"What happened here, Alban?" she asked, and as Pop began his
story, Ma's head moved in sharp, little jerks. "That's it. I've had it.
Our house is full of other people's junk, but a dead man's chair?"

"Lucy, it's a great find. It's real comfy. I tried it out already at the
dump. It's gonna be so good for my back. You know how sore it
gets." He patted the chair. "Don't you worry none, honey. I'm gonna
patch this hole, and nobody'll ever know a bullet went through it."

Ma glared at this man she married in a hard-sprung love that got
her pregnant and hitched within months. She went into their bedroom then Edie's to pack. Ma phoned her sister to pick them up.

Her parents had loud rows before, but Ma's silence frightened Pop.

He begged her to stay and got angry when she wouldn't. He cursed as Ma loaded their bags into the car's trunk. Ma's sister yelled back at Pop. The car sped off, and Edie remembered her father chucking beer cans and rocks against the bumper and back window. Her mother's head was down. Her shoulders shook.

They returned a few weeks later after Ma and Pop made up. Edie was glad. She missed Pop. Her mother did, too. Pop may be a crusty so-and-so, but there was something true about him. He loved them, and they knew it.

About a year later, Ma discovered she had cancer, a sickness so fierce the doctors gave no chance of curing it. Pop, bless him, was good to the end. He sat next to Ma when she took to her bed, feeding and washing her. In the hospital, he stayed by her side. He cried horribly when she died and went on a bender that lasted two weeks. Her two older sisters, long out of the house, hated him for it, but Edie understood. Pop needed to get away from so large a dose of pain.

Edie watched her father eat. His thick white hair fell in front of his eyes. She needed to cut it again.

"What'd you do today?" she asked.

Pop ran a hand over his whiskers. He grunted.

"I straightened up the place," he said.

"That so?"

Edie laughed because the room was filled tightly with junk. The kitchen sink was stacked high with dirty dishes. She and Amber would have to wash them tomorrow.

"When I got sick of that, I got the mower started and tried to cut the grass, but it's gotten so goddamned high. I'll have to use the weed whacker from the highway garage."

Pop cut two short rows in the grass before he left the mower next to the old doghouse filled with gas cans. Edie wasn't surprised. The closest distance between two points for her father was usually a crooked line.

Edie planted a hand on her hip.

"I saw how far you got. It couldn't have taken very long," she said. Pop ignored her.

"I tried to take a nap on the porch, but there was too much hammering next door. Bang, bang, bang, that's all I could hear."

"At Aunt Leona's?"

"Nah, the other side. Doyle's."

The Doyle place was located at the bottom of their dead-end road, closed up after the last Doyle, Elmira, died, and the family who lived elsewhere couldn't decide what to do with the property. It must have been three years ago, and Pop got a few bucks keeping an eye on the place.

"Somebody moved in? Elmira's house has gotten really rundown."

Pop glanced up from his plate.

"I went over to see what's what and met the fella. Damnedest face I ever seen. Scars up and down like somethin' clawed him. He walked with an awful bad limp."

"What clawed him?" Amber asked.

"Didn't bring it up. It's not polite, honey. I'll let your Aunt Leona do it." Pop grinned at his crack. "Friendly guy though. Name's Harlan Doyle. His father, Aldrich, grew up next door. Elmira's boy. He went to Japan in the war, and when he came back, he married a woman and moved south to be with her people. They used to visit the old folks here once in a while. Says he remembers me."

"I saw a man at the ceremony today," Edie said. "He wore sunglasses, but they didn't cover the bad scars on his face. He's tall, but his body was crooked like somethin' wasn't holding him up."

"That's him."

"He says he's gonna fix up the place?" Edie asked. "Is he really planning to live there?"

"That's what he says. Maybe I'll get me some work out of it."

Pop made smacking noises with his mouth. He pointed toward the hutch.

"I almost forgot. I got a present for you, Amber. Go see over there."

Amber went to the hutch. She held a wooden box when she twirled around.

"This it?" she asked.

"Yup, darlin', bring it here."

Pop's eyes grew bigger as he told Amber to twist the crank on the box's bottom, and after she did, the workings produced a tiny, tinny tune. Edie shifted in her chair to give her daughter room. Amber opened and shut the lid. She smiled at the gift and at Pop.

"Thanks, Poppy."

Edie hoped her daughter would never be ashamed of her grandfather. Even though Ma got mad at Pop, she always defended him for working hard for his family. "Somebody has to take care of the dump," her mother said when her sisters complained how horrible their father smelled.

When Ma got sick and after she died, Pop took Edie to the dump when Leona was not available to babysit. She stayed close to her father, or if the weather was bad, she waited in his attendant's shack when he went outside to help a customer. Some people stared, wondering why Benny Sweet brought his youngest to such a place. Afterward, Pop told her about a treasure he salvaged from their load of trash. "People don't realize what great stuff they throw away" was his motto. Or he'd reveal an observation, say, "How the widow living near the store was dumping a lot of vodka bottles lately."

Pop chuckled.

"Do you like the box?" he asked Amber, and after she said yes, he pulled himself upright. "By the way, next time you see Marie, you can tell her for me the chicken was a little dry this year. I'm gonna need a coupla beers to wash it down."

A Familiar Song

Edie stood on the front porch of the Conwell General Store, her arms crossed as she watched her daughter get on the school bus. Amber was up the steps and drifting down the aisle to an empty seat. Her girl's somber face peered through the window. Edie smiled when Amber smiled. The bus rumbled away.

She hooked the outer door to the wall and carried the bundle of newspapers left on the porch to the rack near the checkout counter. She walked through the center aisle, the hem of her skirt swinging against her legs as she passed the shallow rows of cans and boxed food. Her shoes pushed into the soft floorboards. This building has always been the town's only store, and a St. Claire has always owned it.

Her father-in-law without fail was first in the store, an hour before Edie and Amber arrived. When Fred unlocked the back door, the early-risers joined him, waiting at the tables near the deli counter while he made a pot of coffee. Walker was often among them, and sometimes Pop, if he had to get to the dump early, or more rarely, if he had an odd job in town. Edie and Amber usually showed up when most were leaving. Marie was in later.

Now the retirees were settled in. Edie brought a wet rag to wipe the tabletops.

"Edie, your new neighbor was in this morning," one of the men said. "Says he's fixing up the old Doyle place."

"That's what Pop told me. What's he like?"

Another man lifted his cup.

"He's kinda tall and skinny," he said. "He's got brownish hair hanging to his shoulders. He didn't look too old, but it's hard to tell with the scars on his face."

The first man nodded.

"He had a soft, slow way of talking like he was from the South or something," he said.

Her father-in-law spoke.

"Real quiet guy. Odd name." Fred's brows creased as he tried to recall more. "Shoot, he said he used to come here as a kid."

"Pop said his name's Harlan," Edie said. "Harlan Doyle."

"That's it. You meet him, Edie?" Fred asked.

"Not yet. I have to go over and welcome him to the neighborhood," she said.

"Did Benny tell you about his face?" Fred asked.

"He said it was scarred badly."

Fred's eyes shot up and down.

"You're telling me," he said. "I didn't know where to look. No one did."

Edie held the rag.

"I think I saw him at the Memorial Day ceremony when we were at the stone for Gil," she said. "A man stopped to see what was going on. He had a limp, too."

"I wonder what he's doing here. His grandmother's place can't be in any shape to live in," Fred said.

"He told Pop he's gonna fix it up." She shrugged. "Maybe he'll sell it."

The screen door swung open, and Edie gave a hello to the new arrival. She went about her routine getting the store ready. She had done it so long she could manage the small chores without thinking, each one like a note in a familiar song. She went in the back room to get more milk for the coffee. The front door slapped against the jamb. Two men talked with Fred. She recognized their voices, two guys on their way to work, plumbers who had pickup trucks with metal toolboxes attached to the beds and roof racks for piping.

Working men and women would visit the store during the next couple of hours. Edie knew all their names, except for the people passing through. The Conwell General Store was located on a state-numbered route, a busy enough road for those who lived and worked in the hilltowns east of the Berkshires.

Edie cleaned spilled sugar near the coffee area. Water gurgled through the machine. She greeted a man who worked on the town's highway crew.

"When are you guys gonna grade my road? I swear I'm gonna bite my tongue some day driving over that washboard," she said.

The man grinned and tipped his head. His big hand reached for a muffin on the deli counter.

"I'm afraid you'll have to take it up with the boss," he said. "He's the one who makes the schedule."

Edie frowned. Her father and the town's road boss had a long-standing feud because Pop kept taking stuff from the highway garage without asking. Once when Pop borrowed a truck, the two men almost came to blows at the dump, and the board of selectmen reprimanded the road boss for going after an old man. Now the road boss gets his revenge every spring by grading their dirt road last. During the winter, it's the final one plowed.

"Forget it," she said.

"I'm sorry, Edie. You know how it is."

"Sure. See if I dance slow with you anymore at the Do." She pressed a finger to his chest. "Or anything else."

"Edie, don't be like that. You know what a prick he can be."

"So you say."

Her eyes followed the man to the front door. Another one quickly replaced him at the table of retirees. The old-timers would nurse their coffees while they talked over business about the town and beyond.

Edie carried a coffee pot to the table and offered to refill the men's cups.

"What's in the paper?" she asked.

"Check this out." One man pointed to the front page. "This story says a man killed all of his family then himself. Damn country's gone nuts."

"Seems like it."

Edie stationed herself behind the deli counter. This was her spot, making sandwiches and cutting lunchmeat and cheese to order until Amber returned on the bus this afternoon. Then Vera, who worked part-time, or some other woman from town, took over.

Marie showed up mid-morning. Her mouth twitched when she saw Edie, and after a few words to Fred, she went into the office. She didn't come to the store yesterday, the day after Memorial Day. Fred said she was under the weather. Edie knew she was hung over and still grieving for Gil.

She waved Fred over.

"Yes, Edie?" he said.

"Could you watch the counter? I wanna talk with Marie."

Fred nodded.

"That'd be nice of you, Edie." He took an apron from its hook behind the counter. "It hasn't been easy lately. It never is after Memorial Day. She gets so worked up."

"I understand."

The office door was slightly ajar. Marie was at her desk. Her hands were folded on its top. She stared at nothing.

Edie knocked.

"Yes?" Marie asked.

Edie stepped inside.

"How're you doing, Marie?"

Marie's head shook slightly.

"You'd think it'd get easier after these years, but it doesn't. I hope I didn't act too foolish the other day."

"You were fine, Marie."

"Fine." She squeezed her hands, one over the other. "That's a relief."

Edie jabbed her thumb toward the door.

"I gotta get going. I left Fred in charge."

She was nearly out the door when Marie said her name.

"Thank you for asking."

"Sure, Marie."

When Edie returned, the retirees were gone, and workers followed them on their morning break. Mothers with small children and the lunch crowd would be next. Deliverymen would come and go. The day typically passed in a pleasant pace, no surprises, no ups or downs.

Edie bent over the store's sink, scrubbing the cutting board in its deep tub. She peeked over her shoulder when she heard boot heels chop hard against the floor. She recognized Walker's step.

Walker poured himself a cup of coffee before he came to the deli counter. Edie glanced around the store. Usually, he kept a respectable brother-in-law distance, so as not to raise suspicion with his parents or Vera, his wife's sister, and worse, one of the town's real talents for gossip. Walker stood before her.

"Edie, give me a hunk of the cheddar cheese," he said.

"How much, Walker?"

"How about five pounds?"

Her mouth quivered.

"Five pounds is an awful lot of cheese."

"Is it? Just give me a piece."

Edie cut a thin wedge off the wheel.

Walker peeked at his mother, who talked with a customer in front of the store.

"I tried calling you last night," he said so only she could hear.

Edie placed a square of white paper on the scale and weighed the cheese.

"I was at Aunt Leona's playing cards. Was there something you wanted to tell me?"

"I wanna see you tonight. I believe we have some unfinished business from the other day."

Edie didn't look directly at him, but she smiled.

"Amber's home," she said.

"Why don't you find someone to watch her? We'll go somewhere. Just you and me."

She couldn't get away from his eyes.

"How about seven?" she said. "We can meet behind the store."

He nodded as Edie wrapped the cheese in paper, taping the ends, so the package was tight enough to mail. She handed it to Walker, who gave her a quick smile before he left. He stopped to joke with his mother on his way out. Edie made him a satisfied man.

Moments later, the front door slammed hard, and Pop strutted, all-smiles, down the aisle as if he won first prize. He said her name, then helped himself to coffee, and as usual, didn't bother to leave any money in the jar beside the machine. He continued behind the counter.

"Got a little something back there to put in this coffee?" he joked. "Guess what I got in the back of the truck? Let me just say the yard'll be lookin' pretty spiffy by time you get home, thanks to the Conwell Highway Department."

"Shit, Pop, if the road boss finds out, we'll never get our road graded."

Pop snorted.

"Don't you worry none. I'll get it back to the highway garage before the little bastard even misses it."

"No, you won't, Pop, and it'll never get done."

"Jesus, girl, you gotta have more faith in me."

"I know better." She handed him a sandwich she had made for herself. "This is for you," she said, and Pop licked his lips as he took it to a table. She sat beside him. "Do you mind watching Amber tonight? I gotta go some place."

Pop chewed hard on his sandwich.

"Maybe I got some place to go, too."

"I'll drop off a six-pack."

Her father grinned so hard she could see the ground food in his mouth.

"All right, now we're talkin'. Just tell the li'l darlin' to come right over."

A Soft Roll

Edie let her car idle behind her in-laws' store, now closed, while she listened to an old country tune about love lost between a man and a woman. She tipped her head back as she followed its sad lyrics. She sighed. The man was so lonesome for the woman he didn't think he could go on.

She stared at the wooden stairs that rose to the store's second floor, where she and Gil lived before he left for Vietnam. She shut the car's engine and found the key for the lock in her purse.

The apartment was empty, except for the furniture she left behind when she moved next door to Pop. She walked toward the couch. She remembered how she sat here, yelling and slapping the air as if she could fight off the bad news about Gil. Fred, the soldier, and Marie, who stomped shrieking upstairs, stood there unable to do a thing she needed. Walker was the one who sat beside her and spoke in a low rumble while he tried to comfort her. Only one other time she cried as hard, when her mother died, but then it was a child's grief. She clung to Walker, feeling he and Gil's baby were the only ones who kept her from throwing herself down the stairs.

Edie went to a window when she heard Walker's pickup. He was out, searching for her. She tapped the window's glass, and Walker nodded before he took the stairs. She opened the door.

He came toward her for a kiss. His smooth cheek smelled of aftershave.

"What are you doing up here, sweetheart?" he asked.

"Just looking around. I haven't been here in a while. I was just remembering things."

He smoothed his hair behind his ears.

"We don't have to go anywhere. We can stay here."

"Walker."

"You scared of getting' caught? No one can see we're parked behind the store. Nobody's downstairs." He touched her skin above the neckline of her dress. "Is this dress new? I like the way it fits you tight around your waist like that."

If she shut her eyes, he sounded just like Gil.

"I dunno, Walker."

He chuckled.

"You dunno if the dress is new, or you dunno if you want to do it here?"

She didn't have to answer. He came on strong, kissing her hard, backing her toward the bedroom. He bunched the fabric of her dress in his hands, lifting the skirt up and over her head. They tumbled onto the bare mattress as she helped him out of his clothes, and he undid what was left of hers. His boots thumped to the floor.

"Baby, I can't wait," he groaned.

When they were done, Edie stared up at the ceiling. Walker slept beside her. The only light in the room came from what the moon cast inside. She and Gil slept in this bed. They loved each other and made a baby here. She cried herself to sleep after he died.

For years after, Edie stuck to being a grieving, lonely widow. She took care of Amber, seeing only Pop, Leona, or an old school friend. Eventually, Walker stopped coming. She had no time for him. Then he and Sharon got married. They had their twins.

Edie didn't start going out until Amber was nearly four, and only because Aunt Leona or her in-laws took her overnight. She knew it was unlikely she would find true love at the Do-Si-Do, but she had fun. The men knew and she knew no one could ever take Gil's place.

She saw Walker at the Do, and, of course, his parents' store. Two springs ago, when he was renovating a home in the town's main village, he came into the store three or four times a day on a coffee run or for lunch. If he were there with his crew, he'd joke with her like so many of the men. Then he started coming alone, seeking her out.

One afternoon, Walker came into the store's office. He sat on the desk's corner, holding his cowboy hat, his hands rotating the brim, so it appeared he was steering it. He talked about paperwork and being the boss while he stared at the front of her dress. She stood to put a folder in the file cabinet, and as she passed, he grabbed her arm, pulling her so close his breath warmed her. He kissed her, and he kept kissing her. When she dropped the folder to the floor, its papers rustled as if a bird had been flushed fast from the woods.

"What say I come over later?"

His voice was full of breath and moan, and she let him put his hands all over her.

The next day, Aunt Leona asked why Walker's truck drove past her house late at night and didn't go back for several hours. Edie said he was looking at some repairs the house needed. She didn't fool her aunt then, or when she asked several times afterward.

"Back for more repairs, eh?" Leona said with a sly grin.

Walker made Edie feel wanted when they were together, but it would never be enough to fill her. Only Gil did that.

Walker said once it was a huge mistake he married Sharon.

"I dunno why we're even together," he told Edie.

She placed her fingertips over his lips.

Now she slipped her hand from Walker as she tried to get up, but his fingers cuffed her wrist to keep her from leaving.

"Where're you going?" he asked.

"To the bathroom."

"Stay here."

Edie rolled onto her side to face him.

"How's the new job?" she asked.

He frowned.

"Damn New Yorkers. You know who I mean, the couple that bought the old Franklin place on the south end of town. They can't make up their fuckin' minds."

"Uh-huh."

"The woman wants wainscoting in the dining room. The man wants a chair rail. I joked they might have to flip a coin cause one of 'em didn't want what the other one did. Maybe they'll do both. You know how New Yorkers are."

"Uh-huh."

"First, they asked for exposed beams in the kitchen. Now they're not sure it's what they want. They're gonna get back to me on that one."

"Uh-huh."

"On top of that, one of my framers quit mid-week. Couldn't hack the work. Remember I told you about Tom? I had my doubts he'd last anyway, but I thought I was doin' his family a favor. Dumb fuck can't hold down a job for long. I feel sorry for his wife and kids."

"Uh-huh."

"To top if off, the lumberyard messed up my material order. It set me back today. I hate that shit."

"You'll fix it, Walker," she said. "You always do."

Walker sighed. The air came from deep inside him.

"Yeah, Edie, I will. Hey, I see you got a new neighbor. You meet him yet?"

Edie shook her head.

"I heard about him though. I think he's the one who was at Gil's ceremony on Memorial Day."

"I saw him that day, too. Seems like he was in an accident or some-thing."

"I need to go over. Pop and Aunt Leona already have. They say he's really nice."

"You do that. At least, I won't have to worry about him."

"Why do you say that?" Edie asked.

"You haven't seen him up close. He's one ugly son of a bitch. I can't see a woman wanting to be with him for free."

"Walker, you're not being very nice. Suppose he was in Vietnam like Gil?"

"Then I feel real sorry for him." He gazed around the room. "We'll have to do this again."

Edie shifted.

"Not so fast." His hand closed tighter. "What's with you and Lon-ny?"

"Him? We're just having some laughs," Edie said.

"I heard you both left at the same time the other night. You sleep with him?"

"We left at the same time? So what. Walker, you're hurting my wrist."

His lips opened and shut, but he didn't speak. He loosened his grip.

"Tell me more," he said.

"I was having fun, just like you and me are having fun."

"Fun. Is that what this is?"

"What else can it be, Walker?"

"I'm hoping for more."

"More?"

He began kissing her neck. Edie's chest rose and fell in a slow roll as he brought his hand to her.

Real Late

Pop was stretched on his recliner. His open mouth poured out a long, wet snore. His eyes opened when Edie tapped his shoulder.

"Thanks, Pop. I'm gonna bring Amber home." Edie cocked her head toward the couch, where her daughter slept beneath a worn quilt. "Everything okay?"

He nodded.

"Yeah, yeah," he mumbled. "She's no trouble at all."

"Want me to shut off the TV?"

"Nah, leave it. I wanna rest my eyes a bit."

She did as he asked before she woke her daughter. Amber was too heavy to carry, so she guided her next door. The girl clung to her.

"What time is it?" Amber asked.

"Late, real late," her mother answered.

Neighbors

Harlan Doyle sat on the porch of his grandmother's house. His long legs were stretched, and his back rested against the narrow clapboards while he contemplated the day ahead. The rain stopped in the middle of the night, and now the sun drew moisture from the ground. His bad leg ached from it.

He glanced at the sagging tent pitched in the front yard. He salvaged the contents now piled beside him on the porch's floorboards. He didn't relish sleeping here in the open or inside the house, which wasn't worth living in yet although it might be his only recourse if it rained again. He slapped at the mosquitoes, relentless this early hour.

The birds rejoiced in the trees around him. Last night, an owl's call woke him twice, but it was a sound he found interesting.

Harlan was tall and hawk-nosed, with tired, green eyes that made him look as if he possessed wisdom and kindness, and long, brown hair pulled into a tail. He used to have a pleasant face, but scars cut deep ridges along both sides. The accident messed his body, and the doctors in Mexico did a lousy job patching it, but he was done being angry with that and other things.

His parents gave him this house, which his grandmother last owned. His uncle, his father's only brother, reported after a visit last summer the place would fall into the cellar hole unless something was done to save it. The property had acreage, but most of it was wetland. The brothers settled on a price, and Harlan took the house and this chance for a fresh start, back where his family once lived.

When he arrived, the house was boarded, its clapboards stripped to the gray wood. Trash filled the rooms. Anything left behind after his grandmother died was broken. He spent the last few days prying sheets of plywood off the windows, ridding the house of the small animals that lived there, and figuring how to make it his home. It would take work, and he couldn't do it alone, but now he was here, so he'd see it through to the end.

The first time Harlan remembered visiting this town, he was maybe six, and he rode in Daddy's Cadillac from Jacksonville, Florida, one summer. Daddy and Mom took turns. Daddy was a better driver although Mom complained when he used his knees to hold the steering wheel as he rolled himself a smoke or opened a can of beer.

Harlan stayed in the back seat, stuffed alongside whatever they couldn't fit in the trunk. He hardly left Florida, and he wondered how different back home, as his father called it, would look as he stared out the window at the fields, swamps, and forests beyond the interstate's guardrails. He read license plates and listened to the radio, but it was too long a trip, and he found his parents' conversations uninteresting, except when they talked about money and relatives. They started out teasing and fun, but then their voices got sharp edges, and they didn't speak for a while.

Harlan lay on the back seat, tossing a baseball. A couple of times it hit the ceiling, and his eyes met his father's in the rearview mirror.

"Hey, buddy, one more time, and I'm chucking the ball out the window," his father said in a low, even tone that showed he meant business.

His mother turned around. Her hair, so blonde it was almost white, bounced around her shoulders. She kissed the air with lips as pink as petals.

"Mind your father, honey. It's a long ride," she said.

The sky seemed small in Conwell. Daddy said it was because the hills and woods closed you in, but it was green, and the houses were larger than those in Florida. Daddy stopped the car in the driveway of his grandparents' house, and they were stretching the stiffness from their bodies when his grandmother and grandfather came outside to greet them. Daddy grew up here before he went overseas during World War II. He saw fighting in Japan and met Harlan's mother on a hospital base when he came back wounded. Daddy had been back to visit, and Mom, when they were first married, but this time the whole family came on vacation.

His grandfather and grandmother appeared old, not the kind of grandparents who would play with him. His great-grandmother, who sat in a wheelchair, had only one leg hanging beneath the hem of her dress. His father warned him Great-Granny lost the leg because she had diabetes, but she wasn't what he imagined. She was a heavy woman, so the one leg she had left was as stout as a fence post.

"Come here, Harlan. Let me get a look at you," Great-Granny said, gesturing with her finger. "I believe he favors you most, Aldrich."

Harlan stayed a few feet away while the woman waited for her hug. He knew he should, and he was nearly ready when Mom dropped a stuffed alligator onto Great-Granny's lap.

"This is for you," Mom said brightly.

Great-Granny yelped and brushed the gator onto the floor, where it bounced so hard it appeared the stuffed critter was leaping to bite off her last good leg. Daddy started chuckling when Mom tossed the gator onto the coffee table and swore beneath her breath.

"Say, Mother, what do you have there?" His grandfather's eyes went from one person to another. "Isn't that critter something?"

For the next several days, Daddy took Harlan swimming, fishing, and riding around on the dirt roads in his big Caddy, the dirt kicking up behind its back tires. They went to the general store for something cold to drink. A fan from the ceiling pushed air around the store with broad paddles. His relatives complained about the heat since they arrived, but it couldn't touch a Florida summer.

One night he and Daddy played cards in his grandparents' kitchen while Mom watched TV in the living room. His grandparents already went to bed. Daddy drank beer and gave Harlan his own bottle of Coke. He taught him how to play Go Fish and groaned when Harlan managed to beat him.

"You little weasel, you got me that time," Daddy said, and then he blew across the top of his beer bottle.

"Pipe down in there," Mom called from the other room. "There're some old people trying to sleep in this house."

"You don't look so old to me," his father shouted back.

Harlan giggled when Mom came rushing into the room, pretending she was mad at Daddy, but they ended up kissing in the kitchen. Mom twisted away, and Daddy slapped her bottom.

"I'll get you later," he said, raising his eyebrows.

Mom wiggled her hips when she left the room.

He came with his parents to Conwell a few times after that, including once for his grandfather's funeral. He didn't know anyone, except family.

Harlan glanced up when a wild animal broke through the underbrush in the field beyond the large barn. It was a pasture when this was a farm, he remembered from his visits. Now blueberry bushes, briars, and scrubby trees, birch and juniper, sprang from the ground. This was the original house on the road, named for his family, early settlers in Conwell. A century ago, a Doyle built the three houses on this road, but the other two have since left the family.

He met two of his neighbors. The old man, who was supposed to watch the place for his family, was the first. A nosy so-and-so, Benny Sweet stared at him squarely in the face, reading it, as he welcomed the warm beer Harlan offered him. Benny quizzed him on his plans.

A daughter, who's a widow, and a granddaughter lived with him. His son-in-law was killed in Vietnam.

"A real nice guy," Benny Sweet told him, sucking at the inside of his mouth. "Rotten luck it happened."

Yesterday, Benny's sister visited, sounding the car's horn until he came outside. She stayed in the driver's seat, head bobbing, her hair a vicious shade of red. Harlan explained what he was doing, how he planned eventually to convert the barn into a workshop. He told her he built and refinished furniture as a trade. The moving van with his tools and household things should be here next week. Leona Sweet, as she introduced herself, was as forward as her brother, and Harlan felt self-conscious his clothes were so dirty and sweaty.

The power company promised him electricity Monday, and he was still working on the phone. Somebody was coming next week to check the well's pump in the cellar.

Harlan glanced at his watch. He needed to get rolling. He should go to the city, about twenty or so miles away, to shop for a stove and refrigerator, but for now he was content using his cook stove and a cooler. Besides, he needed to get rid of the trash left in this house. He had piles of it. The dump was only open two times a week, Wednesday afternoon and all day Saturday, but his neighbor, Benny, who ran the place, told him he would be there later this morning to move piles of trash around with a dozer. Though the dump wouldn't be officially open, this being Friday, Harlan could bring a couple of loads.

Benny winked when he said, "It'll be just us neighbors."

Harlan looked toward the end of the driveway, where a woman walked along its grassy edge. The hem of her dress swayed as she moved. He guessed she was Benny Sweet's daughter. He couldn't remember her name, but he recognized her from the time he stopped at the center of town on Memorial Day. He had just arrived, pushing to make the final leg of his cross-country trip, so he drove all night, staying at a rest area for a few hours to sleep. He parked the pickup when he saw the crowd. It turned out to be a ceremony. He remembered the woman's pretty face softened by sadness. The girl beside her held a framed picture of a soldier standing near a helicopter.

"Hey, there," she called to Harlan, and when she was closer, "My name's Edie St. Claire. I'm your next-door neighbor."

Harlan pulled himself upright. His bad leg felt dead and useless, so he punched it a bit to get it moving, feeling embarrassed. Edie kept smiling as if she didn't notice. He was on his feet and stretching himself upright. He nodded.

"I'm Harlan. Harlan Doyle."

She stood at the bottom of the steps. She held something wrapped in aluminum foil.

"I know who you are. Pop told me about you. So did my Aunt Leona. I hear your truck go by. I brought you something." Her hand swung forward. "This is for you. Banana bread. I made it myself this morning. It has real walnuts."

Feeling too tall and awkward standing on the porch above this woman, he limped down the steps. He took the bread. It was still warm.

"That was awfully nice of you," he told her.

Edie glanced around. Harlan saw what she saw.

"You got a lot to do here."

"I work with wood."

"Work with wood. What's that mean?"

"I build furniture. One-of-a-kind pieces."

"Fancy stuff?"

"Sometimes." He grinned. "My tools are supposed to get here soon."

Her head tipped to one side.

"You gonna sell the house when you're done?"

"No. I'm planning to live here for good."

"For good? Really? People usually fix up these old places to make money."

She came nearer. Her blue eyes opened wider. He felt himself smile.

"Not me. This house belonged to my family."

She laughed as she gestured toward the tent.

"You'd better hurry up then. Winter always comes faster around here than we think, and your tent's not gonna keep you very warm."

He nodded. Edie only came up to his shoulders. She didn't seem to mind being this close to a man she just met.

"I was going to go into town to find a roofer. I don't have a phone yet. I thought I'd use the payphone near the store." He slapped at his right thigh. "Bum leg. It'd be tough for me going up and down a ladder carrying bundles of shingles."

She studied his leg and then his face.

"Were you in the war?" she asked quietly. "Is that how it happened?"

"I was in an accident."

He glanced away for a moment. Her eyes were still on him.

"You got hurt real bad. Sorry it happened." She paused. "I know someone who can help you. His name's Walker St. Claire. He's my brother-in-law. He does this kinda work, and anyone who hires him gets his money's worth. He could help you find a plumber and electrician, too, if you need 'em. You got a paper and pencil? I can give you his number."

"Come inside."

Harlan stumbled forward, dragging his leg, impatient at his clumsiness, but he made it to the door first, so he could open it for her. The kitchen was a large, square room with wooden cabinets and six-over-six paned windows that would let in natural light once their glass was washed. This was the first room he cleaned. The appliances were long gone, except for an iron cook stove in one corner. The plumbing was missing beneath the sink, but its porcelain was in decent shape. He already fixed the leg on the kitchen table. That and a chair he found in the attic were the only pieces of furniture in the room. He set the bread on the table.

"I liked your grandmother an awful lot," Edie told him. "I work at my in-laws' store. I used to bring her groceries on Saturdays. It was the day she baked, and she always gave me something to take home."

"I'm afraid I didn't know her very well. I only came here a few times when I was a boy."

"That's a shame. Elmira was a wonderful woman, and she was awfully kind to us. I remember she made us all dinner when my mother died. I still have the pink blanket she crocheted for Amber after she was born. Amber's my little girl."

She laughed.

"What's so funny?" he asked.

"Whenever your grandmother hired Pop to help around the house, she made sure he completely finished the job before she paid him. She'd give it a close inspection. She knew my father all right. She'd say, 'Alban, don't ever try to fool an old lady, at least not this old lady'." Edie raised a finger. "I suggest you do the same, Harlan Doyle. I love my Pop, but he's bit of a rascal, if you get what I mean."

He handed her a paper and a stubby pencil from the counter. He watched her write.

"I'll keep it in mind."

She gave him back the paper.

"By the way, if you want to swim, there's a clean, deep river across the road just up a few yards from the end of your driveway. Take a left, then a right onto an old logging road. You can't miss it if you're on foot. The land belongs to my Aunt Leona, but she won't mind if you use it. If you want to wash up, that's okay, too. The closest Laundromat is two towns away, but I bet Pop could hook you up with a washer when you're ready for one. We have a back yard filled with 'em. He'd load up the front yard if I let him, so you'd be doing us both a favor. He might have a refrigerator and a stove, but it depends on your taste. None of 'em match."

He heard himself laugh.

"Thanks. I'll remember that, too."

She nodded toward the door.

"I gotta head out. Amber and I have to get to the store. She catches the school bus there. Stop by the house some day. You can meet her. She's sort of shy, but she'll get used to you."

The door closed, and she was gone. He tucked the paper with Walker's number in the breast pocket of his t-shirt. He thought about the next time he could see her.

Somethin' Worth Somethin'

Harlan inched his pickup over the rutted road. He passed Benny's house, both vehicles gone, and Leona's, buttoned up. Then he was on a paved road to the town's main route, a few miles to the Conwell General Store. He'd been here only five days, and already he knew his way around. The public buildings like Town Hall and the school, plus the Conwell Congregational Church were centrally located. The general store, a garage, and a graveyard, where the Doyles were buried, were a few miles away on the same road. The Do-Si-Do Bar was in the western end of Conwell. A few paved roads crisscrossed the town, but most, like the one where he lived, were dirt.

He pulled his pickup into the entrance of the town dump and then backed the truck to the edge of a large pile of garbage. He had a full load, his second trip today. Benny Sweet came quickly to examine the contents, but once again he complained all he had was junk.

Benny's breath smelled of liquor.

"Looks like your grandmother's place got cleaned out. Hope your family got the good stuff she had," he said.

Harlan flung a lampshade on top of the pile, its side stove-in badly like someone took a foot to it.

"I hope so, too," he said.

"You can't leave an empty house alone without asking for trouble," Benny said. "Kids started hangin' out there, making a mess. That's when your uncle had it boarded up and asked me to watch the place. Kinda too late by then."

Harlan held the racks to a refrigerator no longer in the house and scraps of metal he couldn't identify.

"Want any of this stuff?"

"I'll take the racks. Toss the rest."

Harlan hoisted himself onto the truck's bed. He planned to use a shovel to scoop what was left.

"Thanks again for letting me do this," he said.

Benny winked then pointed to what he had set aside, a couple of lamp bodies and a wooden trunk between his attendant's shack and the dozer he used to move the trash. He leaned against the pickup's fender. He made a whistling laugh through the gaps in his front teeth.

"You won't believe what people dump here. Once I seen a woman grab a wedding dress and veil outta the back seat of her car and toss it onto the garbage. I laughed to bust a gut after she left. Gotta be a story there." He tipped his head. "I seen sad things, too. I wanted to cry out loud the day a young couple who lost their baby threw out their crib."

Benny frowned at the memory.

"I run an orderly dump here. It'll get a bit tricky when it gets hotter, and I gotta keep the flies down. But the dozer does an excellent job gettin' it covered." He spat a yellow wad of phlegm on the gritty ground near a stray tin can. "I get rats, too. Big suckers. Some nights I just come down here with a bottle and my twenty-two and pick 'em off one at a time. My Edie used to come. She's a real hot shot like her old man. You might like to join me sometime."

Harlan leaned on the shovel.

"I met your daughter today. She brought me some banana bread she baked. I ate a slice already. It was really good."

50

Benny made a whistling laugh again.

"She gave you one, too? She's a fine girl, my Edie. She'd make some man a great wife. You might wanna think about it."

Harlan grinned as he scraped the flat-edged shovel across the bottom of the pickup's bed. His leg throbbed, and he moved slower than earlier this morning, but this was the last load today.

Benny squinted.

"Harlan, hand me that copper wire you got back there. Now there's somethin' worth somethin'."

After he returned home, Harlan found the entrance to the path, where Edie told him, and he walked through the forest, following an old logging road until it ended at a river. He scanned the area. No one was here.

He set a bar of soap and a bundle of clean clothes on a dry, flat rock. He stripped off his shirt and pants, both so soiled from work, dirt was on the inside. He sat on the rock in his shorts, stretching his toes into the cool river water. He ran a hand over the ropelike scars on his bad leg and the one on his abdomen. He snorted. His body looked as if it belonged to a monster.

Harlan was glad he came to live here. He liked being around people who got to the point fast. "Were you in the war?" Edie St. Claire asked him. "You got hurt real bad." She said that, too, and she was right.

Tonight he planned to eat out instead of heating food on his camp stove and drinking warm beer. Bennie Sweet told him where to go, the Do-Si-Do Bar, which he passed on the way to the dump. Nothing fancy, the old man told him, but he wouldn't leave hungry. Besides, it was Friday, so there might be a band. He could enjoy a little music.

Harlan yanked off his shorts and stepped into the river until it was high enough for him to let his body go with one long yell. He dunked himself, using the soap on his hair and body, moving fast because the water was cold. He tossed the bar to the shore and dove beneath to rinse off before he swam back to land, feeling like a new man.

The Do-Si-Do

The Do-Si-Do was crowded by time Harlan got there. People were finishing their meals, or drinking and waiting for the band setting up on the stage. Harlan made a lumbering step. Some in the bar took notice. It was to be expected even if he weren't the ugliest man in the place because he was the latest stranger who moved to town. He figured he'd eat alone at the bar, but then he heard a shout. His neighbor, Leona Sweet, slapped his arm as he passed her table.

"You, Harlan Doyle, sit here with Edie and me," she said. "Unless you'd rather eat standing up."

"No, ma'am, I wouldn't."

Leona used her foot to push a chair forward.

"Park yourself right here."

Harlan sat across the table from Edie. She wore a jersey with Conwell Women's Softball stitched across the front.

"Hello, neighbor," Edie said. "We meet again."

"So we do."

"I see you found the swimming hole and cleaned up. You look a lot better than the last time I saw you." She stopped. "I'm sorry. I didn't mean anything by that. Sometimes we Sweets just can't keep our mouths shut when we should."

He chuckled.

"It's okay. I found the river like you said, and it did feel great to get clean again." He glanced over his shoulder to give the waitress his order, a burger and fries, before he turned toward Edie and her aunt. "Edie, do you want another beer? How about you, Ms. Sweet?"

Leona's red hair shook as she made a hooting laugh.

"Ms. Sweet? Ha. You can call me Leona." She bent toward him. "And, yes, we'll take those beers."

He grinned as he raised two fingers.

"Make it two more," he told the waitress.

Edie's head moved with the tune on the jukebox.

"How was your game?" Harlan asked.

She shrugged.

"Eh, we lost. We stunk up the place."

Leona pawed the air.

"It's not Edie's fault. She's the best player on the team."

"Aunt Leona, that's not true. How about Gloria and Patsy?"

Leona waved her arm over the table.

"Shush, honey. Let me tell the story. We were down by one run. Edie was at the plate. First, she gets a ball, then a strike. I yelled for her to wait for her pitch, and she does, sending it where the left-fielder couldn't get it. My Edie had enough time to reach third." She winked at Harlan. "I had my rally cap on."

Edie crossed her arms.

"I believe you're boring our neighbor," she said.

Leona wagged a finger.

"You be quiet, Edie," she said. "Then Vera, that dumbbell of a coach, keeps the first basemen in the game. The woman couldn't run the bases if her shorts were on fire. She does manage to get a base hit, but she's too fat to make it to first." Leona slapped the table. "Game over. We lost."

Edie laughed.

"You can't win 'em all," she said. "But you sure like to."

Leona gave Harlan's arm a playful slap.

"Edie's the best all-around on the team, maybe the league," she said. "She can hit and has a good glove and arm. I never miss a game. You should go. You'll meet people that way."

Harlan chuckled. He was used to quieter people. Certainly, his parents were that way, hard-working folks who gave him enough love growing up, but you had to know they loved you because they would never say it. His ex-wife, Susan, was like them. "Don't you know I love you?" she used to say. Then again, it turned out she didn't. Her little boy must be walking now, and maybe she'd have another. He would have liked starting a family with her although now he was glad he didn't. He would never leave a child behind.

"She's my biggest fan," Edie said.

The waitress brought their beers. Harlan's order would be out soon, she told him.

"Did you call Walker?" Edie asked Harlan.

"Not yet," he said.

"Make sure you do. He'll give you the best price."

The crowd took a couple of songs to get dancing. Harlan drummed his fingertips on the tabletop and hummed to the music. He wasn't a fan of Country and Western, but this was a mixture of old-timey stuff and new, and the band was doing a decent job with this standard.

A tall, blond man stood over Edie and asked her to dance. The expression on her face was playful.

"Why not?" she told him.

Leona arched an eyebrow as she drank from the bottle. She made a point of peering down at Edie's feet.

"Good thing you're not wearing open-toe shoes tonight, honey," she said. "This one's got such huge feet, he might not have much control over them."

"Aunt Leona, shush. You're embarrassing him." Edie looked up at the man. "We're gonna do just fine. Right, Pete?"

"Yup," he said.

Harlan's eyes traveled toward the dance floor, where Edie and the tall blond did the two-step to a lively tune about happy cowboy love. The man rushed her some, but Edie gave him the lead, so they were a smooth-moving couple. Her mouth was open and laughing as he guided her around the floor, twirling her this way and that. Sometimes she sang along.

Edie returned, drinking from her bottle of beer. Her eyes searched the crowd.

"Be right back," she told Harlan.

She returned moments later with a dark-haired man. He extended his large, rough hand. His grip was tight and dry.

"Name's Walker St. Claire. Edie says you might want me to give you an estimate for a new roof. Your grandmother's house?"

"That's right."

"I could come by tomorrow afternoon, say around one, one-thirty. Does that work for you?"

"It does. I wasn't planning on going anywhere. See you then."

The waitress set down Harlan's plate of food, and when he looked up, Edie and Walker were gone.

"Where'd they go?" Harlan asked Leona.

She shook her head and frowned.

"You don't want to know. Believe me, you don't."

Only One

Walker grinned when he saw Edie's car ahead on the town's main road. His twin sons, Shane and Randy, so identical he usually called them "boys", sulked beside him. They were coming from Saturday morning baseball practice, and the boys had been bickering about something the other was supposed to have done. Walker, tired of it, told them to shut up, or he was dumping them alongside the road. Little brats, their mother spoiled them.

Walker flashed his headlights, signaling Edie to stop. He pulled to the shoulder. She did the same.

"Why are we stopping?" one of his boys asked.

Walker checked himself in the rearview mirror.

"I need to talk with Aunt Edie," he said. "You boys behave your-selves, or I'll give you both a smack when I get back." He waggled a finger. "You know I will, right?"

The boys raised their eyes slowly. Walker waited.

"Yeah, Daddy," they said in unison.

Walker reached into the breast pocket of his black t-shirt for a pack of gum. He tossed two sticks onto the front seat.

"Don't leave the truck."

He strolled across the road toward Edie's car, the heels of his boots clicking over the road's pavement. He leaned against her door, feeling happier than he did all day. She wore a rosy scent he liked. Her blouse was open a few buttons at the top. Edie knew how to make him feel welcome.

He smiled at Edie's girl, Amber, his niece, who sat in the front seat with a comic book on her lap.

"Hey, there, cutie pie," Walker said. "How're you doing?"

Amber blinked. Her eyes were the same blue as her mother's.

"Good, Uncle Walker," she said.

"Here. I have this for you." He reached across Edie to hand the girl two sticks of gum. "You can save one for later."

"Thank you," she said in a thin whisper as she slowly unwrapped a stick.

He grinned.

"You're welcome."

Walker ran his hand over Edie's arm.

"What are you doing tonight?" he asked.

She stared at his hand.

"Not sure," Edie said. "Probably hanging out at the Do. You?"

"How about a ride to my camp at the lake? I need to get it open for the summer. Check on things, you know?" He lowered his voice. His eyes shifted briefly toward Amber. "Can you get yourself free?"

Walker glanced toward his pickup. His boys were shoving each other and shouting. But he didn't say anything to stop them. He waited for Edie's answer.

"I can't now, Walker. I gotta finish my route."

Her head bounced toward the back seat filled with boxes of groceries. Edie was making her Saturday morning deliveries to the old folks in town and beyond.

"I see that. What about later?"

"I dunno, Walker."

He ran his fingers through his hair.

"Why are you acting this way?" He lowered his voice. "Are you mad at me for somethin'?"

Edie's mouth stayed open as if the words were stuck in there.

"No, I'm not mad at you."

"All right. Ask my mother if Amber can stay the night at her house. She's crazy about her." He paused. "We can take the canoe out. Just you and me. We'll have a great time. You'll see. And I'll get you back home tonight."

"Overnight? Your mother had Amber last night."

Edie stared through the windshield as if she were expecting someone she knew to drive from that direction.

"Come on, baby," Walker said. "What's goin' on?"

"Nothing," she said. "I'll ask your mother. I'm sure it won't be a problem. When do you want to pick me up?"

"How about two?"

"No, make it later. Two-thirty. Your mother gets off at two."

Walker nodded.

"That'll work. I gotta go meet that crippled neighbor of yours first to give him an estimate on a new roof. I'll pick you up after."

"Walker, don't say that about him." Edie bent forward. "Hey, look over there. Your boys are gonna cross the road."

He spun on the heels of his boots. His sons stood along the road's shoulder. A car sped in front of them.

"You two! Stay right there!" he yelled before he slapped the panel of Edie's door. "See ya later."

Walker marched across the road. Behind him, the tires of Edie's car dug into the dirt as she drove away.

"I thought I told you two to stay in the truck," he growled at his sons.

"We wanted to see Aunt Edie," one boy said.

"Your aunt had to get going. She's got lots of food in the car that'll spoil. She's taking it to all the old people who shop at your grandparents' store."

Walker shut the passenger side door after the boys climbed inside. One boy stuck his head through the open window.

"Ma says you like Aunt Edie too much," he said.

Walker's neck got hot.

"She did, did she? Sometimes your mother can say silly things." Walker kept his voice at a casual tone. "You remember what I told you about your Uncle Gil, how he died in the war? Your aunt and cousin just need a little help cause they're all alone. Sometimes I'm the only one who can do it." He playfully tugged on the lid of the boy's ball cap. "Besides, everybody likes Aunt Edie a lot. Don't you?"

The boys' heads bobbed.

"Yeah," they said.

"All right then, let's get going. I bet your mother has lunch ready."

Worked

Walker was the first one in the house. His wife sat on the edge of their bed, her wide rear end sinking into the mattress. She held a mirror close to her face as she plucked her eyebrows, definitely the woman's best feature. She didn't take her eyes from the glass.

"How'd the boys do at practice?" she asked.

"Great. Coach says Randy's gonna be the starting pitcher next game."

She lowered the mirror.

"Really? He's that good?"

"That's what he says."

She raised the mirror and pressed the tips of the tweezers over a hair. The skin popped upward as she pulled.

"Sharon, I was thinking of going to the camp today to open it up for the season."

She worked on another hair.

"When do you wanna leave?"

"Uh, I was going to go by myself this time." He swallowed. "I need to meet those folks from New York. You know, the Jews who

60

bought the old Hamilton place. Name's Goldberg."

"We could always wait in the truck while you talk with them."

"That's not such a smart idea. Those people are his and her law-yers. I don't want them thinking we're a bunch of hicks." He relaxed as he built his story. "This could be a really big job for us. Really big. I warned these folks before they bought the house it was gonna cost them a bundle to fix, but they didn't care cause they had their heart set on living in an old place in the country. They haven't even mentioned money, so you know they're filthy rich. It could mean we finally go on that vacation to Florida you're always talking about. How about taking the boys to Disney World this winter? They'd love it."

"Florida. Really?" She smiled because he nodded. "Will you be home for dinner?"

"I don't think so. I don't wanna rush it. I gotta handle this just right." He paused. Disney World was the clincher. "Who knows what I'll find at the camp? Last year, I had to get rid of a rats nest."

She made a familiar sour face as she squeezed the tweezers. Her eyes were on the mirror.

"Yeah, yeah, go ahead without us. I'll take the boys to Vera's. Just try not to be too late."

Nice View

Walker climbed the wooden ladder he set against Harlan Doyle's house. He took the rungs easily until he was on top of the roof. Harlan followed slowly, using his arms to pull himself upward, but he stayed on the ladder.

"Yes, sir, you need a new roof alright." Walker stepped over the shingles, which broke easily beneath his boots. "Some of the boards seem soft. They could be rotted. If that's the case, they'll have to be replaced. It's not a big deal. It'd take my crew two days tops for the whole job."

Walker kicked at a shingle.

"How soon could you get it done?" Harlan asked.

"Next week, maybe. We could use a fill-in job right now." Walker crouched on the roof. "Nice view from up here."

Harlan pointed toward the west.

"Those the Berkshires?"

"That's them all right."

Walker turned toward Edie's house. He recognized his mother's car in her driveway. She held Amber's hand. Her head tipped forward as she smiled at the little girl. Walker frowned. He didn't remember his mother being so tender to him even after Gil died, and she should've been.

After they got the news about Gil, the whole family went to the apartment above the store where Edie lived. So many people were there, so much grief, and in the middle of it, Walker tried to help his mother down the stairs to her car, but she pulled her hands from him, squawking for him to leave her alone. She might as well have said, "I hate you. If I lost a son, it should've been you and not Gil." But Walker's draft number was high. He didn't have to go to Vietnam. She never said she was thankful for that, at least.

Walker kicked a shingle and watched it sail off Harlan Doyle's roof into the treetops. He grinned at the man's scarred face.

"Like I said, this shouldn't take more than two days. Let's get down, and I'll write you up an estimate."

Harlan lowered himself so slowly down the ladder Walker muttered, "Poor fuck," and he meant it.

Home Sweet Home

Walker took it slow over his camp's muddy driveway. The property was on a lake in the northwestern part of the state, an hour away, almost to New York.

"I helped my father build the cabin when I was a boy," he told Edie. "It used to be the only one for miles, but now a couple of new places go up every year. Newcomers. They build houses with those big-ass windows and docks for their speedboats. You know, second homes for rich people from out of state."

"It's real nice here, Walker," Edie said.

"My father gave up this camp a few years ago when he lost interest in it. Before that, the men in our family used to fish and hunt here a couple of times a year. We went for a week, living it up on steak, trout, and booze, tromping through the woods, sometimes getting a deer or a bird. It's all mine now."

Edie sat forward as she took in the view of lake.

"It feels so far from home," she said.

"That's why I like it."

Walker usually came with Dean, his best buddy and the foreman of his crew. The two of them talked over the old days and their family troubles. Walker hated his wife and loved Edie. Dean, broke from a divorce and deaf in one ear from Vietnam, lived in a singlewide trailer within walking distance of the Do on the west end of town. Dean had no intention, so he said, of ever getting married again.

"It used to be a lot quieter in the summer," Walker said. "But I know other places around here to fish. We could even go swimming if it's warm enough. What do ya think?"

"Okay, Walker, I brought my bathing suit like you asked."

"Nice, baby." He patted Edie's thigh. "I gotta warn you, it's pretty rough. No electricity. There's just an outhouse. Or you can go in the woods like I do. Nobody ever comes here. Nobody." He smiled at Edie. "There's a bar in Hartsville that serves food, so we could go there for dinner."

"You think we'd be all right?"

"Don't worry, baby. Nobody knows us here."

The cabin, its exterior covered by vertical boards, rose on cement posts above the dried leaves and pine needles of the forest's floor. A shed for his boat and hand tools was beside it. Firewood was stacked in high rows between the maples. Edie followed Walker around his land. Limbs were down from this winter's ice storms, but except for some broken planks on the deck and a busted hinge on a door, his place was in okay shape.

Walker unlocked the cabin and used his shoulder to shove open the swollen door. The camp was too still from being without people. Its tight walls kept the cold and must inside.

"Home sweet home," he joked.

The one-room cabin didn't have much: a galley kitchen with empty shelves and a hand pump in the sink, a two-burner camp stove, propane lanterns on the counter, and a built-in table. A ladder next to the woodstove lead to the attic, which had a few extra beds from when the place was full of hunters. A couch, a double bed, and bureau were behind the ladder. A stuffed pheasant, its tail feathers spread like a

65

fan, was perched on the wall above the bed.

Walker stood behind Edie and circled his arms around her. He kissed the back of her neck. She smelled nice. He touched her front, moving her toward the bed, until she and he fell on its quilt, kissing and pulling off each other's clothes. Sunlight coming through the small window near the bed shined on her body, and he kissed her belly and breasts. He whispered her name and then, "Baby."

Scared

Edie dressed as she walked around the cabin. She kneeled on the couch to study the dusty black-and-white photos of men holding dead game and strings of fish. Walker grinned from the edge of the bed, where he pulled on his cowboy boots.

Her face spun toward him.

"It's Gil and you," she said.

Walker stood beside her. Two smiling boys, wearing plaid jackets and furry hats flapped over their ears, posed with rifles.

"It's us alright. Dad used to bring me and Gil up here when we were kids."

"Look at you two. Just like Shane and Randy."

Edie studied the photo. Walker cleared his throat. He wanted her to look at him.

"What do ya think it would've been like if he lived?" he asked her.

"Well, for one, I wouldn't be here with you."

She smiled. But Walker felt his jaw freeze. His words came from the back of his throat.

"What are you saying?"

"I'm saying we would've been happily married. I wouldn't have been alone with Amber."

"You think so, huh?"

"Course, I do."

"Sure."

"Walker, this is silly."

He clasped her arm tightly and brought his face close to hers. Her smile went flat. Edie cried out, and when he let her go, she dropped the photograph to the floor.

"Yeah? You probably would've had a bunch of kids, got fat, and he'd be cheatin' on you."

Tears filled her eyes.

"Walker, stop it."

She tried to move away. He wouldn't let her.

"I should've had you first."

She was scared, he could tell, but she wasn't backing down. She jerked her head back.

"No, you wouldn't have cause I loved Gil more. I always will."

Walker saw darkness and light flash like a summer squall. His fingers pressed into Edie's upper arm as he rushed her across the room. Her shoes crushed the broken glass, and the hem of her dress flapped around her bare legs. He gripped harder. She cried when her hip smacked the corner of the bedpost as he threw her down on the mattress. She tried getting up, but he shoved her down again and kept her pinned. He slapped her arms and legs, her backside. Her fists hit against his chest. He held his hand high, but Edie covered her face and rolled to the other side of the bed. Sobbing, she stayed that way.

Walker balled his hands into fists as he charged outside to the dock. The lake that spread before him was as gray as his heart now felt. He took the air in short, sharp breaths. He kicked the part of the dock where the boards had fallen away. He should've known better than to ask something like that. Gil was a topic they rarely discussed. No one did, except for Dean, and he was allowed because he brought up stuff they used to do.

"Goddamn it, I really fucked things up back there," he said out loud.

Walker shuffled through dried leaves toward the open doorway. He didn't see Edie. He searched the cabin, saying her name, but she was gone. He went outside, calling again. She didn't answer.

He saw movement through a clearing between the trees. His eyes followed it. Edie ran up the road.

He shook his head.

"Walker, you're such an asshole," he told himself.

Edie didn't stop when he called her name. He flung open the door to his truck and got it started. He kept it in first up the driveway and on the gravel road. He didn't want to scare her any more than he already had, but she glanced back and ran harder.

Walker drove slowly alongside her. He reached over to crank down the window on the passenger side.

"Edie, Edie, please, stop, please. I'm so sorry."

"Go away, Walker."

"Aw, Edie."

She kept going. He pulled the truck to the edge of the road. He jogged to catch up with her.

"Edie, hey, wait up."

She stopped running and bent deeply at her waist. He moved toward her.

"Edie, forgive me, please, baby."

Her lips quivered when he stood in front of her. She took a step backward.

"Honey, it's breaking my heart seeing you like this," Walker said. "I know I deserve it for treating you that way. I don't know what got into me being jealous of Gil. It's stupid." He paused. "I just want the kind of love you had for him. Can you forgive me, Edie?"

Her head was down.

"Can you?" he repeated.

She still didn't speak.

"Come on, Edie, get in the truck. There's no way you can walk home from here."

"I'll go to the restaurant we passed back there, and I'll call Pop to come get me."

"The Lookout's at least six miles from here. Suppose you can't reach him? It's Saturday. He's probably out."

"I'll call Aunt Leona."

"You really want her driving all the way out here?"

Edie thought it over. He wanted to touch her, but he didn't dare.

"Okay," she whispered.

She was silent as they walked back to the truck. He opened the passenger's door.

"Here you go, darlin'."

Walker put his arm around her. She didn't resist. He held the door open until she sat inside. He got in the driver's seat.

"I gotta lock the place up first."

She nodded.

Walker backed the truck until he reached the driveway. He parked beside the cabin.

"Edie, listen to me. I'm really sorry. Believe me." He shook his head. "I was just being a jerk again. You know me by now. Hey, hey, there." His voice was soft and pleading. "Come on, baby. It's all right. That's my girl."

The Lookout

Walker chose a back booth at the Lookout Bar and Grille, the restaurant they passed on the way to his camp. It was a rustic place done in knotty pine, with deer heads hanging off the wall as if a tall herd was ready to dart across the room. A fieldstone fireplace, blackened by smoke, took up one wall. Picture windows overlooked the lake.

The waitress, the wife of the owner, came to their table. She grinned at Walker.

"Hey there, handsome, I haven't seen you in a while," she said. "Who's this pretty lady? You usually come here with a bunch of guys stinkin' of fish."

Walker chuckled.

"This is Edie," he said.

"You have a nice place here," Edie told her.

"Lucky guy," the waitress said, winking. "What'll it be for you two?"

They drank beer on tap as they waited for their order, local trout, he insisted, although next time he'd do the catching.

"I'm gonna make a list of supplies for when we come up here. Maybe you can help me. I'll have to do some work, but we can have some fun, too. I could take you out on the canoe. I bet you'd like that."

He sat back, studying Edie. She was here, but not really. Usually, he'd tell her a joke, and her eyes would get bright as if he were the funniest man in the world but not tonight.

Edie leaned forward. She held her hand over the side of her face.

"Buddy. Buddy Crocker's over there," she whispered.

"Shit," Walker said.

Edie bolted for the women's room.

Walker searched the room behind him. Buddy, Sharon's cop brother, a sergeant in the Conwell Police Department, was at the cash register, reaching into his back pocket for his wallet. Buddy's red hair looked as if it had been cut straight across his scalp with a brush hog. The man's cheese-white face didn't have a whisker. His spine was locked straight.

Walker squinted at the women's room door and lit a cigarette. He waited until Buddy grabbed his coffee and a brown paper bag before he called him over.

"Hey, Buddy, working tonight? You're a long ways from home."

Buddy came toward the booth.

"I'm fillin' in for somebody up here. They're shorthanded in this town." His head tipped forward. "I didn't expect to see you here. What's up?"

"Just opening up my camp at the lake," Walker said. "It took longer than I thought. Kind of a mess there."

"Lake? Sounds nice."

"You should go sometime. You and the family. Good fishing. Got a canoe. Just ask for the key."

Buddy eyed the tabletop, the extra beer.

"You with somebody?" he asked.

"A buddy of mine. His old lady tracked him down, and he had to get home. You know how it is." His boot heels scraped the floor. "Speaking of which, I should give Sharon a call and tell her I'm on my way. I didn't think it'd take this long."

Buddy nodded.

"Sure, sure," he said. "Catch you later."

Walker went to the payphone near the restrooms. Buddy was out the door, but Walker lingered. The cruiser's blue lights flashed through the restaurant's windows when it left the lot. He knocked on the women's room door.

"Edie, Edie, you can come out now," he whispered.

The door opened a crack.

"You sure?" Edie asked.

"Yeah, yeah, Buddy's gone. He didn't see a thing."

She slipped out. She bit her lower lip.

"Oh, Walker."

"It's okay. Our order will be here soon. We'll head on back after we're finished."

Walker smiled, but he didn't feel happy.

Finished

Walker killed the engine in front of Edie's house.

"How about I come in for a while?"

Edie reached for the door handle.

"I don't think so."

"Your little girl ain't here."

"Walker, I'm thinking none of this is a good idea. I mean us."

"Baby, I told you I'm sorry about today. I promise I won't do it again. Honey, I'll make it up to you."

Her chin was up.

"Walker, what the hell are we doing? You're married. You've got two boys. You got a business and a house. You're not gonna leave any of that for me. We won't ever be together. Never."

"Don't you worry about any of that. I'll work things out."

"What about your parents? What would they say about you and me? They're only nice to me cause of Gil and cause I have Amber. They'd blame me for breaking up your marriage. So would the whole town."

"Who cares about my parents or the town?"

"Who cares? I do. I dunno if we love each other enough for it to last all that. Let's be honest for a change."

"Honest?"

"That's right."

She had the truck's door open. He went to grab her arm but held back when he saw the expression on her face. She pushed the door shut and marched across the grass to her porch. Cats scattered quickly from her path. She didn't turn once.

"Come back, baby," Walker said.

He saw her through the kitchen window. The light was on. She stood in the middle of the room. Walker's chest rose and fell. She wasn't returning. He backed the truck slowly from the driveway. Its headlights stretched over the dirt road. The engine cycled. Walker waited to see if she changed her mind, but she didn't.

Another Load

Harlan Doyle motioned to the movers who carried his drafting table and a chair through the kitchen door.

"Same place where you put the tools," he told them.

The driver told Harlan he got lost trying to find Doyle Road until he backtracked to the general store, where a friendly woman gave the crew coffee on the house and drew him a map. Harlan figured the friendly woman was Edie.

The phone company said it would send someone out, maybe Wednesday, but he had no water yet. Getting the well's pump to work was going to cost him more than he figured. At least, everything he owned would be inside this house. He was making progress.

Harlan took the steps down from the porch. He got closer to the van, and after his eyes got used to the darkness in its box, he saw the movers were more than two-thirds done. The load mostly contained his tools and some lumber he couldn't part with, black walnut and English elm. The few pieces of furniture he owned, like the Mission-style bed he built, were unloaded already.

He heard the whirr of bike tires, and when he leaned toward the side of the truck, his neighbor's daughter was near the end of the drive. He remembered her name was Amber. He saw her playing in her front yard or at her great aunt's, and whenever he drove by, the girl watched his truck pass. The last time she gave him a timid wave.

He stumbled alongside the van until he was about four feet from the girl.

"Hello, I'm Harlan. Harlan Doyle. Your name's Amber, right?"

She slipped from the bike's seat, so both feet were planted on the ground. She fingered the plastic tassels hanging from the handle. Gold paint covered the bike's metal, even its spokes.

"Uh-huh, that's my name. Amber Lucille Marie St. Claire."

"Well, Amber Lucille Marie St. Claire, I don't believe I've ever seen a gold bike like yours before."

Her lips formed a tiny smile. Amused was the word that came to Harlan's mind. He recognized the same smile from her mother.

"Poppy painted it for me. He brought it home, you know, from the place he works."

"Your grandfather did a fine job on your bike."

She checked the fenders.

"Yeah, he did."

Amber stared. He knew she couldn't help it. Nobody could.

"I'm glad you stopped by," he told her.

"You have a lot of stuff."

Amber still checked him out. She didn't have so much of her mother's features he could say she looked like Edie, but the expressions were similar, and she had her blue eyes.

"Mostly tools though. I'll need them to fix up my grandmother's house. Do you want to see inside?"

"I can't. Aunt Leona's supposed to be watching me until my Grandma Marie comes to get me. I didn't have school today. The teachers are doing something. Aunt Leona told me I could ride my bike, but she wouldn't want me to go into a stranger's house."

"I guess I am a bit strange."

She giggled.

"That's not what I mean. I didn't tell her where I'm going. I don't want her to get mad at me. I better go."

"Okay, maybe I'll see you soon."

She squeaked out a "bye" before she pedaled the bike forward and made a half-circle back from where she came. Harlan limped toward the house. The movers were coming for another load.

Play Ball

Leona sat in the front seat of Edie's car, giving her niece pointers on their way to her first home game. Her aunt knew softball better than anyone else, and she might have made a smart coach, except she would have argued too much with the umps and made the players cry. Her aunt played when she was young until she ran off to marry her first husband. She always played infield, and her favorite was third base, Edie's position. Only someone with a strong arm and quick reflexes could play third, Leona often said, and in that regard, Edie was just like her aunt.

"You've gotta be more patient at the plate," Leona told Edie. "You need to watch the ball."

Edie had her eyes on the road, but she kept nodding and saying, "Yes, Aunt Leona," so the woman would be certain she was paying attention. An "uh-huh" or a "yup" wouldn't do for her aunt.

"I hear the pitcher on the Wilmot team is just a young thing, so give her a real mean face to rattle her," Leona said. "Like this."

Leona lowered her brow until her eyes were slits. She pressed her lips so tightly, they were like red blisters ready to burst. Edie started laughing.

"Aunt Leona, I can't do that." She glanced in the rear-view mirror at Amber. "You okay back there?"

Amber blinked.

"I'm fine, Ma."

Amber sat there quietly ever since Edie picked her up at Fred and Marie's house.

"You have fun at your grandparents?" Edie asked. "Did you get to eat lots of ice cream and go shopping as usual?"

Amber giggled.

"I did."

"What did Marie get you this time?" Edie asked.

"A bicycle. A two-wheeled bicycle. It's bright red. She let me pick it out."

Edie glanced sideways at Leona.

"You were going to get Amber a bike for her birthday," Leona mouthed.

Edie nodded.

"Really?" she asked her daughter. "How come we didn't bring it home?"

"Grandma says it's for me to use only when I visit her and Grandpa."

Leona twisted in her seat.

"Sounds like she's trying to buy you off, kid." She winked. "But you know your Ma and I love you the most."

Amber giggled and kicked her feet.

"What about Poppy?" she asked.

Leona snorted.

"Him, too."

Amber had been coming to these softball games since she was about eighteen months, plunked in a stroller behind the bench or on Edie's lap. She remembered holding Amber, her fat arms and legs flexing like pistons, her body rigid while she howled to eat. Birdie, their coach then, quipped, "Loud fans. Just what we need to rally this team."

Leona wore a white visor with Conwell Women embroidered in blue on the front so her red hair poked up like sparks over the top. Vera passed out the visors at practice yesterday. Edie snagged one for Leona, who snatched it eagerly from her hand.

"Makes me look like one of the team," her aunt had said as she stuck the visor on her head. "What do you say?"

"Like one of the team, Aunt Leona," Edie repeated.

The old woman's mouth formed a big, red smile.

Edie found a parking space close enough to the field, so Leona wouldn't have to walk too far. Amber carried a folded aluminum lawn chair while Edie held Leona's arm. Her aunt's bones were so twig-like and jumpy, it was like squeezing a cat.

Edie nodded to Amber.

"Why don't you bring Aunt Leona's chair to her favorite spot? You know where."

"Okay, Ma."

They neared the home bench. Vera lifted her eyes from a clipboard and frowned at Edie.

"You're almost late," she said. "I was gonna put somebody else in at third."

Leona grunted loudly.

"Eh, Vera, you can blame it on me," she said. "It takes longer for us old broads to get ready." She raised a wrinkled hand toward the field. "Is that your daughter over there? She's a big girl. I bet she's a hitter like her ma."

"Yeah, she is," Vera said. "She plays ball in high school."

It was slow going over the soft, uneven ground, but Edie got her aunt to her chair. Leona liked to sit to the right of the home bench, so she had a clear view of third base.

"This is just fine, honey." Smiling at Amber, Leona lowered herself onto the chair. "It's a nice night for softball."

"Sure is," Edie said. "Just enough of a breeze to keep the bugs away."

Edie trotted back to the car for her equipment bag and cleats. Most of the girls were already practicing, gabbing so loudly Vera stuck two fingers in her mouth to break them up with one sharp whistle. Edie tied the laces of her cleats with double knots and arranged the visor on her head. She found Birdie's daughter, Patsy, who still played centerfield with the team, and the two of them began throwing a ball in easy lobs to each other.

Edie loved the team's home field at the Conwell Rod and Gun Club, a nice combination of rusty, red soil for the diamond and crisp, green grass. The outfield bordered a cornfield, where at the start of the season, the stalks rose in nubs through the soil. The corn grew as the season progressed. At the end, tassels topped the ears, and they were close to picking.

Birdie used to come here during the afternoon on game days to tend to the ball field. He raked the diamond, and if it was dry, he wet it with a hose to keep the dust down. On the weekends, he loaded his mower onto the back of his pickup to cut the grass. Now the highway crew took care of the field.

"How's your dad?" Edie asked.

"He's hanging in there," Patsy said. "It really bothers him he can't coach this year. He doesn't even wanna come to the games."

"Oh" was all Edie could muster.

The team had lots of family even without Birdie. Vera played first, and her cousins, both divorced, were at shortstop and second, and the three women could execute the best double play in the league. Robin, who was in her thirties, had been catching for the pitcher, Gloria, for years. Gloria wouldn't have anyone else because Robin, her second cousin, held her mitt so steadily, her strikes dropped in its center like fat eggs on a skillet. Their leftfielder, who had bad timing to have a baby in the middle of the team's short season last year, was back. The new girls, including Vera's daughter, played the two other spots in the outfield. Birdie always tried to work everyone in each game. Not every woman could start, but they all played. Vera said at the team meeting a few weeks ago she would do the same.

Patsy grunted when Vera yelled for infield practice, and the players took their places, so she could hit to them. Edie was in perfect fielding position when Vera chopped one her way. It took a tough hop in front of third, but she played it off the bounce. Edie fired the ball across the diamond to Patsy, who was filling in at first, and savored the smart pop it made in the pocket of her glove.

"Nice snag, Edie," Leona shouted.

Leona took a small pad from her purse, so she could keep track of the score. Although one of the players on the bench kept the official book, her aunt said it helped her stay in the game. Besides, she didn't trust the old geezer who ran the scoreboard. Sometimes he got confused, so the score could say something like 57 to 33. That's when Leona would yell at him, and one of the players would have to go over to help him get it right.

Their fans showed up for the home opener between Conwell and the team from Wilmot. Typically, only one or two husbands came because most played in the men's league. Some boys who were friends with the high school girls were here, plus a slew of retired people and some relatives who sat in lawn chairs along the sidelines. Leona joked with the men who brought coolers for their beer. Her aunt bragged she always drank free on softball nights.

The top of the order for the Wilmot team went down one, two, three with pop-ups to the infield. The batters tended to hit that way when Gloria was in top form. Her pivot foot touched the rubber as her right arm swung back then forward before she released the ball in a perfect arc to home plate.

Now Gloria paced behind the sitting players, her black glove tucked beneath her arm. She nodded at Robin, who chewed on the loose rawhide of her catcher's mitt.

"How's he calling 'em tonight?" Gloria asked.

"About as good as he ever does," Vera answered for Robin.

Robin's mouth got rubbery and wide as she let out a horsey laugh. In all the years Edie knew the woman, she hadn't uttered one clever statement. She left that to her teammates.

"That bad, eh?" Gloria squinted at the stands. "Anybody know that guy watching our game? I've never seen him before."

Vera glanced over her shoulder.

"The one with the messed up face?" she asked. "Isn't that your new neighbor, Edie? He's come into the store."

Edie turned. Harlan Doyle sat alone in the stands. He grinned when she raised her glove.

"That's him all right. His name's Harlan Doyle. He's Elmira Doyle's grandson. He's fixing up her house," she said. "Nice guy."

"What the hell happened to him?" Vera asked.

"He said he was in an accident."

Edie paid attention to the game. The pitcher from Wilmot was having a control problem. The Conwell Women's shortstop, frustrated by the lack of opportunities, swung at a cheap one, hitting a fly to the leftfielder. Her teammates groaned.

The team's new baby was asleep in her carriage safely behind the bench. Only Robin didn't have kids, and Gloria's were grown. For the most part, the kids got along. But sometimes a couple of the boys fought, or a kid got hurt, or a crying baby wanted to be held. Those sitting on the bench took care of things while their moms were on the field. Edie always gave the players' kids free penny candy whenever they came into the store. She glanced toward the playground, where Amber hung around some of the younger kids. Later, she would sit on the Conwell home bench.

Patsy was up, so Edie rose, slapping her hand against Gloria's as she took her place in the on-deck circle. She stood with her legs apart, her bat resting on her shoulder. Patsy was tight at the plate, but she managed to get a hold of one, so she had an easy run to first.

Aunt Leona clapped.

"Come on, Edie, it's more fun with two," she yelled.

On the first pitch, Edie hit the ball way beyond the reach of the leftfielder, a home run in this park.

Conwell clobbered the team from Wilmot, typically the league's doormat, so Vera put the new girls in early. On the last out, the Conwell Women jogged off the field, slapping gloves and shrieking.

"Meet you all at the Do," Vera told her teammates.

"What for?" Robin asked.

"Jesus, we're gonna take Gloria out for her birthday," Vera said.

"Gee, I forgot."

"That's why I'm telling you all."

Edie went for the bag she stowed behind the bench and went to Leona. Amber waited with her. She smiled for her daughter.

"You won," Amber said.

"Yeah, we did."

Leona clasped the arms of her chair as she pulled herself up.

"I don't think Wilmot produces too many able-bodied women," she said. "Their pitcher's arm was so skinny, it was a miracle she could throw."

"She fooled us some of the time," Edie said.

"What about the umpire? What kind of man dyes his hair black like that? I bet it wipes off on his pillow. His wife better be careful, or she'll get some on her face."

"Aunt Leona, how much beer did you drink tonight?" Edie asked.

Leona waved her away.

"I lost count after the fourth inning," she said.

Leona's voice was hoarse from yelling. She booed one of the ump's calls so loudly he muttered and glared. At that point, Vera asked Edie to tell her aunt to pipe down. But Edie reminded her it wouldn't make a difference if she did. Her aunt wouldn't listen. She was having too much fun.

"Vera's gotten as fat as a pig. She should go on a diet," her aunt went on. "She can't even bend over to pick up a grounder." She paused to take a breath. "I see our new neighbor came to the game. Harlan Doyle. Nice name, don't you think?"

"He said you went by to meet him."

"I did." Leona nodded. "Too bad about his face. Something or someone hurt him, but you get used to it." She frowned. "And, no, I didn't ask him how it happened. That's what's Alban would do."

"Funny, Pop said the same thing about you."

"The smelly bastard."

Leona clamped her mouth shut. Edie almost laughed, but she held back because it would provoke her aunt into a long discussion about Pop, mostly about his no-good qualities. He still hadn't cut the grass. The weed trimmer from the highway garage lay on the porch. But Edie was tired of nagging her father.

"Shh, there he is," Edie said. "I'll be right back."

Edie leaned her gear against the car and walked toward Harlan. He grinned when he saw her. Aunt Leona was right. You do get used to his face.

"Howdy, neighbor," she greeted him.

Harlan hobbled as he picked up speed.

"You're a really good player," he said.

She smiled.

"I learned everything from my aunt. Besides, it wasn't a strong team."

Harlan shrugged.

"I enjoyed myself."

"Are you still sleeping in your tent?"

"No, I'm inside now. I only live in two rooms, but it's coming along. You'll have to stop by to see what I've done."

His head dipped forward. The skin on his neck reddened.

"I'll do that." She saw over her shoulder that Aunt Leona and Amber waited beside her car. "Sorry, I gotta go."

Edie loaded the gear and her aunt's chair into the trunk. She started the car. Leona chuckled.

"What?" Edie asked her.

"I think he's kind of taken with you," Leona said.

Edie's eyes were on the rearview mirror as she backed the car from its spot.

"Who?"

"The new neighbor," she said.

"Aw, come on."

Her aunt slapped her arm.

"Course, he is. I can tell. I saw his face when he talked with you."

"I just got the feeling he thinks he says too much," Edie said. "But he really didn't."

Leona snickered.

"See?"

She put the car in forward.

"If you say so, Aunt Leona."

Girl Talk

Edie walked into the Do-Si-Do Bar. The team was there to celebrate Gloria's birthday although at first she wouldn't go along. The rule was women only, and only those old enough to drink, so that left out the teenagers. The team invited her aunt, but she begged off. She had her fill of beer tonight. Amber could stay with her. Edie should go and have fun for the both of them. She went home first to change out of her sweaty uniform. Most did the same.

· "I don't like making such a big deal about my birthday," Gloria complained.

"Maybe we do," Vera said.

"Shoot, it's my birthday, and I can do what I want."

"Fat chance on that," one of Vera's cousins said.

They were having pizza and beer, and Patsy paid for the first round, which she said was on Birdie. Edie got the second, and by then everybody was loosened up, talking it up about family and the team.

"Did you see their shortstop split her pants in the third inning?" one of Vera's cousins, the starting second baseman, said in her squeaky voice. "Her butt was so huge, it looked like a crescent moon whenever she bent over. Somebody on her team should've told her."

Robin giggled so hard she sprayed Coke through her nose and mouth. Gloria patted her back while Edie used napkins to clean up the mess.

"At least it wasn't a full moon," Vera said, which made everyone laugh harder.

Edie gazed across the crowded room. Walker drank with his crew at a table, and a few times he and she exchanged looks. A band wouldn't start until nine, so people kept feeding the juke. Then it would get quiet for a while until someone, who couldn't stand being in a bar without music, got it going again. A couple of times, Walker stood over the jukebox, punching in numbers for all the songs he knew she liked.

Patsy raised her bottle in a toast to Gloria, and everyone went along, which made the woman go all smiles. She stretched over the table to give her friends high-fives. They were definitely the noisiest in the joint. Once in a while, a man stopped at the table, but Vera would tell him to take a hike. This party was strictly for girl talk. Walker stayed clear although he gave Edie a wink when she passed toward the women's room.

Gloria pointed her bottle at Robin.

"I like your new hairdo," she said. "Short and spiky. You look like one of those rock stars."

"Go on," Robin gushed.

Gloria waved at Robin.

"Stand up, so everybody can see," she said.

Robin waved her off.

"Shit, Robin, why don't you have a boyfriend?" Vera asked. "You'd make a great catch for some guy."

"Yeah, but it's gotta be the right guy," Patsy said.

Edie scanned the barroom. The place was crowded with so many longhaired guys in jeans and t-shirts, it looked like men's night at the

Do-Si-Do.

"There's gotta be a decent man in here somewhere," Vera said.

"Robin, what do you want in a guy?" Patsy asked.

"Want?" Robin answered.

"For starters, he has to have all the standard equipment," Vera said.

"You mean he can drive stick?" Robin asked.

Vera slapped the table so hard the beer bottles clattered.

"A dick." Vera raised one finger then two. "Can drive stick on a pickup." She searched the room. "Shit, it could be anyone in here. Like him."

The girls laughed when Vera pointed at the old coot playing with his false teeth at the end of the bar.

"Real teeth definitely would be a plus," Edie said, deciding to go along with the fun.

"A plus. I like that," Patsy said. "What else?"

Robin grinned.

"He's gotta have a job," she said.

Vera swept her hand toward the men sitting on the stools at the bar.

"Hell, that cuts out about twenty percent of the room. We're gettin' somewhere."

Everyone on the team was into it now. They shouted suggestions then hooted loudly at Robin's reactions and Vera's comments.

"How about someone who doesn't run around with other women?" Vera's cousin, the second baseman, said because her two-timing husband dumped her last year.

"Yup," Vera said.

"He doesn't fart or burp on purpose in front of you," Vera's other cousin said. "And if he does by accident, he says, 'Excuse me'."

"Shit, that's another," Vera said.

As Edie listened, she realized her teammates were talking about the men they knew and not a special guy for Robin.

"He should remember her birthday and not ask her what she wants for a gift," Patsy said.

The women howled.

Walker strutted across the room to their table.

"I believe you gals are having the best time in the Do tonight. Mind if I join the team?"

Vera gave him an eye.

"Get lost, Walker. This is for women only."

"What the hell."

Vera jerked a thumb.

"You heard me. Beat it."

Patsy bent forward over the beer bottles.

"Since when did you become a fan of the team?" she asked Walker.

"It's got women, don't it?" the second baseman said.

The other women roared at Walker's expense. He glanced at Edie, but she wasn't about to come to his defense.

"I guess I know where I'm not wanted," he said.

"You got that right, Walker St. Claire," Vera said. "Now git."

Noticed These Things

Harlan sat at the bar of the Do-Si-Do, watching the action. The band was back after a break, the guys strapping on their guitars and setting fresh beers on the stage floor. The lead singer lit a cigarette before they played the opening chords of something Southern. Harlan arrived as the women from Edie's softball team were leaving, and Edie introduced him to several of her teammates before he escaped to a stool. He grinned when Edie came from the payphone to the bar.

"All right, I can stay longer," she said to the bartender, and then she smiled at Harlan. "Howdy, neighbor."

"I met your daughter today," Harlan said. "She hung around for a few minutes."

"I heard. Amber's on the shy side until she gets to know you. She takes after the St. Claires. I've never known a Sweet to give up the end of a conversation. She did say you had nice things. Lots of tools."

"Yeah, I do."

Edie's head jiggled to the song's beat.

"The band's pretty good, don't you think?" she said.

"I'd say so."

"Do you dance?"

"I used to before the accident. Maybe I could if it was a slow song."

Edie came closer.

"We should try it sometime," she said in a low voice, and he felt heat rise from his neck to his cheeks.

A new song started, and a tall man with a heavy beard asked Edie to dance. She raised her eyes at Harlan, but she told the man yes, and after a quick swig of beer, she left. Harlan followed her around the floor, and when the song was over, she danced with another man who asked.

Walker took the stool next to his.

"Put two beers on my tab, one for my friend here," he told the bartender, and then he turned toward Harlan. "We'll be at your house early Monday if that's all right with you," he said, all business, but then his tight face softened when Edie reached between them for her bottle.

Walker grinned.

"Hope that guy didn't break any toes."

"It wasn't so bad."

"You were lucky."

Walker didn't take his gaze off Edie. His voice took on a warm, teasing tone. He whispered in Edie's ear, but she shook her head and said, "No." He asked if they could go outside, and again she said no. Harlan noticed these things. Edie went across the room, sitting with a group at a table until she danced with yet another man. Walker pressed his lips, and then he slapped his hand on the bar top.

"I need to head out early. I gotta see about a job tomorrow morning. Some folks from New York want to fix up an old house they bought. His and her lawyers. It's more house than two people need, but I won't refuse 'em." He downed the rest of his beer. His head bobbed toward Edie. "Something else, ain't she?"

"Yes, she is," Harlan said.

It was close to last call when Edie was back at the bar. Her arm brushed Harlan's when she asked the bartender for another beer.

"Put it on my tab, will ya, Mike?" she said. "I'll settle with ya later."

"Having fun?" Harlan asked.

She leaned against Harlan as she drank. Enough buttons on her blouse had come undone, so he saw the lacy edge of her red bra.

"It's okay, but I'm not going home with any of them." Her words moved like ball bearings over a wooden floor. She pointed to a dark-haired man. "He sure wants me to." She pointed to two others. "Them, too, but I'm not interested." She laughed hard, nearly tipping off her stool, but Harlan caught her arm to save her. "Thanks." Her voice was breathy.

"Let me give you a ride home."

She patted his shoulder.

"No, I'm fine. I've driven home a lot drunker than this. Besides, it's not that far."

Edie was off her stool, walking unsteadily toward the door. Harlan hobbled after her, but by time he stepped outside, her car was gone. He got in his truck and followed the sway of her car's rear lights up the road. He drove slowly, so as not to panic her, but she sped up. When he turned onto Doyle Road, he found her car hung up on a stonewall at the first curve. He moved so quickly from his truck, he hopped.

Edie opened the car door, laughing and taking his hand as if this was a planned part of her night out. He reached past her to turn off the engine.

"It's you again. Hello, neighbor."

She kept laughing as he used the strength of his arms and his good leg to hoist her into the cab of his pickup.

"That curve sure snuck up on me," she said. "But Pop can get my car out. He can borrow chains and a truck from the highway garage.

He can leave 'em in the front yard with the weed trimmer and the mower. Might as well have everything from the highway garage at our house. We already got the dump out back."

Her laughter was loud and high. Harlan laughed with her as he parked the truck in her driveway. The headlights swept across the back porch, where cats' eyes shined green and glassy.

Edie patted his arm.

"So, Harlan, what do you think of our little town? We haven't scared you away to wherever you came from, have we?"

"I'm from Florida, then Washington State. And, no, I haven't been scared away."

He shook his head. She was smashed.

"Glad to hear it. Pop and Leona say you're okay, so that's a good sign. I liked your grandmother. Know what she used to do? She'd get three cords of firewood dropped off in her driveway in the spring. Every time she went in, she carried one or two logs into the shed off the kitchen."

"What shed?"

"That's long gone. It caved in one winter. Your uncle paid Pop to clear it away. The pieces are in our back yard with everything else." She made a high-pitched laugh. "If somebody came to see your grandma, she yelled out the window to bring in some wood. When fall came, all of it was inside." Edie giggled. "How old was she when she died?"

"Ninety-three."

"Ninety-three." She twirled a finger. "And sharp till the end."

The porch light came on, and a bare-chested Benny Sweet walked outside. He hitched his pants and squinted at Harlan's truck. His work boots were untied.

Benny poked his head inside the truck.

"What's the matter with her?"

"I believe she drank a little too much." Harlan hooked his thumb toward the road's entrance. "Her car's stuck on a stonewall back there."

Edie stared at him, and then her father.

"Not again," Benny said. "You all right?"

"I'm fine." Her mouth spread into a teasing grin. "Pop, where were you tonight? You missed a good time at the Do. All the ladies were asking about you."

"Which ones?"

"All of 'em."

Benny laughed through his nose. Harlan laughed with him.

"Yeah, well, there's always next time," her father said.

Benny opened the truck door. Edie smiled at Harlan as she slid to the ground. Benny's arm coiled around his daughter. He took her purse from Harlan.

"Honey, let me get you inside. The skeeters are kinda bad."

"Sure, Pop. You finally cut the grass, and you did a really nice job this time." Her voice moved up and down as if it was set to music. "I can't believe it."

"Watch your step," her father said, and without looking back, he gave Harlan a large, friendly wave of his hand.

True

Pop crouched next to Edie's car. She watched him take different angles on its undercarriage and the stonewall.

"I feel stupid missing that curve, Pop. Is my car gonna be okay? I gotta do my delivery route this morning."

Pop stood and wiped the dirt from his hands on the back of his pants.

"Yeah, yeah, I'll get you out. You were damn lucky, honey. Nothin' looks broken underneath. I think I can drive it back down the way you got it up there. Now move outta the way."

Pop yelled about a lot of things and people, but not about anything she or Amber ever did. The rest of the world, including his resentful older daughters, was the source of his problems, not those he loved best. He cranked the engine, and using the mirrors, he inched the car backwards. Edie gave him a cheer when the four wheels were on the ground. He grinned at her when he got out, and then he circled the car, inspecting its condition. He whistled a short, busy tune over and over.

"Just a couple of scratches," he said. "Be more careful next time.

Get a ride, will ya? Or I'll come get you. You should've let Harlan do it."

She winced.

"That was sure embarrassing, me acting like a loud drunk from a bar in front of him. What must he be thinking?"

"Aw, honey, we all act foolish once in a while." He chuckled. "Even your old man."

Edie kissed her father's cheek.

"Thanks, Pop. What would I do without you?"

"I keep askin' myself that. When your Ma died, I was a broken man. Maybe if I'd been younger, I'd a found another wife, someone to help me raise you."

"Oh, Pop."

"Don't 'oh, Pop' me. You need to get yourself a man, Edie. I ain't gonna be around forever."

"You sound like Aunt Leona."

"Yeah, well, she's gettin' on like me. We wanna go in peace," he said. "See ya later. I gotta open the dump."

"Thanks again."

Pop sucked at his teeth, and then he walked to his truck in a bowlegged gait Edie could pick out of a crowd.

Edie drove to Leona's. She took her hands from the wheel to see if there was any pull in the steering, but thankfully the car drove straight. She parked in her aunt's driveway, but Amber was already out the door. After they were done delivering groceries, Edie was taking her to the fair at the Conwell Congregational Church.

Amber clutched a five-dollar bill.

"Look what Aunt Leona gave me," she gushed as she got in the front seat.

"Does she wanna come?" Edie asked.

"No. She said lightning would hit her if she went near the church." Edie honked the horn as she backed the car into the road.

"It just might."

"What did she mean?"

"Aunt Leona likes to pretend she's a wicked person. But we know different, right kiddo?"

Amber waved the bill.

"Uh-huh. She gave me this to spend."

Hours later, Edie walked with Amber among the tables of crocheted and sewn stuff the church's old ladies made to sell. A bored teenaged boy led a pony along a line of maple trees.

"You wanna go on the pony ride?" Edie asked her daughter, but Amber wrinkled her nose. "No? Maybe you'll change your mind later."

People said hello. Most she saw every day at the store. It was one of the nice things about living in such a small town: just about everybody was good for five minutes of conversation, but if she wanted more, many were happy to oblige.

They stopped at the cakewalk game. Wooden squares were placed in a circle on the grass for the players. It was like walking on flat stones in a river. Before each round, one of the church ladies in charge made everyone turn around and shut their eyes while she placed a silver dollar beneath a square. She started the record player again, and when the music stopped, whoever was standing on the lucky square got their choice of the homemade cakes on display.

Winning a cake at the fair was a Sweet family tradition. For years, Pop came before he opened the dump to try his luck at the cakewalk, begging the old ladies to start the game early for him. Sometimes he won on the first or second tries, so he chose the largest cake and went happily to work. He ate most of it in his attendant's shack, carving off chunks with his jackknife.

When the game didn't go his way and Pop was hung over, he wouldn't give up so easily. He cursed the winners and yelled when they took the cakes he wanted. By time he succeeded, vehicles had formed a long line outside the dump's gate and people complained. One time, the Conwell Board of Selectmen called Pop into their meeting to reprimand him. Edie went with him. Pop gave his version of the story, acting like a country lawyer in his defense. After he was done, one of the selectman quipped, "All that for cake? Benny, next time I'll bake you one myself."

The problem was solved the following year when the minister banned Pop after he shoved a boy to the ground. Pop said it was an accident. He lost his balance. But Edie got him to admit it wasn't true. The little cheater was peeking, Pop knew, because he was peeking, too.

Edie and Amber studied the players as they stepped deliberately from one square to another. They stopped when the old lady picked the needle from the record. A teenaged girl gave a gleeful shout when she saw she won.

Edie reached into her purse and handed Amber a couple of bills.

"Go win a big one for Poppy," she said, and Amber smiled at the happy thought.

Bob

Edie heard shouting from inside the house, and when she checked the kitchen window, the road boss and Pop were going at it near the highway department's idling pickup. The man's face was red and his fingers punched the air in front of her father. Pop, just home from the dump, had been hauling his booty into his shacks out back. Amber, she was relieved to remember, took off on her bike to Leona's.

Edie stepped onto the porch, but the men didn't notice her until she was beside them. Pop, his overalls caked with dirt, smelled sour and rusty like the inside of a garbage can.

"I told your old man to keep his hands off the highway equipment." Spit flew from the road boss' mouth. "Who in the hell does he think he is?"

"Leave Edie outta this," Pop growled.

Edie didn't like the look on the road boss' face. She had seen enough bar fights, and her father, although a scrapper, was no match for a man his size or age.

"Take it easy," she said. "Pop took care of the trimmer. He didn't mean any harm."

"That's not the point," the road boss said. "It don't belong to him. All of this is town property."

"I'm a taxpayer and a town employee, ain't I?" Pop said.

Edie cringed.

"It don't give you the right, you stupid little fuck," the road boss said. "Stick to the dump where you belong. I don't go taking your crap."

The road boss' belly jiggled beneath his chambray work shirt as he stepped onto the porch to get the trimmer. He cursed loudly when he noticed a gas can and tools belonging to the Conwell Highway Department. Pop cussed back while the man loaded the stuff into the back of the pickup. Her father trailed him, making certain he didn't take anything of his, and in his agitation, he tripped. The road boss sniggered as Pop fell to the ground.

"You fucker," Pop growled.

Edie bent over her father. Pop was too angry to take her hand although he managed to scramble to his feet when the pickup's tires spun away. Pop jogged after the truck, and Edie relaxed. She knew he'd only run a few yards before he'd be out of breath. This episode would be over until Pop was brazen enough to borrow something else from the highway garage. The board of selectmen would never fire Pop because no one else wanted his job. Besides, he was popular with the townspeople, especially the newcomers who thought he was a colorful and helpful character.

Edie waited for Pop to give up when she heard the squeal of locking brakes, the stutter of tires over the road's hard ridges, and a thud as metal hit something soft and large. The loud, pained howl of an animal followed.

She ran past Pop to the road where Leona's dog, Bob, lay near the wheel of the highway department pickup. The poor animal thrashed and moaned on the dirt. The road boss got out of the truck, and Pop hurried.

"You stupid fuck, you ran over my sister's dog," he yelled.

"What in the hell was it doing in the middle of the road?" the man yelled back.

"Hell, if you graded it, you would've been able to stop in time."

The dog was going to die, suffering to the end if nothing was done. The two men were too locked in a rage to care, so Edie ran to the house. Pop's twenty-two was where he normally stowed it, in back of his bedroom closet, and she checked to see if it was loaded.

When Edie returned, the highway department pickup and Pop's truck were gone. The dust they made lingered over the road. She didn't have time to be angry because the dog panted and made sharp, sad cries. His eyes circled in pain.

She aimed the twenty-two at the dog's head. Tears came to her eyes. She held a deep breath.

"Edie, let me do it."

Startled by the voice, she almost pulled the trigger. She didn't hear Harlan arrive, and she was grateful when his hands took the rifle. He held it steadily, firing one shot close-range at the dog, whose body jumped as if it were charged, and then it did nothing more. His head had one red hole.

"It looked as if you couldn't do it," Harlan told her.

"I would've if I had to. Poor Bob."

Edie knelt before the dog and touched his fur. His body didn't resist when she stroked it. Edie's eyes swept toward the side of the road, where she saw Harlan's idling truck. She squinted at the man.

"How bad is that leg of yours?" she asked.

"My leg?"

"Think you can help me move him?" She fingered the dog's smooth ear. "There's a soft place out back where we could bury him. I don't want Amber to see him, and I don't know when Pop will be back. Do you mind helping me?"

"Of course, not. Why don't you take this rifle back? I'll shut the truck's engine."

They rolled the dog onto an old cotton spread Edie got from the house and dragged him slowly over the road then the uneven grass. Edie kept checking Harlan to see how he handled the work. She stopped once, but he waved her on.

"How much farther?" he asked.

"We're almost there."

Harlan waited while she got two shovels from one of the shacks. A gray cat sat in the sunlight, blinking at them.

"We have to dig a hole at least three feet down. I don't want coyotes getting to Bob."

"Okay."

She pushed the shovel's point into the ground.

"My mother had a garden here years ago." She threw a shovelful of grass and dirt to the side. "Pop and I tried one ourselves, but the weeds took over. We might've gotten a couple of tomatoes out of it. Pop's not much of a farmer. I guess neither am I. Ever have a garden?"

"No, but I might want to make one here."

Harlan grimaced.

"Is this digging too hard for you?" she asked. "I can take care of this myself if it is."

"I can manage all right, Edie."

"Sorry, I just don't know you well enough."

Her eyes bounced up, checking for Amber.

"Where'd your father go?" Harlan asked.

She pressed the shovel's point into the dirt.

"My guess is he and the road boss are either killing each other at the highway garage, or they patched things up and are having a drink at the Do."

"Really?"

"Yeah, really." She kept her head down, watching where she dug. "I don't usually get so drunk by the way. I'm talking about last night."

"You should've let me give you a ride home."

Edie bent to throw a large stone to the side. She stood straight and wiped the dirt from her hands.

"You and me leave together? That would've got everybody talking." She smiled when Harlan's face reddened. "I didn't mean anything by that. My car's okay, I'm okay, so everything ended up okay. Too bad about Aunt Leona's dog though."

"If there's a next time, ask."

When the hole was deep enough, she took the spread's corners and tied Bob inside. Harlan helped her push the dog's body and cover it with dirt. Edie stood over the spot when they were done.

"Bob was a good, old dog," she said finally. "We're gonna miss him."

Harlan's eyes were kind on Edie.

"What are you going to say?"

She tipped her head.

"That he got hit by the road boss' truck but died right away. I believe a lie would be nicer, don't you?"

Harlan made a humming sound through his nose.

"You're probably right."

Her lips set into a smile.

"This will be our secret, okay?"

"What about your father and the man?"

"I'll handle those two," she said firmly before she smiled again. "Tell me, Harlan. Do you always do this sort of thing? Be in the right place at the right time to do the right thing?"

"Truth is hardly ever."

"Is your leg bothering you? I saw you rubbing it. Come sit down for a while. We'll kick the cats off the porch, and I'll get you a drink. Is cold water, okay?"

"Sounds good to me."

Minutes later, the door hinges creaked, and Edie came out with two large glasses of water and a plate of brownies. She handed a glass to Harlan, who sat on a rocker, moving it slowly.

"It's all we have in the house, but we got some brownies from the church fair. With real walnuts," she said before she set the plate on a table between the two rockers.

Harlan took a long drink.

"That's good-tasting water," he said.

"There's more where it came from. I let the tap run." Edie watched him grin as he reached for a brownie. "Did Pop tell you about my Gil? Yeah? He's the one who gave Bob to Aunt Leona. He was only a puppy, just a teeny, yellow thing. My aunt was feeling blue, and Gil thought the dog would be good company. He was right. You should've heard Aunt Leona when he put Bob in her lap. She squealed like a little girl." She paused. "My aunt made fun of the dog, but it's just her way. She's gonna miss him a lot. I will, too, probably cause of Gil."

"Your father said Gil was a great guy."

"He was."

"I'm sorry he died in Vietnam."

"Me, too." Edie's eyes studied him over the glass. "Harlan, why'd you come here?"

"I was supposed to meet your father. He has a washing machine he wants to sell me."

Her right cheek dimpled.

"Oh, that. I mean why'd you move here?" She took another drink. "There're two kinds of people living in Conwell, and I don't mean the summer people. I'm talking about folks like me who were born here and don't leave cause they don't want to or they don't know how. Then there are those who move here cause they expect things will be better. What's your story?"

She kicked off her sneakers and pulled up her legs, so her feet rested on the rocker's rung. She tipped the chair in a steady back and forth.

"Better. That would be nice." He paused. "If you really want to know, my wife left me, and things got worse after that."

"Before or after your accident?"

"Before."

"You wanna tell me about it?"

Edie's rocker tilted back and forth.

"I was in Mexico," he began.

"What were you doing there?"

"It was the end of a terrible year between my wife, Susan, and me."

"Your wife?"

"Ex-wife. She stopped being in love with me. We were married eight years." He shrugged. "Let's just say I didn't take it well."

"Really? In what way?"

"I got pretty desperate. I did things. I got drunk a lot. Did drugs. I kept bothering her. I'm not proud of that." He paused. "I decided to leave it all behind. I shut my shop and drove as far south as I could in Mexico. I learned enough Spanish to get around. I eventually got used to the idea my wife didn't love me, but I'd be okay. I had my accident on the way back."

"How'd it happen?"

"All I remember was walking across the street late at night. I didn't see the truck coming, but it hit me when it was going fast. The doctors said it was a miracle I survived. Maybe so, but I do wish they fixed me better."

"I'm sorry."

He took a drink of water.

"Me, too. Susan came to see me in Mexico. She helped bring me back to Seattle, where we used to live. She stayed with me a short while to help me recover." He touched the longest scar on his face. "I made a mistake. I thought she was in love with me still. One night I kissed her, but she shrank away. She told me she loved another man. She was having his baby." His finger rubbed the scar. "After I asked her to leave, my parents came to visit. I didn't tell them how bad off I was from the accident. My mother cried when she saw me." He

107

dropped his hand. "I eventually went back to work. I stayed clear of my friends who were hers, too. I heard she got married and had a boy. Anyways, my parents told me about my grandmother's house. They said I could have it if I wanted. They thought it might help me get over all of this. You know, a fresh start and all that."

Edie stopped rocking. Her bare feet were flat on the floorboards.

"So, how are you now?" she asked.

He raised the glass.

"Much better. Thank you for asking."

A Matter Of Time

Edie helped Amber carry her bike onto the porch. Harlan went home minutes before.

"Aunt Leona wants me to ask if you've seen Bob," she said. "I can't find him anywhere."

Edie took her hand.

"Sweetie, I've got something to tell you. Shoot, there's no easy way to say this, and you're old enough. Bob got run over, and he died. It was an accident. The man from the highway department didn't mean to, but Bob was in the middle of the road, and he didn't see him."

"Bob!" Her daughter burst into tears. "Bob died?"

"Uh-huh. It was a highway truck, and Poppy was here," she said, picking what was useful from the story. "Our neighbor, Harlan, came by just in time to help me bury him."

"Where is he?"

"In the back yard. I'll show you."

They went to the spot, and Amber, weeping, squatted to run her fingers over the freshly broken soil. Bob was playful with Amber when he was younger, and in his last years, a steady companion who didn't ask too much.

Edie crouched beside her.

"We'll miss the old guy, won't we?" she said, feeling teary. "It was Daddy who gave him to Aunt Leona. He was still in high school. Daddy and I just started seeing each other. Shoot, now we have to go tell her."

They walked to Aunt Leona's, swapping stories about Bob, like how he used to sleep on the couch on Pop's side of the porch. He chased rabbits, hated cats, and no food unguarded was safe from him.

Leona napped in an easy chair, but she snorted awake when Edie said her name.

"You two," she said gruffly. "Who died? Was it Alban?"

"No, it wasn't Pop," Edie said. "But I do have sad news, Aunt Leona. It's Bob who died. He got hit by a truck."

Her aunt frowned.

"Bob? My Bob died? That's too bad. I'll miss that old mutt." She reached for a tissue in a box on the end table. "Don't mind me."

"It's okay. Amber and I feel awful about it," Edie said.

Amber sat beside Leona. Her small hand patted her great-aunt's shoulder. Leona smiled at the girl, and then she eyed Edie.

"Be straight with me. Tell me exactly what happened to my Bob," she said. "Was it Alban?"

"No, no, it wasn't Pop. The road boss hit him. It was an accident. Bob died right away. At least, he didn't suffer."

"Thank goodness for that at least. I guess it's the way to go," Leona said. "I hope I don't see it coming either."

"Stop talking like that, you and Pop."

Leona waved her away.

"Maybe it's a blessing. It was only a matter of time when I would've had to put him down. His back legs were going." She smiled at Amber. "Bob had a fine life with us. Right, honey?"

"Yes, Auntie."

Leona squinted at Edie.

"You can tell that fathead road boss, I want an apology from him. And I'd better see the highway department grader and a truckload of gravel here first thing Monday."

Edie took the seat beside Amber. Her daughter's cheeks were flushed. She touched her tongue to her forehead.

"Feel her. She's burning up," she told Leona.

Her aunt placed her bony hand on the girl's face.

"Definitely a fever. Let me see your tongue," she ordered Amber. "You're sick all right. Edie take this girl home right now and put her to bed."

Certain

The bartender gave Walker another beer and a shot as he sat at
the end of the bar at the Do-Si-Do. It was ten-thirty and Edie still
wasn't here. He'd been looking forward to tonight. He thought about
it while he watched his boys play ball and when he went about his
Saturday chores, which included a trip to the dump, where Benny
Sweet took some windows he was throwing out. He half-listened
to the useless, old man. The only worthwhile thing he ever did was
father Edie.

Although the Do-Si-Do was close to home, it was crowded and
casual enough he and Edie could talk. They might even dance a fast
one. Nobody cared. She was his widowed sister-in-law. Afterward,
they left separately and met back at her place if her little girl wasn't
there. No one knew about them, except Dean, his best buddy and
foreman, who sometimes covered for him, and maybe Edie's busy-
body aunt. If Benny Sweet suspected, he didn't let on, but the man
was pretty sharp-eyed.

Sharon wanted him to go to a cookout at her younger sister's house
tonight. He lasted a couple of hours, nursing some rotgut whiskey

his brother-in-law bought before leaving, but not without some angry words with his wife. Even if he wanted to be with Sharon, he didn't have any use for his brother-in-law, a man who kept hinting he wanted a job. The man couldn't even cut a board straight for Christ's sake. His sister-in-law wasn't any better, as fat as his wife and their other sister, Vera, and just as bossy. The three of them could run the town. His in-laws had four kids, and the only one he liked was the youngest, a girl with a purple birthmark that spread over half her face.

"I wish you paid as much attention to me and your family as you do that damn bar," Sharon said tonight as they argued inside his in-laws' carport.

He was certain their argument became a topic of conversation after he left, which suited him just fine. Good thing he thought ahead of time to go in separate vehicles.

The band was on a break, so people milled about the Do, holding lit cigarettes and longnecks. He searched the crowd, but still no Edie. He finished his shot and asked for another. Walker nodded when Dean took the stool beside his. He glanced over his shoulder again.

"You see Edie here?" Walker asked.

"No, you have plans?"

Walker's head moved as if he were shaking off a thought.

"She's always here Saturday. I tried talking with her last night, but she kept putting me off."

"Something up between you two?"

"We kind of had fight at my camp, but things are okay now between us," Walker said.

"You two had a fight? What about?" Dean asked.

"Gil."

Dean shook his head.

"You should know better than to bring him up." Dean leaned forward and spoke to the man sitting on the other side of Walker. "You see Edie here tonight?"

"Edie? I think she was in here earlier, but she left with somebody," the man said.

Walker held his jaw tightly.

"Who'd she leave with?"

"Does it matter? Edie'll go home with anybody."

The man chuckled as he enjoyed his joke. But he stopped when Walker gripped the neck of his t-shirt and dragged his face close to his. The man let out a high-pitched fart.

"You watch what you're saying about Edie. She was married to my brother. You know the one killed in Vietnam saving your stinkin' ass. I was the fuckin' best man at their wedding."

Dean placed his hand on Walker's shoulder.

"Relax, Walker. He didn't mean nothin' by it," he said.

Walker glared at them both. He shoved the man to the floor.

"You're wrong by the way," Walker said, standing over the man. "She'd never go home with you, asshole."

Dean touched Walker's shoulder.

"Take it easy, buddy," he said.

"Shut up, Dean."

Walker settled his tab and was out the door. He sat in his truck and reached beneath the seat for a bottle of Jack Daniels. He took a swallow while he watched people come and go. Men had arms around their women. Everybody wanted a good time.

He took another swallow. His head felt as if someone was cracking it open with a tool. He started the truck's engine.

He drove slowly by Edie's house, half of it lit, her end. Only her car was in the driveway. He watched the windows and listened for noise. He saw and heard nothing. He took another swig before he parked behind her car.

Edie answered the door in a white nightgown, the fabric so thin he saw skin and hair.

"Walker. It's after eleven. I was going to bed."

She eyed the bottle in his hand.

"Where the hell were you?" He made his way past her. "I've been waiting for you at the Do. You had somebody here?"

"No, nobody. Just Amber. She's sick, and I couldn't send her like that to Aunt Leona's," Edie said slowly. "It's been a lousy day, Walker."

"Tell me about it."

Walker paced around the room. His head stabbed this way and that, hunting for clues. The bottle of Jack hit the edge of the table, but it didn't break, so he set it on top.

Edie's blue eyes blinked fast as if they were signaling him.

"Walker, what's wrong?"

"You know what's wrong. Who was he?"

"What are you talking about?"

He glared at Edie.

"It wasn't that shit, Lonny, again, was it?"

Walker grabbed Edie's arm and dragged her into the bedroom. She cried, but he didn't stop until he threw her onto the bed, its covers pulled tightly to the pillows. She got to her feet, and he shoved her down again.

Edie moved around, fighting him off, but Walker straddled her, so she couldn't get away. He slapped her arms and legs, and the rest of her. She pushed back. She begged him to stop. Then he let her have it hard across the face. Her head whipped to the side as his palm shot against her cheek. She shrieked when he did it again.

Then she went still.

Walker followed Edie's gaze to the doorway where Amber stood. The girl glanced from him to her mother. Her lips trembled when she said, "Ma."

He moved off Edie.

"Shit," he said.

Edie rushed toward Amber, shielding her daughter from him. She wiped tears and blood with the back of her hand.

"I have to take care of her, Walker. I want you to go. Now." He opened his mouth, but she gestured toward the door. It was a tone he had never heard her use. "Walker, get out. I don't want to see you ever again."

Edie took Amber to the girl's bedroom. Walker followed them to the hall, and behind the door, he heard Edie's voice rise and fall, her mother's voice.

"Ma, you're hurt. There's blood on your face, on your nose and lips. Oh, no, Ma."

"Shh, shh, I'm okay."

"No, you're not. I heard you scream."

"Uncle Walker was just upset, and I couldn't calm him down. I'm sorry if he scared you. Uncle Walker's a good man."

"Not if he hits you, Ma."

"Shh. Give me that towel over there. Thanks. Let's lie down on your bed."

Walker knew Edie wouldn't leave the room as long as he was here. So he went.

Little Comfort

When Walker slipped into bed, his wife moaned softly and shifted onto her back. If he'd been in love, he would've touched her, getting her warm for him, making her feel she was his. But he wasn't, so he let her be, snoring lightly through her open mouth. Beads of sweat clung to the hairs above her upper lip.

The scene at Edie's kept pouring into his head. He wanted to drive to her house, but she wouldn't welcome him back so soon. He punched at his pillows. He'd have to find a way to fix things with her. He'd make her forgive him for going crazy like that.

Enough moonlight shined in the room that he saw his wife's face, so white and motionless she could have been dead. He imagined her body turning blue, then black, and rotting away. He saw flies and maggots feeding off her, and he found a little comfort there.

Distant And Small

Edie woke up in Amber's bed. Her arms cradled her daughter. Walker left hours ago, but she didn't feel like sleeping in her own. She only left to wash the blood off her face and get ice. The dishtowel she used was wet on her pillow.

Amber talked in her sleep. Edie couldn't make out what she said, except for "Ma." Her words were distant and small as if she spoke through fog.

"Was Uncle Walker the man you went to see?" Amber asked before she fell asleep. "Did he come here, too?"

"Your uncle and I are very close," she told Amber. "He and Aunt Sharon don't get along."

Edie touched where Walker struck her face. She should get more ice. Her body ached in spots when she shifted her position. She placed her tongue on Amber's forehead to test her temperature. She felt cooler.

Her daughter was growing fast, and Edie hoped it wasn't too late to give her a family, a mother and a father. She knew people who grew up fine without either, including herself, but this is what she wanted for her daughter. Amber was lucky to have people who cared for her, but the men in her life, her grandfathers, were old. Amber often asked about her father, begging for stories, wondering what it would be like if he was alive. Edie read from the letters Gil sent on thin, blue paper from Vietnam. Gil wrote about his hopes for them, the love he had for his wife and unborn child.

"Daddy loved you even though he didn't meet you," Edie told her.

Typically, Amber smiled although one day she asked, "How could Daddy love me? He never saw me."

"A mother and father's love can be that strong," Edie told her.

Walker was right about one thing. She and Gil would have had more children.

She thought about the time Harlan's grandmother, Elmira Doyle came to see her after Gil died. Amber was a few months old, and Edie rocked her, trying to get her to sleep when she heard the sound of someone climb the stairs to her apartment. She didn't recognize the footsteps. In those days, it was mostly Walker, Pop, or Aunt Leona, sometimes her in-laws, who came to see her.

Edie carried her baby to the door and watched Elmira, who was in her late eighties, make her way in halting steps. She brought a baby blanket she crocheted in three shades of pink. Edie, who got teary over the gift, let Elmira have the rocker. She wrapped Amber in the blanket and set her on the woman's lap. Elmira kept the rocker moving, declining an offer of tea or anything else. Amber slept.

She remembered Elmira saying, "This is a hard time for you, Edie. Gil was a special man. He'll be a hard one to replace. But you have to get through it. Do it for his child. Do it for him."

Harlan said he hardly knew his grandmother. It was too bad. She was a woman worth knowing. Edie would have to tell him the story some day.

"Do it for his child. Do it for him. " She held onto Elmira Doyle's advice when things were hard.

Gil was so excited when she told him she was pregnant although he worried because the baby would be born before he returned. He was going to miss things. They were coming back from telling his parents about the baby when Gil said, "Listen to me, Edie. If I don't make it back, count on my parents to help. My brother, Walker, too. You won't even have to ask."

Edie put her hand over Gil's mouth.

"Don't talk like that," she told him.

A truck pulled into the driveway. Pop cursed loudly when he worked at his door. He was home briefly in the evening to announce, as Edie predicted, he and the road boss worked things out, first at the highway garage, and then at the Do. The highway crew would be grading the road Monday. Leona would get her apology.

"Leona must be the most powerful woman in Conwell," he said. "The guy's scared shitless what she'll do when she finds out about the mutt. I don't blame him. I'd be, too."

Amber's eyes fluttered open. Her fingers plucked at her mother.

"It's only Poppy come home. Wait till he sees the cake you won him," Edie told her, and she smiled when Amber settled back to sleep.

Tripped

Pop knocked once.

"Thanks for the cake," he shouted as he came through the kitchen door, but he stopped when he saw Edie. "What the hell happened to you?"

Her mouth hurt when she tried to smile.

"Nothing, Pop. I tripped over something in the middle of the night."

Her father came nearer. He scowled.

"That's not from a fall. Someone smacked you hard across the face, someone with a big hand." Pop pointed to the bruises that wound around her upper arm like a tattoo. His lips twitched. "Who in the hell did this? I'm gonna kill the son of a bitch."

"Take it easy, Pop. It was nobody. Like I told you, I tripped," she said, but her father kept staring. "I know I look like hell, but I don't wanna talk about it, Pop."

She tried to get past him. He stepped in her way.

"It was Walker, right? Don't give me that. I ain't blind."

"Oh, Pop," she said when her father hugged her.

"Did Amber see you like this?"

"Yeah." She raised her face. "She's with Marie and Fred at church. I asked her not to tell them. I'll do it myself tomorrow."

"What the fuck, I'm calling the cops."

Pop went for the wall phone. Edie touched his arm.

"Pop, don't, please. Walker didn't mean to. I bet he's really sorry."

"That's what they all say." His breath whistled through his teeth. "He smacked you hard, honey. You gotta tell me what happened."

Edie raised the towel holding ice to her face. The phone rang. She jumped.

"Don't answer it, Pop," she said. "Somebody called twice already this morning. I bet it's him."

"Edie, I don't like the sound of this."

"Listen to me, Pop. Last night, Walker was at the door, acting like a maniac. He came over drunk thinking I had some guy here. I didn't. Only Amber. But he didn't believe me."

"Amber?"

"She came in at the end. She didn't see him hit me, thank God. She's confused, and I didn't know how much to say without scaring her."

"Honey, your Ma and I had some terrible fights, but I never touched her. Any man who puts a hand on you this way doesn't really love you. Never mind who he is. Never mind he's married and has kids." He lowered his voice. "You can do a lot better than him."

"Pop."

"Gil, he was special. I was so happy when you and him got married. I couldn't ask for a better husband for you." His chest rose and fell. "Your life would've been golden if it wasn't for that lousy war."

"Pop, stop." Edie started to cry again. "I don't wanna hear it."

"Maybe it'll make you think."

Pop went to the phone. He dialed the numbers fast.

"Leona, you gotta come over here," he said. "That fuck Walker beat the crap outta Edie last night. You should see her face." He paused. "Yeah, yeah, you need to talk some sense into her."

In Trouble

The woods gave off a creeping kind of heat as Harlan walked the path to the river's edge late in the afternoon. He stopped for a peek back at his house, glad he chose a slate color for the shingles. He'd ask Walker to recommend a painter when he showed up tomorrow. He wanted it done by fall. He had in mind a warm gray.

Harlan was nearly to the river when he heard female voices bounce between the ledge and water, and when he got closer he saw they belonged to Edie and her daughter. They sang that silly Hank Williams song about a man who lived in a doghouse after he got in trouble with his wife. Their voices were loud with fun.

Harlan glanced down at his bare legs, hesitant to join them, but Edie noticed him before he could retreat.

"Amber, look. We've got company," she said. "Now over half the neighborhood is here."

Harlan grinned and sat on a boulder to remove his black canvas sneakers. He took his time, pondering his slow, awkward traverse into the water. He watched the girl jump off a boulder into the darkest part of the river. She called to her mother before she scrambled back onto the rock.

Edie stood in water up to her waist. She wore a two-piece suit, the fabric pink and flowery. Her breasts shook above her top when she laughed at what the girl said.

He held his breath.

Edie's head twisted from the girl to him. Her face and arms were bruised. Her lips were swollen and cut. He wanted to ask what happened although he was afraid to hear the answer.

Harlan rose, stripping off his shirt, before he stepped carefully across the river's stones. Edie kept talking to her daughter although at one point, when she checked Harlan, she lingered on his leg and torso. Her eyes pinched in pain.

Finally, he was in water deep enough to let his body fall, groaning as his flesh released its heat. He swam a few strokes to where he couldn't see the river's bottom.

"This is a nice spot," Harlan said.

Edie and Amber treaded water.

"It sure is. My sisters and I went swimming here as kids with Pop. He did belly flops off the boulder for laughs. You know my father." She shook her head. "When I was a teenager, we had drinking parties down here. We had lots of fun." She pointed at Amber. "I don't want you doin' any of that."

"Aw, Ma," Amber said.

Edie told her daughter, "Amber, show Harlan how far you can swim under water." She grinned. "I swear she's part fish."

"Wanna see?" Amber asked.

"Go ahead. I'll watch," Harlan said.

Edie kept count as Amber dove beneath the water, swimming a straight line until she came to the surface, gasping for air.

"How'd I do?" she asked her mother. "How'd I do?"

"That was the longest ever. I counted to twelve."

"Yes!"

Edie smiled.

"Amber, we're gonna head home now. The bugs are awful, and I gotta make dinner," she said. "I'll see you, Harlan."

"Wait up," he said. "You're right about the bugs."

Amber went ahead, collecting her things along the water's edge. Edie lagged behind.

"By the way, the town's highway crew is supposed to be here Monday," she said. "They're gonna finally grade the road."

"That'll be nice. The road is rather rough."

Edie held out her hand, and Harlan took it to give himself some balance when he stood on the bank.

"It's too bad it took a dead dog." Edie lowered her voice. "Thanks for helping me with that."

"No problem." He paused before he spoke again. His eyes curled downward at the corners. "Edie, are you all right? Are you in trouble?"

Edie shook her head.

"I'm fine, Harlan. Really," she said although he could tell she wasn't being true.

A Dad Out with His Sons

Walker glanced at his boys asleep in the cab of his pickup. They were flopped against each other, their cheeks red from being on the lake so long. He blew the smoke from his cigarette out the window, feeling a little beat himself. His foot tapped the brake pedal when he spotted the eyes of a wild animal shining in the darkness. It stayed on its edge of the wooded road, so he kept going.

He chucked the butt out the window and took a swig from the beer bottle he held between his thighs. He tried calling Edie a couple of times this morning when his wife went to the store, but no one answered.

Instead, he took his boys fishing, which tickled his wife, and he rushed them from the house before she got preachy about it. He let the boys fool around in the water while he did repairs on his camp. He rowed them in his canoe to his special fishing spot, where he caught the limit, including a trout measuring twenty-one inches. He had some good moments, letting the boys take over paddling and showing them how to clean the fish and ice them down. His father used to do the same with Gil and him. After his brother died, Dad didn't want to come here anymore. He lost interest in the camp and a lot of things.

Walker brought his boys to the Lookout Bar and Grille, where he and Edie ate, for burgers, and he gave them money to play the pinball machines. He was just a dad out with his sons today. The only hitch was when the waitress asked about Edie. He told the woman she didn't come on this trip and hoped the boys were too busy with their food to hear her.

His sons weren't bad boys, a lot like him and Gil at that age, impossible to stay with one thing very long, fighting about the dumbest things. He really should spend more time with them. How old were they now? He thought they were younger than Edie's girl, Amber. He wondered how much he scared her last night, yelling and going after her mother, how much she saw. He remembered Edie trying to get away from him as if he was going to hurt her more. He loved Edie, for God's sake.

Walker didn't bother hitting the directional when he made the turn onto Doyle Road. He nodded when he saw Edie's car parked in her aunt's driveway and the front rooms lit. He knew she visited her aunt to play cards. There she was safe and sound, and he turned the truck around in Edie's driveway to get home, whistling all the way.

His wife waited for them. She helped him put the boys to bed and unload the fishing equipment, actually being nice about it. He had another beer in the kitchen, checking the messages Sharon wrote on a paper, all of them business.

He took a shower, and when he was done, he found Sharon in their bedroom. Only one lamp was lit, but it was enough light to notice his wife wore a blue nightgown, and she had put on makeup. She came up to him, her belly pushing the fabric as if she were pregnant, but it was impossible since she got her tubes tied after the boys were born.

"What do you say, Walker?" Her voice was low. "We haven't done it in a while."

She rubbed against him.

127

"Sharon, I'm pretty beat. It's been a long day with the boys."

"Walker."

Her hips moved. He didn't know whether to feel pity for her or disgust.

"Is that a new nightgown you're wearing?" he asked.

"Uh-huh, I bought it just for you."

She made a humming noise as Walker got under the covers. She pulled back the sheet and moved close to him, touching him through his shorts, pulling the waistband down, so she could get at him. He was soft until she used her hand. He'd have to be dead not to feel anything when a woman does that, but there he was ready with the wrong one.

Walker positioned himself above her, lifting the bottom of her nightgown and putting his hand on her. Sharon lay there, letting him do whatever he wanted, and she moaned when he got inside her. He thought about Edie, the way she moved against him, the things she said, how her body felt. Walker pushed faster and harder, punishing his wife until he had enough.

The Lie

Edie was at the deli counter Monday morning. She sighed when she heard her mother-in-law's voice. The bruises and busted lip were awful, she knew, because she checked them enough times in her bedroom mirror. She wore a long-sleeved top on purpose.

Marie's hand flew toward her mouth.

"Edie, what happened to you?"

"I tripped over a footstool in the middle of the night. I was going kinda fast, so it was a bad fall."

Marie came closer.

"Maybe you should've stayed home."

She thought about it before, but Walker's crew was working next door on Harlan's roof. She didn't want him coming over to see her.

"I know how I look, Marie," Edie said. "Everybody's been asking what happened."

Her mother-in-law studied her.

"How about covering it up with makeup?"

"I tried, but it turned out lousy. Anyway, nothing's gonna fix this mouth."

Marie nodded solemnly. She gave a wary eye to her husband, who stood near the coffee machine. They probably thought she was drunk. Aunt Leona had warned Edie when she saw her yesterday.

Marie's forehead bunched above her brow.

"Are you still going?" she asked.

"To Amber's school? Course, I am. She'd be disappointed if I didn't. You?" Edie saw doubt in her mother-in-law's eyes. "It's okay, Marie. I wasn't doing anything I wasn't supposed to when it happened."

She let Marie drive her to the elementary school in her Thunderbird. Edie and Gil went to the same school when they were kids. As she and Marie walked through the hallway of the one-story wooden building, Edie recalled where her desk had been in each classroom. She remembered where Gil sat, in the back with Dean, the two of them fooling around, throwing stuff at her. Walker was in a grade younger.

Tomorrow was the last day, so the school had an assembly in the cafeteria, which tripled as the auditorium and gym. The classes were going to perform, and Amber was supposed to have a small solo when it was the second-graders' turn.

Aunt Leona, who had already arrived, saved two seats in the second row for them. Edie knew all the mothers, and as she expected, they checked her out. Sharon sat to the left with her younger sister. Their heads pecked as they talked.

Leona squinted through one eye.

"Sorry to say, Edie, but you look like hell," she said.

"Thanks a lot, Aunt Leona."

"Not much you can do with bruises like that. I should know. I had one husband who was a beater." She patted Edie's knee. "Be brave, honey."

"I'm trying."

Edie ignored the stares of the other mothers.

"The road crew showed up after you left for the store," Leona said.

"Christ Almighty, I had the darnedest time getting out with all those trucks in the way."

Marie nudged Edie as the children filed into the room. Edie picked out Walker's twins from the kids in their class. Amber acknowledged her presence with a tiny wave. The poor girl still wasn't feeling well, but Edie figured it had more to do with worry than a stomach bug.

"Amber, Amber," Leona said in a hoarse whisper until the girl smiled, and then she was back in Edie's ear. "By the way, I got my apology."

"Already?"

"Yup, just before I came here. I decided to go the highway garage instead of waiting for the road boss to come over to my house. I wasn't about to have that grease monkey dirtying up my floors." She shook her head at the thought. "I got myself all dressed up like I was going to church although heaven knows I'd never do anything like that." She winked. "That's why I'm dolled up this way. Pretty fancy, eh?"

"I noticed."

"Anyway, I told that man it was a lucky thing my dog died right away, or I'd be seeing the board of selectmen about getting him fired." She spoke so loudly people noticed, and Leona fired them all one of her mind-your-own-goddamn-business glares. "I swear the man went white as a ghost. The weasel did a little dance and said he was sorry for hitting my Bob." She snorted. "Just to rub it in, I pretended I was hard of hearing, so he had to repeat everything but louder. I wasn't going to let him off easy."

"Aunt Leona."

Leona worked her red lips, relishing the memory.

"He said I might have noticed the highway crew was working on our road first thing this morning. I asked the son of a bitch what it'd take to get our road graded earlier next spring. Is he going to have to run me over?" She laughed ahead of the punch line. "You know what he said? No, but Alban will do just fine."

Edie laughed softly through her nose at her aunt's silly story.

The kindergartners were first, reciting a poem, and Leona poked Edie in the arm, whispering the boy on the right held his pecker the entire time. Marie bent forward and pressed a finger to her lips as if it would stop her aunt. Leona's thin eyebrows rose so high they looked like they'd slide up to her hairline.

The second-graders sang a round then a folk song. Amber took a step forward. She wore a new dress Marie bought her. Her dark hair was pulled back in two French braids that hung to her shoulders. The teacher, who played the piano, bowed her head, and the other kids fell silent. Amber's voice spread through the room like the call of a solitary bird in the forest. Edie cried at its beauty.

Too Damn Hot

Walker yelled to Dean who worked the backside of Harlan Doyle's roof. Dean's head was down as he sliced shingles to size with a razor knife, but eventually he held his hammer mid-air and glanced Walker's way.

"Where in the hell's that kid?" Walker's words came out strained. "I sent him down to get a bundle of shingles twenty minutes ago. Christ, what was I thinking hiring him? That's what I get for doin' somebody a favor."

Dean pulled a few nails with heads the size of shirt buttons from his leather tool belt. He squinted at Walker.

"Jesus, Walker, you've been on the kid's case all morning." Dean used the hammer's claw to raise the brim of his Red Sox cap, stained by oil near the Boston B. "He probably went in the woods to take a shit. He'll be back. You got a problem?"

Walker glared. The other two men on his crew hammered the roof's front.

"Whose side are you on anyway?" he barked at Dean.

"Shut up, Walker. Talk to me when you're in a decent mood again, will ya?"

Walker scooted to the ridge. He peered over the other side, and two sweaty, sunburned faces stared up at him. Damn, it was too hot for this kind of work although they'd be here a while longer. Early this morning, the crew used barn shovels to scrape the brittle shingles off the roof, letting them fall into a dump truck below. He told Harlan it must have been forty or fifty years since the roof was last touched.

The house was old enough that wide planks had been nailed beneath the shingles instead of plywood. Most likely they were milled from the trees on this lot. A few would have to be replaced. Rot, Walker said, and Harlan, who wasn't about to go onto the roof to test the theory, took his word. Later, when the crew tossed the boards to the ground, the man could see for himself they were shot. He would know Walker was honest after all.

Now the crew hammered long rows of shingles in place over tarpaper. He figured they had another full day ahead. Walker watched the weather report this morning. A late-afternoon thunderstorm was the only threat.

"Guys, take a break," he said. "It's too damn hot."

Walker lit a cigarette before he tossed a butt and lighter to Dean. He sat by himself as the other men climbed down to get a cold drink from the cooler. Below him, the town's highway crew was on the road, grading and trucking in stone, raising dust that nearly reached them on the roof.

He thought about seeing Edie at the store when he and Dean made a coffee run this morning. His gut twisted when he saw the bruises fanned across her cheek, and her split, swollen lips. She kept her eyes lowered. She barely spoke to him.

She whispered, "Not here, Walker. People are watching. Your parents."

"Can I see you later? We need to talk," he whispered back.

"No."

"Can I call you?"

"No."

"Come on, Edie, let me explain."

She went away without another word.

His mother and father took him aside to ask about Edie, but it was clear they didn't know he had any part in it. His neck and face heated anyway.

"Does she get drunk a lot?" his mother said.

"Jesus, Mom, she said it was an accident. Didn't she?" he told her.

When Dean asked Edie what happened, she lied about falling. It was the only time she looked directly at Walker. Dean saw it, too, because in the truck he asked what was wrong.

"She sure wasn't happy to see you." Dean squinted at Walker through the corner of his eye. "What a mess on her face. Must've been quite a fall."

Walker kept silent. He hated hearing what Dean said because it made him feel worse. She wasn't answering her phone either.

He flicked the butt over the edge of the roof before he climbed down the ladder. His crew talked with Harlan. The man stepped back to check the roof's progress. He had a towel slung over his shoulder, and he wore shorts, so anyone could see hard stuff tore into his body. But if Harlan was self-conscious, he didn't let on. Walker reached into the cooler for a bottle of Coke. The boy came from the woods, tugging his belt, and Dean gave Walker an expression that said he was right.

"Heading out for a swim?" Walker asked Harlan.

"Yeah, to the river across the road. This heat came on so fast, I've got to cool off."

"I know what you mean," Walker said.

The boy fished in the cooler for a drink, but Walker had lost interest in the kid. Instead, he watched Harlan make his way down the driveway. His weak leg chopped the ground. Walker would hate to be a cripple like him, but the man whistled, so it couldn't hurt that much.

So Sorry

Walker was parked in Edie's driveway for at least twenty minutes before she came home with her daughter.

"Amber, go inside," Edie said, and when the girl gave her mother a worried look, she nodded. "It's all right. I need to speak with Uncle Walker for a few minutes."

His heart began a hard rush as he left the truck. He rehearsed what he wanted to say while he waited. Edie waved at Amber until she stepped away from the screen door.

"Is this an okay time?" he asked. "I tried calling you, but… "

Walker removed his cowboy hat and bowed his head slightly. He planned to keep his voice warm and low.

"Go ahead, Walker."

"Baby, I'm sorry, so sorry I hit you. I was way outta line." He exhaled loudly. "Some idiot at the Do said you left with another man, and I believed him. I should've known better. It just made me crazy to think about you with somebody else. You gotta forgive me. Please."

"You hurt me, and you scared Amber. She doesn't understand

what's going on."

"It won't happen again. I promise. I'll make it up to you."

He reached for her arm, but she yanked it back.

"Don't touch me." She paused. "We shouldn't see each other any-more."

Deep lines creased Walker's brow.

"You don't mean it."

"I do. Nothing good's gonna happen for us. People are gonna get hurt."

"I told you already I don't care about that." He dropped his voice. "We have a great time together. Don't I make you feel good?"

"It's wrong, all wrong," she whispered.

Walker kissed her tenderly on the corner of her mouth, but she shrank back.

"Edie, don't."

"We shouldn't have done it in the first place."

"I'll leave Sharon today. I wanna be with you."

"I know that, but would you love Gil's girl like she was yours?" she asked. "I have to think about her, too."

Walker was silent.

"Yes," he finally said.

Edie's eyes filled with tears.

"It's not true."

Benny Sweet's truck pulled into the drive. Walker snorted when the old man rocked in his seat.

"You'd better leave," Edie said.

His eyes were stuck on her.

"We're not done. I mean it."

Walker was in his truck and gone before Benny Sweet's feet were on the ground.

Three Strikes

Edie dug the toes of her cleats into the dirt in front of the visitors' bench while she watched Vera's daughter chase a high one by the pitcher from Hartsville. It was her second strike, and her mouth hung open when the ump called the third on a perfect pitch she watched. The girl stomped to the bench.

"Call that a strike? The ump must be blind," she whined.

"It was a strike," Edie said. "Next time, try standing back in the batter's box. You can see the ball easier."

The girl huffed off and sat on the bench beside her mother. Before long, the two of them had their heads together.

"Hey, Edie." Vera spat her gum onto the grass. "Mind your own business and let me do the coaching."

Edie didn't answer. Instead, she clapped for the next batter. Patsy sat beside her on the bench.

"What's going on?"

Edie shook her head.

"I'm not coming back if Vera's coaching next year," she said.

"Edie, don't say that."

"I don't care about losing. I've been on losing teams before. But the fun's gone."

"You can say that again."

"All I hear is bitchin' about who makes a bad play. The worse is Vera and her cousins, and that daughter of hers."

Aunt Leona noticed it, too. After the last game, their third loss in a row, she announced in the car, "The team's going down the toilet with a giant flush from that woman."

Patsy sighed.

"You're right. It's not the same," she said.

The next player hit a pop-up to the second baseman from Hartsville, so they trotted onto the field. Edie punched her glove and got into position at third. The first two outs were easy, but Gloria missed a dribbler, and one of the outfielders bobbled an easy fly. The bases got loaded on a line drive. Gloria kept rotating her shoulder while she walked near the pitcher's rubber. The girls from the other team, sensing her fatigue, squealed on the sidelines. Edie peeked at the scoreboard. It was eleven to three in the fourth. Conwell was losing again. She blew air through her lips.

Edie checked on Aunt Leona, who swatted mosquitoes and pouted in her lawn chair. Her drinking buddies didn't make the long ride to Hartsville, a new team in the league, and so it meant a dry game for her. Amber was at the playground, pumping herself high on a swing.

Gloria lobbed one the batter smacked out of play although the high school girl in leftfield made a go for it. The second pitch hit the plate, called a ball by the umpire, and so did the next. Robin chucked the ball back to Gloria, who spun around to study her team. Gloria appeared to be figuring out something before she got back in place.

Leona put her two hands together to holler, "Hey, Gloria, throw her the funny one."

Gloria laughed to herself as she brought the mitt and the ball upward as if she were going to kiss them. Her right hand swung back and forth before she released the softball in a perfect arc. The batter connected, but Edie, reaching, snagged it. Afterward, she slapped gloves with Gloria.

"I'm getting way too old for this," Gloria told her.

Edie trotted to the bench, where Vera leaned toward her, "I'm putting in one of the high school girls at third. You can sit the rest of the game."

"What? I never sit the bench this early," Edie said.

"Maybe it's about time you do. I always thought Birdie played favorites. Anyway, I'm the coach now." Vera rose with the scorebook in her hand. "I'll tell the other team about the sub."

Edie stared straight ahead, silent, stewing on this while she brushed off stares from the other players. She pressed her fingers lightly against her bruised face, enjoying the sensation. The marks had faded, so they appeared as if someone had painted her skin with a light wash of purple, green, and yellow. Soon they'd be gone. Walker wasn't giving up so easily, however, calling every night to ask her forgiveness, and each time, she told him they were through. She couldn't let him hear any doubt in her voice. She had to be strong.

Aunt Leona kept talking about Walker. The last time she said, "Walker's bad news no matter how good the sex was. I mean it's why you were with him, right? The sex."

"Some of it," she answered.

At the store, Walker gave her a hand-dog expression as if she was the one to wrong him. She made a point of staying out of his way, ducking out the back if she heard or saw him. Her mother-in-law complained once she couldn't find her, and the woman blushed when Edie said she had cramps.

Edie came home one afternoon to find a small velvet box on her doorstep that contained black pearl earrings to match the necklace he once gave her. The next day, while Walker was in the store, she snuck out to put the box, now containing the earrings and necklace, in the front seat of his truck.

That night Walker phoned her. His voice was wrung by grief and anger.

"Keep 'em, Edie. They're for you," he begged.

"I don't want 'em."

"Damn it, at least hold onto the necklace. I gave you that before."

Her throat got tight.

"Walker, leave me alone. Just leave me the hell alone."

"Or what?"

She put the receiver down.

For the past two nights when Edie looked out her bedroom window, Walker was parked outside, spying on her house. She didn't tell Pop, of course, or Aunt Leona.

When Walker called next, she asked him to stop. He laughed.

"It's a free country, baby," he told her.

She began locking the doors at night.

Edie watched her teammates take the field. A couple of the veteran players gave her questioning looks, but she waved them off.

Amber tapped her shoulder.

"Ma, why aren't you out there? Aunt Leona said to ask."

"Vera put somebody else in my place."

"You look mad."

"I'm mad, but I'll get over it. It's not important." She smiled. "Tell Aunt Leona I'll give her the whole scoop later."

In the end, the game was a rout. Conwell lost by one run short of the mercy rule. Players grumbled as they stowed their stuff. Edie, who had already packed her gear, went to help Leona.

"Edie, get your butt over here," Vera yelled. "We need help with the equipment."

Edie brushed her off.

"That Vera has a goddamn nerve," she mumbled.

She stopped when a woman jogged toward her.

"Edie, right? We met at the Lookout. I waited on your table. Remember? You and Walker were there one night." She grinned. "Walker here by any chance?"

"No, he isn't."

"He was in not that long ago with your boys. Cute kids. Twins, right?"

Edie's heart beat harder when she saw Vera standing nearby. The woman squinted, rolling her lips as she savored this moment.

"Sorry, I gotta go. Nice to see you again," Edie said.

She escorted Aunt Leona to the car. Amber went ahead with the chair. When she glanced back, Vera was talking with the woman.

She moved faster, pushing her aunt so quickly, the woman complained, "Jesus, Edie, where's the fire?"

Owed Him

Back from guarding Edie's house, Walker got a beer from the refrigerator. He smelled Sharon's cigarette when he went into the living room. Her eyes were beaded by anger.

"Just comin' from your girlfriend's?" she said through her teeth.

Walker froze.

"What'd you say?"

"You heard me. Your girlfriend, Edie." She made a scornful laugh. "Christ, Walker you should see yours face."

"You don't know what you're talkin' about. You're acting goofy, Sharon. You got your period? That why?"

"Shut up, Walker. Just shut up." She spat her words. "Vera called me about the waitress from the Lookout who was at the Hartsville game tonight. She told Vera she saw you and Edie all lovey-dovey the day you went to the camp a while back. She thought you two were married. She even thought our boys belonged to her."

Her lips curled into a sneer.

"My brother, Buddy, figured something was up the night he saw you eatin' there. You told him you was meeting some guy, but I bet it was her. My brother's smart. He thought somethin' was fishy. I should've listened to him."

Walker didn't move. He felt his anger strobe while his wife continued to talk.

"What's the matter? You got nothin' to say? I sure got plenty. All these years, you helpin' her out, feelin' sorry for her. Vera told me how you come into the store, talking with her, sniffing around like a dog. No wonder you don't touch me."

Her voice was so shrill, he wanted to slap her mouth. It was a miracle their sons hadn't woken up.

"Pack your stuff and get the hell outta here. Me and the boys don't need you." She laughed hard. "Maybe that little slut will take you in. Or did you hit her so hard she doesn't want you anymore? Ha, that'd be rich."

Walker stepped closer, clenching his hands. Sharon saw it, too.

"Go ahead. Hit me. I dare you. I'll just call Buddy and get you arrested." She gritted her teeth. "You don't know how much I hate you right now."

It was then he saw the revolver on her lap. She patted the gun as if it were a pet. But he didn't think she had it in her to fire it. It probably wasn't even loaded.

"I hate you, too, you fat bitch. Only reason I married you was cause I knocked you up, and then you lost the baby. I should've left you then."

Sharon snorted.

"I got news for you. I was never pregnant. Fooled you, didn't I?"

Walker went for the lamp on the table beside her chair, yanking it, so a flame shot from the socket. Sharon raised her feet and shrieked when he smashed it to the floor. He rushed through the darkness to their bedroom to pack a couple of bags. Dean would take him in, he was certain, and he'd come back later for the rest after he worked things out.

A Place To Crash

Dean swung open the door to his singlewide mobile home. A small flap of belly hung over his white Jockeys.

"What's going on? Why you here?" He yawned. "It's pretty late."

"I need a place to crash for a while. Sharon threw me out." He looked past Dean's thin, hairy body. "What? You got somebody inside? A woman?"

He stepped back.

"Ha, I wish. Come on in."

Walker threw his sleeping roll and two duffle bags beside the door. The place was a mess, smelling like old beer and cigarette smoke. He tipped an uncapped bottle of Jack Daniels toward Dean, who took a swig before handing it back. Dean swept clothes, papers, and other junk off the couch onto the floor. Both men plunked themselves down.

"The fat bitch got wind of Edie and me. She threatened to call that cop brother of hers. She even had a gun." Walker fished for the pack in his shirt pocket. "You're not gonna believe this one. She faked being knocked up, so I'd marry her."

Dean took a butt, keeping his good ear toward Walker, a habit that made it appear he was a bit unbalanced.

"You're shittin' me. Too bad you didn't know sooner." He exhaled. "You could've saved yourself a lot of trouble and money."

"Don't rub it in." Walker's eyes narrowed. "I gotta find me a lawyer, but I'm sure as hell not using yours."

"What'd you mean by that?"

Walker's head swiveled for effect.

"How many years were you married? All you got out of it was this trailer and the junk you have in it."

"What'd you expect? She got the house cause her daddy gave us the money for the down payment." Dean shrugged. "I walked out with my dogs, the clothes on my back, and enough dough to buy this trailer. Glad we didn't have kids, or I'd have to pay for them." He flicked at the peeling label on the Jack. "I'd say I actually made out pretty good considering."

Walker scowled.

"I'm not gonna get away so easily." He reached for the bottle. "Right now, I don't give a shit. Help yourself by the way."

"Sure, Walker."

Walker took another drink before he passed the Jack to Dean. He found the bottle at home and drank from it on his way here. At least Dean had a spare room, and the man did owe him. No one else wanted to hire him, broken down after Vietnam, drinking and drugging too much, and here he was first man in charge of his crew. Too bad he blew his money at the Do.

"Shit, I have to meet those New Yorkers tomorrow to go over the money," Walker said. "I'll just have to see her later to give her the news."

"You talking about Edie?" Dean's eyebrows shot up and down. "Nobody's seen her lately. People at the Do have been asking."

"Yeah, I know what you're thinking, so you don't have to say it. I think about it all the time."

Found Out

Edie knelt before a row of cartons in the center aisle of the general store.

"Amber, Mrs. Brewster wants a can of coffee and one of the sweet milk," Edie read from her list. "I think that's all. No, wait. She wants a box of rice. Get the kind she likes."

Her girl scooted around the corner.

"Okay, Ma," she shouted.

The old-timers called in their orders the day before. If Edie didn't answer the phone, they insisted on speaking with her because they knew she'd write everything down carefully and let them ramble a bit about themselves.

It took all Saturday morning to finish the route. She and Amber would have to bring in the boxes, and for some of the sickly ones, put everything away. She checked around the house to see if they needed anything done. Many offered them something to drink, wanting her and Amber to stay a few minutes more, to hear the news in town, and for their company.

"How about some cold water? I'm real thirsty. So's Amber," Edie would say, and the man or woman would go to the sink to let the faucet run until the water got as cold as it was in the ground.

Amber learned quickly that well water was all they would accept because many had less than them. But they wanted these people to feel they could give them something. What was better than a cold glass of water?

Edie was pleased her daughter wasn't shy with any of them. Then again, she had been coming along since she was a baby, and Edie set her down on the lap of an old folk while she brought in the groceries. They wanted to hear how Amber was doing in school. They asked her to show off her Halloween costume and to tell them what she wanted for Christmas and her birthday. They kept saying Edie should find a husband, how her precious girl needed a man as fine as Gil to be her father. These people became part of their extended family, and it saddened them when any got so feeble they had to go into a home. They grieved when each one died.

Edie's hand was on her hip as she checked the list.

"I need three rolls of toilet paper, two boxes of corn flakes, and one of oatmeal." Amber scurried to the next aisle. "There and there." Edie pointed to the right boxes when she returned. "Go ask Grandpa to put the cooler in the car. He should be done marking the packages of meat."

She went behind the register, where Vera rang up an order. She ignored the woman's probing glance as she collected nip bottles, candy bars, and small packages of pies to tuck in the boxes.

"Who ordered that stuff?"

Edie pretended not to hear. If her in-laws insisted, she would pay, but she didn't think Fred and Marie would begrudge a few extras for these old-timers, their store's most loyal customers. She bent over the boxes, double-checking the lists before she carried them through the store's back door to her car. The cardboard boxes with the dry stuff went in the trunk. The rest was stacked in the back seat and on the floor. It was a full load.

Edie tucked the folded paper in the pocket of her dress. Amber was back.

"We're almost done, kiddo," she told her daughter. "The last box is missing a can of baked beans and a jar of relish. Hurry up. We gotta get going."

Edie frowned. Sharon was in the store. The woman stopped to talk with Vera, but her small, dark eyes were pinned on Edie. She guessed what was coming. The waitress at last night's game told Vera about her and Walker being together at the Lookout, and naturally she told her sister. Edie felt trapped as the woman's heavy footsteps vibrated through the floorboards. Sharon held her purse as if she was strangling it.

"Don't you go anywhere, Edie. I got something to tell ya," she announced loudly. "I know all about you and Walker. Him cheatin' on me." She dug her free hand into her hip. "What's the matter? Didn't think I'd find out? What kind of a sister-in-law are you?"

Edie was silent. Customers gawked. Her in-laws were somewhere in the store. But she thought only of Amber as she searched for her.

"Look at me. I'm talking to you. I threw the worthless piece of crap out last night. I gave him two sons, twins, and this is how he treats me." Her voice rose higher. "Everybody in town felt sorry for you cause of Gil dying in Vietnam. No father for your baby. Truth is no one thought you deserved him, especially his parents. Right, Marie?"

Sharon gestured toward the end of the aisle. Marie held her hand to her throat as she croaked Gil's name.

"Benny Sweet's daughter marrying someone like Gil. Your old man runs the dump for Christ's sake." Sharon made a scornful laugh. "Then you go try to steal his brother, my husband. You pig, I hope you want what's left when I get through with him."

Amber came around the corner, taking a few steps before she stood beside her grandmother. Edie shooed the girl away, but she stared dumbly, and Marie stood there, useless, shocked about her and Walker.

Sharon's head shook as if she were having a stand-up fit.

"I heard all about you picking up men at the Do. Edie, you were no different in high school. You let anyone get in your pants. How you got someone as nice as Gil to marry you, I'll never know."

Amber bit her fingernails.

"You done yet?" Edie asked in a low hiss. "No? Too bad. Take it with up Walker. I have nothing to do with him anymore."

She stooped for the last box and moved past Sharon to her daughter. She whispered to Amber, "Put the food on top. That's right. We gotta get going."

Edie nodded as Amber went forward, but she made one quick peek over her shoulder at the stunned faces of the customers. Sharon kept screaming.

Shame

Edie backed her car into a space behind the store.

"I want you to stay here," she told Amber. "I'm gonna give the money to Grandma."

Her daughter's blue eyes blinked fast.

"Can't I come?"

"Not this time, honey. I need to talk with Grandma. Grownup talk."

"All right, Ma."

Amber had been upset for hours, and it seemed whatever Edie said came out wrong. She swallowed hard.

"I'll only be a few minutes. I'll leave the car running, so you can listen to the radio, but don't take it for a drive."

Amber smiled weakly at the joke.

In the office, Marie peered over her spectacles as Edie placed the envelope of checks and cash on the desk. The muscles on her mother-in-law's neck were tight. She dropped her pen and patted her hair, permed and dyed a brassy yellow.

"Edie, I don't have to tell you how disappointed I am in you and Walker. You hid it well. I'll give you that." The diamonds rings on her thin fingers glinted as she swatted the air. "I didn't know about Walker and Sharon either. It was awfully embarrassing to learn about it in the store, and Amber having to hear all that. The customers, what must they be thinking?"

Edie felt her face go red.

"I'm sorry, Marie."

Her mother-in-law squinted.

"This thing between you and Walker. I understand what kind of a man my son is, selfish, uh, very persuasive. He's nothing like Gil." A swallow passed beneath the crepe-like skin on her throat. "Fred and I have been very generous to you, considering. I think out of respect you should've controlled yourself. I mean, what kind of an example are you setting for Amber?"

"What are you saying?"

"You know very well what I'm saying. And poor Sharon."

Edie's regret receded, and anger slid in its place. She heard this shaming tone before. She and Gil sat on the couch in his parents' living room. She wore her best dress. The two of them held hands as Gil tried to make them happy about their wedding.

"Mom, we just love each other so much, we can't wait to be together," Gil said. "I love Edie. I hope you feel the same way about her."

"Of course, dear." Marie's voice dropped. "But you're both so young, only out of high school, and there's no time to plan this right." Marie glanced at Fred, and then Edie. "You're not, uh, expecting, are you?"

Now Edie gave Marie a cold once-over in the store's office.

"I'm not a bad example to Amber. I love her more than anyone."

Marie shuffled papers.

"I understand it's not been easy bringing up a little girl all by yourself. I'm sure it's been lonely for you. But you have to think about Amber. And what about Gil?"

Edie pulled back her shoulders.

"Believe me, Marie, I think about them all the time."

She left the office.

A Satisfying Shatter

Walker used a pry-bar to bust open the back door of his house. Sharon already changed the locks, probably had one of her brothers do it, but he wasn't going to let that stop him. He figured rightly she'd be driving the boys, normally his job, to their baseball practice. He jimmied the bar until the jamb splintered beneath the metal claw and the door popped open. He felt like doing the same to his wife's thick skull.

Sharon left a message at Dean's place that the rest of his clothes was in the garage, but now he searched for his valuables: his guns and fishing gear, his hard liquor. His tools were safe in the shop he rented.

Walker tracked dirt on purpose across the beige wall-to-wall carpeting while he hauled stuff to his pickup. He took the strongbox of cash he hid in the basement before he went through the house for one last sweep.

He paused in the living room, studying the curio cabinet holding Sharon's collection of statues, the elf kids with thumbs in their mouths and dopey poses. He marched into the boys' room and returned with a baseball bat he held high before he whacked the cabinet. The glass cascaded to the carpet in one satisfying shatter, but he went on swinging, hurling the figurines against the walls. When he tired of that, he raked them onto the floor and bashed them to pieces.

Walker thought about his wife's reaction when she got home, and he felt glad for the first time in days.

Officer Buddy

Walker sat drinking with Dean on lawn chairs in front of his friend's singlewide. He came back in a reasonably pleasant mood after smashing his wife's things. His stuff was stashed safely in Dean's extra room now that the two of them agreed on rent until he found something more permanent. He wore jeans and his third-best cowboy boots, but no shirt as he soaked in the summer sun. His dark hair hung in waves along the back of his neck.

"Dean, you'd have a pretty nice view of the town and the Berkshires, except for that pile of tires and the junker you got in your front yard," Walker said. "That the pickup you crashed last winter? I bet you ten bucks I could pick out the tree on this road that fits the crease in the front end."

"Very funny, Walker. But you're right. It's the maple on the last curve here."

Walker thrust an uncapped bottle of Jack Daniels toward Dean, who took a swig before handing it back. They were half in the bag and high from the joint they shared.

"Why don't you start fuckin' Sharon, get her to fall in love with you, and I'll give you a big, fat raise," he told Dean.

"Shit, Walker, I'm not taking your sloppy seconds."

"She might not be much to look at, but she keeps a real clean house. And she's a halfway decent cook. Come on, Dean, who else you fucked lately?"

"On second thought, she don't look too bad," Dean joked, plucking a pack of smokes from the pocket of his unbuttoned flannel shirt.

"Now you're talkin'."

The phone rang inside the trailer.

"Jesus, who keeps calling?" Dean said. "That's about the fifth time that damn thing's rung. No one ever calls here, except you."

Walker chuckled.

"Maybe it's my dear sweet wife finding the surprise I left for her at home."

Dean gave him a sideways glance.

"You sure you don't want me to get the phone?"

"Nah, there's only one person I wanna talk with today. I'm gonna go see her later and tell her myself about me and Sharon."

"Let me guess. Edie?"

Walker wagged a finger.

"Who else?"

Dean's hounds tied in the back yard started howling. Blue lights flickered through the trees.

"Seems like we got us some visitors. Looks like pigs to me," Dean said. "What'd you do with the roach?"

"You mean this?" Walker sniggered as he chucked the snuffed end in the bushes.

The cruiser stopped, and Sharon's brother, Buddy Crocker, and another cop, both part-timers since Conwell was such a hick town, got out. Buddy's red hair shined in the sun.

"Well, well, well, if it isn't Sgt. Buddy," Walker said in the mocking way he always greeted his brother-in-law. When he wasn't a cop, Buddy worked in an auto repair shop. "What can I do for you today?" He reached for a can of Bud from the six-pack near his feet and popped the top. "Care for a beer, boys? Something stronger? Too bad you're both on duty." He gestured toward the driveway. "Maybe you could change the oil on those pickups over there. I believe mine's overdue. What about yours, Dean?"

Buddy cleared his throat, all police business. Dean was silent.

"I need to ask you a coupla questions," Buddy said, reading from a notebook. "I hear you broke into my sister's house and smashed her valuable collection of ceramic figurines."

Walker held the beer can against his thigh as he snorted at Buddy.

"You're tryin' to tell me I broke into the house I built, that I paid for, and that's in my name? That I broke the things she bought with my money? Since your sister hasn't worked in seven years, any money she uses is money I made. Ain't that right?"

Buddy glanced at the other officer.

"Um, I don't know."

"You don't know. Here's how it goes. While I work my tail off, your sister sits on her fat ass, getting fatter. You know how it works, right, Buddy? You're married to one of those, too." Walker chuckled as Buddy stepped forward. His hand was on his holster. "Gee, I hope you're not planning to use that gun on me."

Buddy's partner gave him a warning look.

"You think you're so smart, Walker," Buddy said. "My advice to you is to watch your step. I've got my eye on you."

"I hate to disappoint you, but I'm an upstanding citizen."

Buddy sneered.

"That's not what I hear from my sister. She told me about you and Edie."

Walker's jaw tightened.

"Yeah? Why don't you go ask your sister if she has a permit to carry a firearm? Seems to me she didn't when she pointed a gun at me last night. It was one of my guns by the way. Maybe I should file a report with the police."

The other officer tapped Buddy's arm, telling him they should hit the road. Walker leaned back in his chair, watching them leave. He chuckled.

"I think I got more weed in the truck," Walker told Dean as he chucked his beer can into the pile of empties beside the tires. "Wanna smoke another joint?"

Falling Stone

The bartender at the Do-Si-Do announced last call. Walker pointed to his beer and raised two fingers since Dean, who was using the toilet, would want another.

The bar was dead. The band was a no-show, so disappointed music lovers drifted in and out, some playing pool or pinball, or having a couple of drinks before they moved on. Diehards like Walker and Dean stayed all night.

The bartender placed two longnecks in front of Walker.

"I'm surprised Edie isn't here tonight," the man said. "It's not like her to miss a Saturday night at the Do. She on the wagon?"

"Edie? Nah," Walker said. "Maybe she had some other place to go. Family stuff."

Dean returned to his stool.

"Thanks for the beer."

Walker glanced up when he felt a friendly slap on his back. One of the guys from his crew greeted him and Dean.

"Just got back from the track in upstate New York," he said. "Didn't have much luck on the horses. I was hoping to get laid tonight, too, but it doesn't look like I'll have any luck with that either."

Walker glanced over his shoulder. The only single women were a middle-aged divorcee on the verge of losing her looks and a couple of homely girls just over the legal drinking age.

"Yup, pickin's are pretty slim for women tonight," Walker told him.

"Boy, that was something else between your wife and Edie at the store this morning," the guy said.

Walker frowned.

"What are you talkin' about?"

"You didn't hear?"

"No, I was with Dean most of the day."

The man's eyes jerked from Dean to Walker.

"Your wife went up to Edie in the store and tore into her something awful. I was there for it. You should've heard the things she was saying about you and Edie. The whole store did. No one told you?"

"What kinds of things?"

"You sure you wanna hear this?"

"Yeah, I do."

The man licked his lips.

"Sharon said Edie wasn't good enough for your brother, Gil, and she tried to steal you away. She said she kicked you out last night when she found out. There was other stuff."

"Shit, she did all that at the store?" Walker asked.

"I didn't know about you and Edie. She's real special. You're a lucky guy."

"Yeah, I am." Walker swallowed hard. "How'd she take all that?"

"Eh, Edie acted cool and blew past Sharon with her little girl, but I could tell she was shook in front of all those people." The man's head jerked side to side. "Your parents went nuts after she left. I'm surprised Edie didn't tell you about it. It was kind of a big deal."

"I haven't had a chance to talk with her yet," Walker said. "I'll see ya Monday. Okay?"

Walker waited until he and Dean were alone.

"Did you hear all that?" he asked Dean.

"Yup. Sounded like a bad scene."

"I stopped by Edie's place earlier, but she wasn't home. I wanted to tell her myself about me and Sharon." Walker frowned. "You think she's the one who kept calling your place today?"

"Dunno." Dean downed the rest of his beer. "Let's head out. Looks like they wanna close up the joint."

They were about a half-mile down the road when the lights of a cruiser flashed behind them. Walker swore when he checked the mirror.

"It's that dumb fuck of a brother-in-law." He steered the pickup onto the road's shoulder. "Let's see what that asshole wants."

Walker thought he was sober enough, so he felt smug when he rolled down his window. Buddy Crocker shined his cop light inside the cab.

"Anything wrong, officer? Excuse me, sergeant."

"Don't get smart with me, Walker. Your pickup swerved when you came out of the parking lot. I'd like you to get out."

"Sure, Sgt. Buddy."

Buddy put Walker through the usual tests, making him touch his finger to his nose and asking stupid questions any moron could answer.

"I told you I was sober," Walker said.

Buddy waved his flashlight across the pavement.

"Go ahead. Walk in a straight line," he said.

Walker shook his head at Dean, who stayed inside the truck as Buddy ordered.

"What an asshole," he said to himself.

"Did you hear what I said?" Buddy said in his cop voice.

"Sure did, Sgt. Buddy. So, what'd your sister say about the gun permit? Or was she too busy gluing the pieces of those dumb statues of hers? Those eyes and noses and little dicks all over the rug.

161

Must've been a sight seeing her bend over to pick 'em up." Walker chuckled at the grim-faced cop. "You could've charged tickets and made some money."

Buddy Crocker gestured for Walker to begin, but after a few steps, he used his boot to trip him. Walker fell onto the road, the pavement scraping his jaw, but he was on his feet fast, flying toward Buddy. Too late, when his fist hit Buddy's jaw, he realized it was exactly what the man wanted.

He shoved Walker to the ground, beating his flashlight against his shoulders and back. Dean hollered as he tried to pull Buddy off Walker. Buddy began hitting Dean, too. Walker crawled forward, reaching for the cop's legs. There was a knock on the back of his head, and he felt as if he had gotten stuck beneath a pile of falling stone.

Behind Bars

Walker stared at Buddy Crocker through the bars of his cell. Dean snored on the cot beside him. The city cops let the country cops put their prisoners in their jail, but they had to guard them until they made bail. Walker had enough money on him. He was waiting for one of his crew to give Dean and him a ride home.

"I bet your dumb ass sister put you up to this," Walker growled. "Am I right?"

"Shut up, Walker."

"You ain't gonna put a hand on me in this cell, are you? It was easier on a dark road back home. You can't get away with it here. I believe they call it police brutality. Wait till I get me a lawyer."

"I said shut up."

"I always thought there was a close family resemblance between you and Sharon, especially around the mouth. You know that mustache of hers? She plucks at those hairs and puts white crap on them, but they keep growing back."

Buddy didn't change his expression.

"Walker, you're such an asshole," he said. "What in the hell did my sister see in you anyway?"

"More than I ever saw in her."

Best Man

Walker found Dean already up and dumping grounds in the coffee maker in the singlewide's kitchenette. It was nearly noon.

"You look as shitty as I feel," Dean said.

Walker tugged on his t-shirt. His head and body ached.

"That makes two of us. Got enough for me?" he asked as he stumbled to the bathroom.

He was finishing up when Dean yelled he had a phone call. It was one of his boys.

"Daddy? You coming to our game today? It's the all-stars. We called and called yesterday, but nobody answered."

Walker heard anxiousness in his son's voice although right now he couldn't tell who this one was. They looked, sounded, and acted so much alike. Fortunately, they wore numbers on their uniforms.

His boys asked him to come to their game. This could be a wicked setup by their mother, but maybe the boys needed their father. He worked hard, so they wouldn't go without. He'd been at most of their baseball games and practices since they began hitting off a tee. Walker recalled the fun time they had last week at his camp, how they showed off for him. They even fought for his attention.

"You both want me to come? I'll be there. What time does your game start?"

After he hung up, Walker formed a plan as he drank coffee and smoked. He knew he was going to make some lawyer richer, what with the divorce and, now, getting arrested. He and Dean had to go to court tomorrow. He felt obligated to help Dean. The man didn't have to take his side last night, and they had been friends since they were kids, he, Dean, and Gil. Walker was the best man at both their weddings.

He remembered Gil and Edie's wedding, how beautiful she was in her long dress made of white cotton lace. She carried a bouquet of tiny, pink roses with thin, white ribbons dangling nearly to the tops of her shoes. It was an odd detail for a man to remember, but he focused on her hands during the church service. The two of them, Gil and Edie, were so much in love. It hurt to see them happy.

Afterward in her aunt's back yard, Walker wanted to stop Gil when it was time for them to leave for their honeymoon. Edie acted shy when Walker kissed her cheek then her closed lips. He felt like fighting them all off and stealing her away.

"He'd better be good to you," Walker whispered, and Edie gave him a curious stare. "I mean it."

Walker snuffed out his cigarette. He'd clean himself up and go to his boys' game. He'd avoid his wife and any of her kin. He'd try to see Edie afterward. He'd make things right.

All Stars

Walker parked his truck near the ball field. He drank from the bottle stashed beneath his seat. He needed a pick-me-up before he ventured into the crowd of happy families, one more and another. He was ready.

He nodded when he saw his boys' team throwing and catching. One of his sons, Randy, number three, the starting pitcher, was off to the side, warming up. Walker grinned. He cupped his hands around his mouth.

"How's your fast ball today?" he called, and his boy's game face changed into a son glad to see his dad. "Where's your brother? Oh, I see him over there."

Shane, number six, who played leftfield, talked with the coach. The boy was the best hitter on the team. If he made his two boys into one, he'd have an outstanding ballplayer, better than he ever was although he did teach them everything about the game. He managed to talk the coach into taking his boys a year early. There was no use having them still swat a ball off a tee.

Walker whistled sharply through his teeth, and Shane, recognizing the sound, twirled around. The brim of the boy's baseball cap bobbed as he called back to him.

Walker checked the stands. His wife was with her family. She wore sunglasses as if she were some fat, has-been movie star. He saw no sign of Buddy Crocker. He must be out making the world a more miserable place.

He found a seat on a bench of planks built along the edge of the forest. Most people didn't sit here because of the mosquitoes and the poor view, but Walker preferred the spot. He could smoke and stand to follow a play if he wanted without bothering anybody.

He looked to his left when he heard small feet pound the ground. Shane, number six, came running. He wrapped his arms around Walker.

"What's up?" Walker said.

He looked down at his son, feeling a little choked by the hug. Tears were in the corners of the boy's eyes.

"Dad, why'd you have to go?"

"Your mother and I don't get along. Maybe she told you about it."

"Ma said Aunt Edie is your girlfriend, and you didn't love her anymore."

"That's what she told you? Your mother's a real class act." Walker grunted. "But don't you and your brother worry. I'll take care of you. I'll still see you when I can." He raised the boy's cap to ruffle his dark hair before he reached into his jeans pocket for a package of gum. "Give some to your brother."

"Dad, you got hurt."

Walker pointed to his bruised face.

"This? Eh, got into a small scrape with your Uncle Buddy. It's nothing."

"Ma says you got arrested."

"She did? There's just a little mix-up." He raised his chin. "Looks like your coach wants you. Your game's gonna start. I'll be right here watching. Hit one for me, will ya?"

"Yeah, Dad."

Walker kept standing as a guy holding a bullhorn announced the names of the starting lineups, and then a teenage girl squealed the national anthem as if she were in pain. He took his seat, but he wasn't alone. His wife charged toward him, and in case Walker lost it, he supposed, one of her brothers although not the jerk cop who roughed him up last night. This brother, Jim, who worked on the town's highway crew, was an okay guy. Sharon probably made him.

Walker stared straight ahead as the team captains did the coin toss. The light sparked off the coin when it spun and fell. The players stared at the dirt until the ump said his boys' team would be home. Walker raised a fist.

"Hey, you, we gotta talk," Sharon said.

He noticed the grass was brown in the outfield, probably because of the dry spring. The town should put some money into these fields. His boy playing leftfield would have to be careful about bad bounces out there.

"Walker, look at me."

His other boy, Randy, a leftie, was on the mound. He raised a knee and brought his arms close to his chest the way Walker showed him. His practice pitch, right over the shoulder, made a nice pop into the catcher's mitt, a dead-nuts strike. The catcher rose from his squat to send the ball back. Walker grunted his approval.

"I need to talk to you about money."

Walker let Sharon fume. His eyes were nearly shut when he turned her way.

"What are you gonna do? Sic your dumb ass brother after me again. I know you had something to do with that. You think you're so smart, don't you?"

A smile flickered briefly on her lips. He wanted to slap it off.

"I'm smart all right." She glanced at her brother. "What about money?"

"Send the bills to my office, and I'll pay 'em." Walker lit a cigarette.

"I've been thinking this is a good time for you to go to work."

"Go to work?"

"I'll pay for the boys, but I'm not paying for you to sit on your fat ass."

She huffed and moved around. Her brother didn't make a sound.

"I'm gonna get myself a lawyer."

"You do that, sweetheart," he said without any affection. "I'm not paying for that either."

It was his son's last practice pitch, and then the catcher threw the ball over the mound, where it got to the second baseman's glove in one hop. The boys made high-pitched war hoops and slapped gloves. Walker jabbed his head toward the field.

"The boys asked me to come, and I wanna watch them play. I don't appreciate you tellin' 'em about you and me. They're just little kids."

Sharon paced on her tiny feet. It was amazing a woman so large could balance on them, but then cows walked on hooves. Of course, his wife wasn't always like that. She was cute when she was younger, or he wouldn't have had anything to do with her.

"By the way, I heard what you did in the store to Edie. Stay away from her. It's not her fault we hate each other."

"Right, be a jerk. Too bad she wants nothing to do with you no more."

Walker made a low, dismissive laugh.

"Shut up, Sharon."

The first player stepped into the batter's box. He held his bat over his shoulder as he waited for the pitch. His boy was ready, too.

"Go ahead. Laugh." Sharon's head shook. "What's the matter? Nothing to say? I've got plenty."

Walker took a drag on his cigarette. It felt as if the smoke in his mouth came from a place deep inside like fire spreading along the roots of a dry, pine forest. If he could get away with it, he'd kill this woman. He didn't care she was the mother to his sons. His boys would be better off without her.

"Did I tell you how much fun I had smashing those statues of yours? Shit, I pretended each one of those fuckers was you."

Walker flicked the half-smoked butt near Sharon's sandal, and he gave her a black look that sent her and her brother back to the bleachers.

At the bottom of the fifth inning, Walker leaned over the chain-link fence. His boys' team was winning easily, so he figured he'd head out. His sons sat together on the home bench, their mouths working on large wads of gum. They smiled when he patted their heads.

"You two, good game. You boys know how to play baseball. Who showed you how?"

"You did," they said in unison.

Chuckling, Walker slid his hand into his back pocket for his wallet and gave each a ten.

"Get yourselves some ice cream. You can keep the rest. I gotta get going."

Randy, the pitcher, knelt on the bench, so he faced Walker.

"Dad, don't go."

Walker shook his head.

"Sorry, son," he muttered as the crowd cheered for what was happening on the field.

Crazy Talk

Walker grunted when he sat next to his father on the patio of his parents' home. His father drank a Seven and Seven. Moisture coated the cold glass, except where his fingers smeared it.

"Dad."

"Son."

His father watched Edie's daughter play on a swing slung from the large, low bough of a maple tree on the far edge of the lawn. The girl twisted the ropes into a tight screw and made a happy shriek when she twirled with her head dipped back. The corner of Walker's mouth twitched. He did the same thing when he was a boy.

"Makes me dizzy just seeing her," his dad said with a fondness Walker rarely heard.

"She sure is pretty. She's just like Edie at that age," Walker said.

The ice in his father's drink clinked when he brought the glass to his mouth.

"What's this I hear about you and her?"

Walker squinted at his father although it hurt where Buddy Crocker hit him.

"I guess it depends on what you've been hearing."

"Don't give me that smart mouth stuff. Save it for that dopey friend of yours." His father's voice had a hard edge. "How come you didn't tell us you and Sharon broke up? And this thing about Edie."

Walker was trying to get a handle on his father when his mother came onto the patio. A wet stripe went across the front of her apron. She stood near his father's chair, her hands wringing a dishtowel. She nodded at his father. He knew what the look meant. It was them against him.

"What can I say? We don't get along. Never have. It shouldn't come as a shock to anyone, but I'm sorry you had to learn about it that way. Her coming into the store."

"It was most embarrassing," his mother said.

"I did try to make it work," Walker said.

"Obviously, not hard enough. I mean you have two boys. Think about them," his father said.

His mother made a small, dry cough.

"Every marriage has its troubles, Walker. You and Sharon could still work things out."

"Yeah? Last night she had her brother, Buddy, arrest me. What do you think about that?"

His mother clutched the towel to her chest.

"Arrested? You?" she cried.

Walker gave her such a withering glare she went silent.

"It was a setup. I was coming back from the Do with Dean, and he stopped my truck. I hit him, but he tripped me to the ground first. I'm sure Sharon was behind it." He bent forward. "He beat the crap outta me. See? See, what he did, Mom?"

Her fingers twisted the towel.

"What are people in town going to say?" she said.

"Jesus, Mom, is that all you ever care about?" His voice cracked. "Aren't you gonna ask how I am?"

"Walker," she said.

Walker clawed his chest, so tight he couldn't breathe.

"Thanks a lot, Mom." He pounded the arm of the lawn chair. "You know she tricked me into marrying her? Remember the miscarriage she supposedly had? It was a fake. Don't look at me that way, Mom. She told me the other day. I've wasted my life so far with that horrible woman. I could've been with Edie all this time."

The towel flicked as his mother's hands flew up.

"Edie. Why does it have to be her? First, Gil, then you. It's like she has a spell over you boys."

Walker's eyes were nearly shut.

"You think that's what it is, Mom? You don't think maybe I've loved her for a long time, but I didn't do anything about it? Huh? I loved her before Gil did, but he's the one who got her."

"You're talking nonsense, Walker," his mother said.

"Edie makes me happy. She's the only one. You know what I'm gonna do? I'm gonna beg her to marry me, and that little girl over there's gonna be mine. My daughter." He pointed at Amber. "You both better get used to the idea."

"Fred, try to talk some sense into him," his mother said.

His father's fist pounded the chair's arm.

"That's enough, Walker. You're making your mother upset."

"Dad, we're talking about me right now. I'm the one upset. Me." Walker thumbed his chest. "In case you forgot, you have two sons, and I'm the only one who's still living."

"Walker, stop it," his father said.

"No." He jumped to his feet. "It was always Gil this and Gil that. When he died, I could see it in your eyes, Mom. You, too, Dad. You wished I was the one. Admit it. Go ahead. Tell the truth for once. I dare you."

His father's lips twitched.

His mother cried.

"Why are you doing this?" she wailed.

"You know, Mom, I've seen you with Edie's girl, holding her hand as you walk, the way you smile at her. I don't remember you being like that to me even after Gil died. You had one son still alive, but you didn't give a shit. Did you, Mom?"

"Calm down, Walker. This is crazy talk," his father said.

Walker got to his feet and flung his chair against the house. His mother danced back, shouting his name. He stared through her. His father stood, and Walker rushed toward him, nearly bumping his chest.

"Crazy? You think I'm crazy?"

"Walker, we're just worried about you. That's all," his father said.

"Well, don't be. I'm doing just fine without you, Dad." Walker shook his head. "I came here looking for a little support from you two for a change, but it seems like I came to the wrong house."

Walker stepped off the patio in long, hard strides. He gave one glance back at his parents. His mother fled into the house. His father stayed on the patio, calling him back. Walker searched for Edie's girl, but she was gone.

He left the yard, feeling hot and more lonesome than when he arrived.

Cornered

Monday morning, Walker spoke sparingly to Dean on the ride from the courthouse. He was hung over still from last night, but it was being in a place where Buddy Crocker was respected and he, a successful builder, treated like a low-life that silenced him. The charges against them sounded idiotic when they were read aloud because he didn't get a chance to explain how the cop baited him.

Dean was so nervous in the courtroom that his leg jiggled as if it were a loose piece of machinery. He kept asking Walker questions, and because he couldn't hear a darn thing, Walker had to repeat whatever was said in the courtroom. He and Dean pleaded not guilty, of course, and now he was in the market for a lawyer. He frowned when he thought about his name being in the paper. His mother was right about one thing. It'd be bad for business, and it'd make his enemies, including his wife and her family, happy.

"Hey, Dean, stop at the store for coffee," he said loudly because Dean's good ear was on the other side of the truck. "Let me buy you one. Get yourself something to eat, too, and put it on my tab."

Walker threw his tie on the front seat and unbuttoned his white shirt, still creased from the package. He smelled the stink beneath his arms. The rest of the crew was supposed to be framing a porch. Without Dean or him, he wondered how much was getting done. They'd have to go back to Dean's to change into work clothes, but it was on the way to the job site, the only break he cut so far today.

Dean parked, and boot heels clattered against the floorboards as the two men went through the front door. Edie was stocking shelves, but she quickly left the aisle as if suddenly she had something more important to do. She rushed past the deli counter to the rear of the store. Walker winced. A short time ago, she would've waited for him to pass, giving him a smile and a giggle, maybe a secret touch.

Walker flicked his head toward the tables.

"Sit down, Dean, and drink your coffee. I got somethin' to do."

He went out the front door and around the back of the store. Edie wasn't outside. When he opened the screen door and slipped past the storage room, he found her in the office, her back to him. She spun around.

"Edie, sweetheart, don't be afraid. I only wanna talk. I drove by your house last night, but you were at your aunt's. I wasn't gonna bother you there. But I wanted to tell you myself Sharon and I are through. I heard what happened at the store. I'm sorry about that." He paused. "I just got back from court. You might've heard I got myself in a little jam. But I'd sure feel a whole lot better if things were right between us. I miss you, baby."

Walker spoke in such soothing tones he could have been negotiating her surrender. Edie stared, saying nothing as tears slipped down her cheeks. He kept up his talk while he made a creep toward her so slowly she didn't seem to notice. She wore a blue dress he liked, deep at the neckline and narrow at the waist. She nearly always wore dresses or skirts. It was another thing special about her.

"How's your little girl? I saw her at my folks' house yesterday. Did she say? She's such a cute little thing. You know I always wanted a daughter."

"Walker."

She stepped back, and Walker followed her in this tense little dance.

"I know things have been hard lately, but I'll be free soon, a little broke, but so what? I started with a box of tools, and look where I'm now. Even after I give Sharon half, it's more than when I started. I could make us a good life."

"I told you I can't see you anymore."

"Course, you can."

He pulled a handkerchief from his back pocket and dabbed her cheeks.

Walker positioned himself in front of Edie. Her back was to the wall, and her breath came in short bursts. He felt dreamy and shameless as he pressed his body against her. He got a whiff of the rosy scent she wore, mixed with her salty sweat. He wanted to lap her neck and arms. Surely, that would ease his pain.

"Baby, you know I'm right."

He pushed back her hair and kissed her neck. Again, she resisted. Her eyes were bright with anger or fear, or both, and he chuckled.

"Let me go, Walker. This isn't funny."

"No, it isn't, baby. I love you, and you love me. That's the way it's supposed to be." His hands were on her. "I understand about Gil. Who didn't love my brother? I sure as hell did. But now I'm the one. I'd do anything for you."

Both turned as the door flew open. His mother blinked fast, calling their names and asking what they were doing. Edie bolted from the room. Walker tried to get past his mother, but she moved in his way like an irritated bird. His mother was yelling, "Walker, what's the matter with you?"

Choices

Edie ran up the back stairs to the second-floor apartment, flinging herself against the door until it popped open, and then she locked it. She pressed her hands over her thumping heart, trying to breathe. She waited for Walker's footsteps, but all she heard was the pulse of the store below.

She went to the window overlooking the road in front of the store. Walker talked with Dean near his truck. He jerked his head. His face was so mournful she felt another cry come on. Edie retreated into the apartment, so she wouldn't have to see him.

Edie waited to go back to work when she was sure Walker was gone. Someone finished stocking the shelves, and Marie was at the deli counter trying to handle lunch orders from the workingmen lined up in front of her. She washed her hands and took a place beside her mother-in-law, whose only acknowledgement was to give her room.

"What can I get you today, handsome?" Edie said to the man across from her. She tilted her head to the one behind him. "Hey, Bobby, heard your daddy's coming around. When's he getting out of the hospital? Tomorrow? Tell him hi for me."

She kept up her banter as her hands filled slices of bread with each man's request. She made more until everyone got what they wanted, and then Marie was lathering her hands at the sink's deep tub. Her rings, their diamonds so large they seemed fake, were stored on the counter. Edie came beside her.

"What happened back there, it's not what you think. I don't see your son anymore."

Marie concentrated on scrubbing her hands. She wiped them with a towel and reached for her rings.

"It looked pretty bad to me. It makes me wonder what goes on at your house. Maybe it's not the best place for Amber."

Edie pressed her lips. She glanced back at the full tables.

"You and Fred have been good to Amber, but if you're planning to make my daughter choose between you and me, then you don't love her the way I think you do." She leaned, so her head nearly touched Marie's. "And Gil would hate you for it."

Marie warbled, "Oh," and her hands shook so wildly, her rings clattered into the sink. She gasped as Edie caught them before they fell into the drain.

"Marie, you better hold onto these," Edie pressed the rings onto her mother-in-law's hand. "They probably cost Fred a pretty penny."

Marie squawked, "Thanks."

Without another word, Edie returned to her spot behind the deli counter. She was ready to quit although her shift wasn't over. She had enough of this family, Walker, his wife, and now his mother. She played Marie's words inside her head as she cleaned.

But she glanced up, smiling, when she heard Amber's voice. She ran down the aisle with Pop strolling behind. Edie left Marie to greet the girl, so giggly a couple of the men remarked. Pop wore a sly grin as he peered over the counter, checking to see whether Edie had any food for him. He winked when she angled her head toward Marie, who stared pucker-mouthed.

"You both look like you've been up to something," Edie said. "Are you gonna make me guess?"

"Our lips are sealed." Pop winked at Amber. "You'll just have to find out at the Fourth of July parade." He waved to the lunch crowd. "You all will, so get a front row seat." He winked at Amber. "Right, sweetie pie?"

It was a joke because the town's Fourth of July parade was so small, it really should go twice around to qualify as one. The town fathers and veterans marched, as did the American Legion Band. Kids decorated their bikes with ribbons, and the old-timers got their antique cars running.

"Wait till you see, Ma."

Edie smiled at her giggling daughter. Amber kept on even after Marie came around the counter.

"Are you all set for sleepover camp?" Marie bent for a kiss from Amber. "Did you pack your new things yet, Amber? You did? That's fine. Edie, dear, why don't you get our girl something to eat?"

Split Vote

Edie stared at the softball field and gripped the steering wheel of her car. She wanted to bang her head hard against it, but Aunt Leona sat next to her, saying, "Buck up, Edie."

"Patsy told me the team's gonna vote whether to kick me off the team," she told her aunt. "She said it'd be close."

Leona grunted.

"That's gratitude for you. You're one of the team's best players," she said. "Always have been."

"You and I both know it's got nothing to with that. It's this thing with Walker."

Leona's lips formed a deep, red frown.

"Sharon does have powerful allies on the team, what with family, but there might be a couple of swing votes. I bet you could twist Robin's arm a little to get her on your side."

Edie turned toward her aunt.

"Aunt Leona, truth is I really don't care about Robin's vote or staying on the team. I'm planning to quit before they kick me off. If I don't, half the team is gonna walk. Then there's no team."

Leona raised an eyebrow.

"Edie, you okay?"

"No." She shook her head. "It's Walker. He won't leave me alone. He keeps calling. Now he's parking outside my house."

"I thought I heard his truck. Child, why didn't you say something?"

"What's that gonna do? The other day he cornered me in the store's office. He came through the back door. He scared me bad. Marie walked in on us, and now she thinks I'm a terrible mother."

Leona's red hair shook as if it were on fire.

"What!"

"If I was really in love with Walker, I'd be happy his wife threw him out. I'd be hoping he'd be a good step-daddy to Amber." She rubbed the back of her neck. "Right now, I just want him to stay the hell away from me."

"I don't like the sound of this at all," Leona said.

Edie sighed.

"Don't worry. I'll find a way to take care of it."

Edie peered over the steering wheel. The rest of the team was gathered with Vera at the home bench. Some of the players stared at her car. Robin nibbled her nails.

"Looks like they're waiting for you," Leona said.

"Uh-huh. I'm gonna get this over with."

"Shoot, Edie."

"Maybe next year, things will be different. Vera won't be coaching. Or I can join another team." She shrugged. "Maybe Amber would like to play ball, and I can help out. We could go to her games instead."

"I see you've made up your mind. Well, hold your head up high, Edie. We Sweet women are good-looking and tough."

Edie smiled.

"You wanna wait for me in the car? It shouldn't take very long."

"Nah, I wouldn't miss it. Amber's with Alban, so I can make a complete fool of myself if I want without her being here to see it."

Edie got the lawn chair from the trunk and walked with her aunt toward the team. She wore her uniform as if she were suited up to play. Her teammates watched their slow approach.

"Hell, make 'em wait," Leona snarled.

Edie got her aunt settled in her chair, a couple of feet from the bench, and then she approached the team. Her eyes went from one woman to the other. Aunt Leona was right. The vote would be close. Vera stepped forward to speak, but Edie cut her off.

"I'm gonna make it easy on all of you. I heard there's supposed to be a vote about whether I should still be on the team." Edie paused. "I'm gonna disappoint you, Vera. I know this is all your idea." She narrowed her eyes. "I quit. It's not fair for a player to do it mid-season, but it's better than half the team. I wish you all luck."

A few of the girls hugged Edie. They went up to Leona, who told each one, "Atta girl." The rest stared dumbly or walked with Vera to the diamond, ready to play.

"Edie, what about the uniform?" Vera yelled.

Edie flipped her off. Leona's red lips were clamped tightly as she nodded.

"You did just fine, Edie. I'm proud of you. Let's hit the road. I could use a stiff drink. First one's on me."

"Sounds good. I'll race you there," she said, as she put out her arm for the old woman to clutch.

Angel Doll

Walker left the crew mid-day and drove to his camp. He sat on the dock drinking beer and watching boats glide across the water. This place seemed so far from everything happening to him. It was that way when he was a boy, and his father took Gil and him to hunt, fish, and just be guys. They swam or went out in the canoe. Walker's arms and back were strong, so when he paddled, the canoe moved quickly, its bow pushing the water in steady thrusts.

He was always disappointed going home.

Walker didn't mind the cabin was crude, but he might sink some money into the place. This could be just the spot for Edie and him to get away. He hummed as he thought about her sitting across from him in the canoe. Her dress would flutter above her thin, white thighs. Her smile would be encouraging.

On the way back to Conwell, Walker stopped at Ray's Tavern, a bar he spotted along the way, nothing more than a shack in the woods. He didn't recognize anyone among the haggard faces fixed on the TV set above the rows of liquor. People left him alone, and it was the way he liked it until a woman, maybe in her early forties and still decent enough in the room's dim light, played her eyes on him. She came from the other end of the bar when he nodded hello. Her round bottom rolled onto the stool next to his.

"I was sitting there wondering why a man as handsome as you should be drinking by himself. You seem kinda lonely over here," she said. "Maybe I can fix that. What do you say, darlin'?"

It only cost Walker five bucks worth of booze to get what he needed: a quick wrestle with her top off in the cab of his pickup, her big tits pushing into his face, and then a blow job. It was nothing like sex with Edie, but it helped curb the edge. The woman didn't mind when he brought her back inside, and to be a good sport, he bought her a cocktail before he left.

"I'll look you up when I'm driving through again," he told her.

Walker killed the headlights of his truck when he drove past Leona Sweet's house and let the wheels roll to where he parked the night before. This location gave him the best view of Edie's bedroom windows. He checked his watch. It was after ten. He tried calling her earlier from the Do, where he went after Ray's Tavern, but he hung up when her daughter answered. He stayed put at the Do, drinking himself into another foul mood.

He lit a cigarette and watched the lights in Edie's house, the shadows passing behind the drawn shades. She mostly stayed home these days with her daughter. He smiled.

Edie caught on right away what he was doing, spying on her, and she told him off the next time he called. She wouldn't let him talk as if she was afraid he'd say something that might change her mind. She was hurting him worse than what he did to her. He couldn't stop thinking about Edie, even when he was working, and yesterday he dropped a hammer on the new kid's foot.

He swiped at the mosquitoes on his forearm, rubbing them, so their bloody bodies burst and smeared on his skin. He thought he saw Edie peek out the window.

"Baby, just give me another chance."

He lit a joint as he set the bottle between his thighs. He stowed his handgun beneath the seat. He was supposed to take his boys to the dinky Fourth of July parade tomorrow, and he didn't want them to find the gun rifling around the glove compartment for gum or change. Good kids, but dumb enough to point it at each another. Walker didn't know why he brought the gun. Was he expecting Edie to have someone over? No one was with her tonight or any of the nights he parked here. So far, so good.

He laughed, feeling goofy from the weed, as he pictured his nutty mother getting in his way in the store's office the other day. Edie acted so skittish when he rubbed against her, like a schoolgirl who'd never been with a man. He exhaled. Edie was just a bit confused right now.

Walker sat for hours, smoking and drinking, keeping his vigil at Edie's house. The only sounds came from the small critters in the woods. The lights inside stayed off. He got out of his truck and moved forward in an unsteady march to her bedroom window, where his boots crushed the brush below. Heavy chintz curtains hung over the window, but he could see her bed through the crack where they parted. A small lamp from the hall gave Walker enough light for a glimpse of her face, pretty and peaceful. He murmured her name and called her, "My angel doll."

He snuck back to his truck.

Walker thought about climbing into her window, finding her in bed, naked and waiting for him. She opened and closed her legs. "Do you like this game?" she asked him. He unzipped his pants in awe of his lust for her.

The second time, he fantasized she wore a nightgown when she walked to his truck. She begged him to follow her inside the house, and then she lay back on the kitchen table, pulling up the fabric.

"She's asleep, so we can't make any noise," she whispered.

He glanced up when headlights shined in the rear-view mirror. The pickup belonged to Harlan Doyle, and the man slowed, staring at his truck although he didn't stop. Walker decided he'd better leave.

Fourth of July

Walker swore and pounded his pickup's horn although the noise hurt his head. His boys weren't coming from the house fast enough, and the last thing he wanted was to go to the door. He reached into the glove compartment for a fresh pack of smokes and hit the horn again, but still there was no sign of the kids. He held the lit butt in his lips and put the truck in gear. Finally, after driving several yards, his boys, dressed in their baseball uniforms, came flying from the house, yelling for him to stop.

They got the truck door open, and their identically worried faces stared up at him. He scowled while one boy then the other climbed into the cab.

"I told you two to be ready."

The son closest to the door held a shaking pile of papers.

"Ma said to give you this."

"What is it?"

The truck's engine idled while Walker read the messages in Sharon's handwriting. The his and her lawyers from New York had been trying to reach him. Now they would find someone else to renovate the old house they were buying. The lumberyard called, and so did the building inspector. There was a letter from a lawyer, hers. He chucked the papers on the floor.

"Shit, you boys stay right here and don't touch a goddamn thing."

His sons' eyes lit up.

Walker stormed the front steps and tried opening the aluminum door, but his wife had locked it. He banged with his fist until she appeared behind the door's screen.

"Let me in." His pointed boots made deep dents in the aluminum panel when he kicked at the door, and he kept at it until its bottom caved in. "I'm gonna break this fuckin' door down."

"No, you'll hurt me," she whined.

"If you don't open the door, I sure as hell will."

The door shook as he gave it two hard kicks. He heard a click, and Sharon slipped outside to the cement stoop. She wore a blue, flowered housecoat that gaped at her breasts. Her head chopped forward like an old hen pecking worms. She backed to the door when Walker poked the lit end of his cigarette near her nose.

"What are you tryin' to do? Fuckin' ruin me? I just lost work because of you." He tapped a finger to his temple. "Get it through your thick, fuckin' head, if I don't work, I don't make money. I know that's something you might understand."

He flicked the butt into the bushes near the door. Sharon's lips flapped open, but nothing came out.

"Anybody needing to talk or see me, you call me at Dean's until I say different. You have the fuckin' number?" Walker got close enough to feel her belly against his belt. His wife whimpered. "Got it now? Good."

Walker charged back to the truck, driving it at a reckless speed through town. His boys clung to each other, sliding around the front seat until finally one pleaded with him to slow down. He glared. Both were on the verge of crying. He let up on the gas.

"What does she say about me?"

"Ma?" the closer one asked as he checked his brother. "Ma says you've got yourself in a lot of trouble. Uncle Buddy took you to court for being mean. She said Uncle Dean says you've gone crazy."

The blue light of a cruiser flashed ahead as a cop directed traffic. He took a hard right onto a dirt road.

"He did, did he? Some friend that asshole is."

Hick Parade

Edie found a spot in the shade for Aunt Leona, who relented last minute to go to the hick parade, as she called it, but only because Amber begged. She wanted her great-aunt to see Pop's surprise, and Leona said, "Huh," in the back of her throat.

"You must be the only person left in this world who isn't disappointed in anything that man does," Leona told her.

"Disappointed?" Amber said as if she had never heard the word before.

Leona let Edie fuss over her, making sure she had enough space in front of her chair, so Amber could sit on the grassy shoulder. Her aunt's head chopped forward. She glanced at Amber sitting on the curb.

"Tell me, Edie." Her voice was low and even. "What's Walker St. Claire still doing on our road at night? I hear his truck go by."

Edie shook her off.

"Maybe it belongs to Harlan coming home late."

Leona made a choking laugh.

"I know the sound of his truck's engine by now. Don't you give me that look, Edie. Nothing good is going to come of this."

"I told you I don't wanna talk about it."

"Maybe you should."

Edie nodded at a couple, super-regulars at her in-laws' store. Her aunt waited.

"He parks there at night. He must be watching my house, seeing what I will do. I could call the cops, but they're not gonna do a thing." Edie shook a finger. "Remember that girl I went to school with, the one who married a beater? You know who I'm talkin' about, Melanie."

"Yeah."

"She used to shop at the store all banged up somethin' awful," Edie said. "She told me the cops said they had to catch her husband in the act. He nearly killed her one time. Then she and her kids were gone. They left town. It was the only way." She sighed deeply. "I can hear the chief saying Walker's only parking on the side of the road. There's no harm in that."

"What if he comes inside your house?"

"He's not gonna."

"How do you know?"

"Cause if he wanted, he would've already done it."

"Shoot, if I were ten years younger, I'd go out there myself and tell him off." Leona's hair shook. "I just hope Alban doesn't."

Edie held a finger to her lips.

"I'm figuring he'll get tired of it and move on. Please, don't tell Pop, please."

"All right, I won't. For now."

"Thanks."

Two men were setting up the PA system on a flatbed trailer decorated with red, white, and blue bunting parked across the road in front of the veterans' memorial. The roadsides were filled with people, most from town, but many from elsewhere, because Conwell was the only one around to have a Fourth of July parade. The town put on a chicken barbecue, and the Conwell Women's Softball Team had a game, the first she'd miss since she came back after Amber was a baby. There would be fireworks tonight at the ball field.

Edie kept saying hello to people she knew, and her aunt, in her fashion, made wise cracks, especially about the men.

"I wouldn't mind some fireworks tonight," Leona said with a dirty cackle. "Yup, fireworks, the kind that makes you feel like there's an explosion going off inside you." Leona pointed across the street. "There's our neighbor. I bet he's got all the right equipment. Maybe a little banged up, but still working. What do you say, Edie?"

"Aunt Leona, shh."

"Don't mind me. I'm feeling a little extra something today."

Harlan made his lumbering way behind the row of people staked out across the street.

"I see him over there," Edie said.

Leona slapped her arm.

"Go get him, will you? I bet he doesn't know a soul here." She slapped Edie again. "What are you waiting for?"

"Maybe he wants to be alone."

"Nobody wants to be alone. Besides, I got a feeling about Harlan. He's a decent man. You don't see many of them in Conwell. You might want to give it some thought, Edie."

"You sound like Pop."

"Yeah? For once, I agree with my brother. Get going."

"Okay, okay. Amber, you wanna come?"

She crossed the street with Amber. It didn't take long to catch up with Harlan, and he stopped when she called his name.

"I see you made it to the parade. My aunt wants you to join us."

He closed one eye.

"What about you?"

"You don't have to be so shy around me, Harlan. Besides we've got the shady part of the street and room for one more."

He grinned.

"All right. I'll join you then."

As they walked across the street, Harlan stopped the man selling parade souvenirs.

"What would you like?" he asked Amber.

"Me?"

"Yes, you, Amber."

After weighing her choices, Amber picked a stuffed, purple snake, and because Harlan insisted, a red balloon larger than her head. Edie took the balloon from Harlan, so she could tie it to Amber's wrist. She touched his hand, the skin warm and roughed up from work. She got a feeling, like Harlan could be a hard-working man spending his day off with his family and liking it.

"What do you say?" she told Amber.

Amber smiled.

"Thank you very much, Mr. Doyle."

"You're very welcome, Amber. But you may call me Harlan," he said. "So, Amber, what can you tell me about this parade? I'm new in town."

Her girl jabbered about the parade, moving quickly in small arcs around Harlan as he walked in large, hobbling steps. Leona watched with a satisfied smile. Edie knew what her aunt was thinking. This is what their girl needed.

Amber sat on the grass shoulder. Leona offered Harlan a chair, but he declined. He stood instead beside Edie.

People were settling along the parade route. Her in-laws waved to Amber from across the street. Edie was listening to Harlan talk with Aunt Leona when she spotted Walker hike down the center of the road, rushing his two boys toward the start. He smoked a cigarette. His head was down as he barked at his boys, "It's your goddamn fault if you're late. Move it."

Edie held her breath and let her eyes pass over Walker as if he were a stranger. But he turned her way briefly, and she caught the expression in his eyes. His body went forward, but his heart stayed with her. Finally, she saw only the back of him.

Everything began to swirl: her family, the town gathered for this silly parade, Walker's dark love for her.

She glanced up at Harlan.

"Don't blink, or you'll miss the whole thing," she heard herself say.

"That's what everyone keeps saying," he said, and then he whispered, "What's wrong, Edie?"

"Nothing, Harlan."

Down the road, the American Legion Band played a raggedy rendition of "Stars and Stripes Forever" to get the procession going. The color guard of flag-holding veterans was first, followed by the usual waddling lineup of town officials. Teams of baseball players, guarded by their coaches, marched in uneven, bumping lines. Harlan laughed about the kid who nearly poked a teammate in the head with a baseball bat and the spooked pony that tried to make a run for it.

"This is great stuff," he said close to her ear.

Edie nearly cried, searching for Walker. She closed her eyes as she listened to the noise made by the rolling wheels, the marching feet, and clapping people.

"Yeah," she said faintly.

Amber tugged at her arm.

"Ma, Ma, here comes Poppy. Wait till you see what we did."

The laughter started farther down the road, and when Edie bent, a DPW truck lurched forward. She began to laugh with the crowd. The hood of the red dump truck was trimmed with strings of triangle-shaped flags, bouquets of dirty, plastic flowers, and a hand-painted sign that read: 35 YEARS WORKING AT YOUR DUMP. One of Pop's drinking buddies was at the wheel, tooting the horn and smiling as if he were set for life.

The truck towed a small trailer holding an outhouse, with the door open, so everyone could see Pop sitting in his red union suit on a toilet. Around the outhouse was an assortment of junk, from wagon wheels to dressmaker's mannequins, to make it resemble the town dump. At one point, Pop stood. The back seat of his long johns hung open, and he saluted the howling crowd as he let loose a roll of toilet paper.

Amber waved to her grandfather when the truck inched past.

"Li'l darlin', how are you?" Pop shouted to Amber. "Hey, Leona, lookin' mighty fine today."

Leona puffed up in her chair.

"Jesus, Alban, what in the hell are you doing?"

But from the crowd's operatic roar, Leona was clearly outnumbered. A photographer from the local paper took Pop's picture, and one of the emcees joked over the PA system, "I don't know about you, but I'm grateful Benny isn't the town's gravedigger."

"Pop sure outdid himself," Edie said, laughing with her father's fans.

Harlan bent over with happy tears in his eyes. Leona reached up to yank his arm.

"You think this is so funny? Enjoy it now, Mr. Harlan Doyle, but if my brother didn't ask the road boss to use that stuff, we can forget about having a highway truck on our road for a long, long while."

Stand Up and Say It

Walker kicked Dean's boots as he napped in a lawn chair in front of his singlewide. The man snorted and glanced around.

"Shithead, whose side are you on anyway?" Walker growled. "You told that fat bitch I'm going crazy."

He kicked the chair again, this time hard enough that Dean almost fell.

"Jesus, Walker, what're you doin'?"

"You saying you didn't tell Sharon I'm going nuts?"

The ball in Dean's throat moved up and down. He exhaled hard through his nose.

Walker glared.

"I can tell what kind of mood you're in, but I'm gonna say it anyway," Dean said. "This thing with Edie is outta control. You're scaring her, and I'm worried about you. Sharon asked, so I told her. She's worried about you, too."

"Since when?"

One of Dean's eyes dropped shut.

"We've been friends, how long? All our lives, right? You have it in your head you gotta have Edie, and shit, Walker, she don't want you. Why don't you face up to it?"

Walker saw Edie at the parade, but after he dropped off his boys, people jammed the roadsides. By time he found her, she was helping her aunt into her car. Her girl was close by.

"Stand up and say it," Walker said.

Dean got to his feet. He studied Walker.

"I'm saying this cause I'm your friend. Back off. Edie's been through enough."

Walker's right fist glanced across Dean's jaw as soon as the man went silent. But Dean stayed upright. He withstood a second punch, then another. He wasn't even fighting back. Dean took a few steps to get his balance. He waited for the next. It made Walker hotter.

"You never stuck up for yourself," he told Dean. "It's pure luck you wasn't killed in Vietnam." His next punch sent Dean sprawling to the ground. "You're wrong. You're all wrong about her."

On The Run

Edie's car was parked in her driveway, but she wasn't home. Neither was her foolish old man, Walker was relieved to see. An orange cat kept sentry on a couch at the other end of the porch. It could keep the smelly thing.

Walker hated cats anyway. Give him a dog that stuck by you no matter what. He hadn't had a hound in years, but maybe he'd get one of Dean's puppies when he moved into his own place. The boys would like that. He could take them all hunting at his camp. Maybe Edie's little girl would want a puppy, too.

"Git," he snarled at the cat, but the animal stayed in its spot, its green eyes winking.

The door to Edie's house was unlocked, naturally. Nobody locked their doors in Conwell, except maybe his parents since they owned valuable things, and newcomers, of course, because they're afraid of the locals taking their stuff.

Walker went inside to use the toilet, and afterward he wandered into her bedroom. He opened her dresser drawers, fingering her clothing, the lacy things, and the packets of rubbers. He held one of her black panties to his lips before he stuffed it in his shirt pocket.

He searched her closet, taking a shoebox covered by wrapping paper off the shelf. Inside, he found blue envelopes, airmail from overseas, all from Gil, and snapshots of his brother and Edie. He slid the box back into place.

Walker stood still, scanning her room, eyeing her bed before he left.

He kept the heels of his boots on the porch's railing as he tipped the rocker slowly. He lit another cigarette while he worked it out again. He'd tell her he'd be a free although poorer man. He would promise never to hurt her again. She would say, "I forgive you." He'd say no one else could love her as much as him, and Edie would tell him, "Of course, Walker."

He stopped rocking. He swore he heard her voice in the distance. It was definitely Edie, but she sounded farther down the road. He ran his thumb along his smooth chin. There she was again.

Walker remembered the place on the river where they used to swim. When they were kids, they parked their cars and pickups near Edie's house, and then hiked quietly down the road, so old lady Doyle wouldn't call the cops. Lots of fun went on there during the summer. He hadn't been back in years, but Edie told him she went swimming with her daughter when the weather got hot.

The back of the rocker hit the house's clapboards as he got to his feet, startling the cat, which leaped to the porch's floorboards and flew over the steps. Walker strolled down the road, using Edie's voice as a target until he found the path's opening, across the street from Harlan Doyle's house. Walker used to be able to drive his truck through here, but now the way was overgrown with pucker brush and saplings. The air was rich with swirling bugs. New growth shined bright green on the tips of the trees.

He stepped quietly toward the river's edge, where he heard Edie sing. He stayed within the trees, wanting to spy on her first.

Walker swore. Edie wasn't alone. She was with her daughter and

Harlan Doyle. The girl was on the shore, stacking river stones into towers. Edie and Harlan Doyle treaded water while they talked. He didn't hear what they said. But she laughed. He laughed. Walker saw Edie's happy face, and once again, everything good slipped fast from him. He saw them together at the parade. He wanted to rush to the river and yell at the ugly cripple, "She's mine!" He wanted to drag him to the shore and beat him.

His eyes filled with tears as he leaned against a tree. He banged the back of his head, cursing. How stupid he was. He wanted to hurt him and hurt her. Anyone. Anything. He headed off, thrashing through the underbrush like a wild thing on the run, his boots kicking, until he reached the road.

Clearer View

"Edie, it's Dean. Did I wake ya? Sorry. I know it's late, but is Walker there?"

She held the phone. Dean's voice was rough and halting like a stalling engine. Finally, she said, "No, he's not here. I'm not going with him anymore."

Dean blew into the mouthpiece.

"Shit, Edie, I'm worried about Walker. He's getting himself in trouble. We got into a fight today. He accused me of stuff, and he's been talking crazy about you. I just wanna make sure you're all right."

"Crazy?"

"You hear he got arrested after Sharon threw him out."

"I heard."

"He's drinking and doing worse since. I talked with Sharon about it. That was a mistake." He blew air into the phone. "He thinks I'm against him. He was here for a few minutes getting some of his stuff before he took off again. He kept saying he saw ya."

"What's he talking about? I didn't leave my road after we came home from the parade. I did take Amber into town later to see the fireworks. That's all. I didn't see Walker. Is he talking about the parade when he was there with his boys?"

"I dunno. He kept yakking about you and Harlan Doyle swimming together. It didn't make any sense."

She sighed.

"He must've seen us at the river. Amber was with us," she said. "Hold on a minute."

Edie pulled back the curtain and was relieved when she didn't see Walker's truck. She put down the phone to check the other side of the house. She shook her head. Walker was in a new spot.

She lifted the receiver to her ear.

"He's parked outside."

"He's what?"

"He does it every night. He just sits there for hours," she told Dean, her words catching. "I lock my windows and doors."

"Edie, that's not right."

"What else did Walker say?"

"More stupid shit. About you being his. Some other stuff. I don't wanna scare you, Edie. I tried to talk some sense into him, but he doesn't wanna listen."

"Dean, I should never have gone with him." Her words were long and mournful.

"It's what he's always wanted, Edie." There was the click of a lighter. Dean inhaled and exhaled. "You should've heard him when we were kids."

Edie remembered Gil teasing her, "I believe Walker loves you more than me," and her response was, "I only love you."

She was so serious Gil kissed her.

"Please, stop," Edie told Dean.

He didn't.

"After Gil died, he was so pissed he married Sharon. He used to cheat on her somethin' awful." Dean blew smoke in a windy stream.

"You were different. You made him happy. He used to tell me things." His voice fell. "He felt like shit after he hurt you. He knew he blew it. All he talks about now is finding ways to get you back."

"It's not gonna happen," she said firmly. "Don't worry, Dean. He won't come in, and Pop's sleeping next door if I need him. I'm gonna hang up now." She paused. "Thanks for calling."

Edie wandered through the dark house, quiet except for the refrigerator's motor and the well's water pump cycling in the cellar. It was too hot to lock the windows, but maybe she should, at least the ones easy to reach from the ground.

A swarm of fireflies sparked near her bedroom window, and the moon, although waning, gave her enough light to see Walker's pickup a short distance on the road. She chose another window for a clearer view. Walker's head was tipped back against the seat. She thought of what Dean said and got her sneakers.

Edie slipped around the back of the house, past where her aunt's dog was buried, to a large tree near the road. The air rang with insects.

She studied Walker, who appeared to have not moved since she saw him from her house. She stepped closer, peeking carefully through the passenger window. She ducked when his eyes opened briefly.

Walker snored with his mouth open. His fine jaw was elongated as his head tipped back against the seat. The neck of a liquor bottle rested against his thigh, its contents nearly gone. He appeared harmless, almost comical, passed out like that, and she almost smiled until she saw a handgun on the seat. Its handle was within Walker's reach. Edie shrank behind a tree when Walker swiped at the insects biting his face. She took a deep breath and stepped as quickly as she could without making a sound.

Back inside, Edie locked the doors and windows, except for the ones in her daughter's room. Walker wouldn't be able to break in there without her hearing him. She got in bed with Amber. She pulled a sheet over them. Tonight she took her to see the fireworks, like a good mother would. Her daughter was leaving soon for sleepover camp, thanks to her in-laws.

Edie put her arm protectively over the sleeping girl. She kept waiting, listening, and hoping Walker didn't find a way in until she, too, fell asleep.

A Heart Sour And Dark

Walker sat on an upholstered chair he dragged from inside the camp onto the dock. His feet rested on a wooden crate turned upside down. By his best guess, it was around three. He must have left his watch at Ray's Tavern, and he supposed the next time he went he'd find it on some drunk's wrist. He didn't care. It was only a gift from his parents.

He drank, first coffee then beer, thought about fishing, but did nothing about it. He couldn't recall when he last ate a full meal. Maybe he'd drive to the Lookout Bar and Grille to get dinner, but he'd have to clean up first.

Two speedboats flared across the lake, slapping water against the bottom of the dock's boards. Lots of people appeared to have taken the week off. He needed a vacation, too.

Walker pulled a joint from the breast pocket of his unbuttoned flannel shirt. He had been here since the Fourth of July. He only went back once to check on the crew, but now he was staying put.

He slept most of yesterday. He didn't know he was so tired. He probably would have kept sleeping, except a woodpecker drummed its beak against a tree. He went outside to take a leak, amused to find the sun past its highest point in the sky.

Later, he stopped at Ray's. The woman from the other time found him quickly. He couldn't remember her name, but she was satisfied to be called "darlin'." He would have taken her out to his truck, but she smelled like dead fish, and he couldn't bring himself to touch her. He bought her a drink and left.

Walker squinted at the sun reflecting off the lake. He squeezed the joint between his lips and reached for the framed black-and-white photograph on the dock. The glass was gone. Two boys posed with rifles. They wore plaid jackets and furry hats with flaps over their ears. When he and Edie were here, she got excited when she recognized Gil and him in the photo. They had that stupid fight, and she took off.

"What the hell was I thinking?" he said out loud.

Walker nodded slowly. He planned to fix up this camp, make it year-round, and turn it into a real home. He bet Edie would like it here, nice and quiet, her girl, too. His boys could visit on the weekends. They'd be his happy, little family.

He took one last look at the photo and flung it far into the lake. He couldn't compete with his brother even dead.

Walker's head fell back against the chair. He took another hit from the joint. He and Gil tried once to see how far they could swim across the lake, and their old man had to fetch them in the canoe before they drowned. He thought it might not be a bad way to go. He could just strip and swim until he got so tired he couldn't stay afloat. In the end, though, it seemed too much of an effort.

A truck pulled into his driveway. From the rattling muffler, he knew it belonged to Dean, who had put off fixing it for over a month now. The truck door slammed, and Dean's boots thudded over the packed dirt and dock. Walker cocked his head.

"You seem rather comfortable there," Dean said.

Walker crossed his ankles, the toes of his cowboy boots spread in a V. He offered the last of the joint to Dean, but his friend eyed the beer can on the deck.

"Want one? There's more in the water. Sorry, it's as cold as it's gonna get."

"You?"

"Sure. See the fishnet over there?"

Dean retrieved two cans of beer from the lake and tossed him one. Walker used his foot to push the crate toward his friend. He flicked the roach into the water.

"Take a load off your feet."

"Thanks, Walker."

Dean popped the can and sat down. He took a drink. Walker shifted in his chair. Last he saw Dean, he stopped by the job site, where his crew sheathed an addition's frame with plywood. Dean was in charge, and after a while, Walker told them, "I guess I'm not needed," and he drove away.

"I'm figuring you didn't drive all this way for a friendly conversation and a warm beer," Walker said. "You look too worried for that."

Dean cleared his throat.

"You're right. Job's going okay, but I need some money to pay the crew and lumberyard." He paused. "Sharon called about the mortgage."

Walker listened with some interest. He didn't want to go back, but he wasn't about to throw away his business or his house. He worked too hard for that.

"I'll give you a check before you leave. I'll put a little extra in it for your trouble."

Dean gave him a grateful smile.

"That's good, Walker, real good."

Walker studied his friend's unshaven face, checking for signs he hurt him when he punched him back at his trailer. He found only a bruised cheek.

"I apologize about the other day. I acted like a real asshole."

207

"It's okay." Dean's face crinkled. "By the way, your boys keep calling."

Walker finished the beer.

"Yeah? What about Edie?"

"Jesus, Walker, I don't wanna talk about her."

"I guess you don't, but she pretty much drowns out everything else for me." He reached into his shirt pocket for a cigarette. "I used to hate Gil for marrying her. I was almost glad he got killed, and I loved my brother. Pretty sick, huh?" He waved the unlit cigarette. "You don't have to answer."

The bottom of the crate scraped against the boards as Dean plucked two more beers from the water.

"Gil's the only one who'd understand how I feel about her," Walker said. "My parents sure as hell don't." His voice faded as he lit the butt. "She always dressed up nice for me. Her hair shined and smelled good. When she laughed, the sound bubbled up from a sweet spot inside her." He took a drag. "You ever see the way she talks with the people in the store? I've seen her give an old barfly at the Do her ear for an hour. She lights up everything and everybody, including me. That's why my brother loved her. That's why. Jesus, the last time he was home, he didn't want to leave her for a minute. I had to shame him to get him up here with me."

Walker shook his head and snorted.

"Gil and I spent the night drinking and talkin' about old times. He was afraid for Edie and the baby while he was away. He wanted me to watch out for her." The corners of his mouth turned upward. "We fried up steaks and went skinny-dipping. God, that water was cold."

He laughed, and Dean joined him.

"Two days later, I drove Gil to the bus station. He was on his way to Vietnam. Edie came with us." Walker murmured. "She was trying to give my brother a good sendoff, but I knew she was scared to death for him. At the station, Gil reminded me all over again to take care of her until he got back." He clicked his tongue. "My brother was somethin' else. He thought of everybody else first. I sure ain't like that." His voice trailed off. "You should've seen those two. I lost count how many times they kissed, and after, when the bus was moving, she ran with it, waving and crying until she reached the street. It just killed me."

"Yeah, Walker, everybody took it hard when Gil died."

"I'm not talking about that. I'm talking about the way she loved him."

Walker spoke this way until the sun slipped behind the trees on the far edge of the lake. Everything around him was heavy and slow. He couldn't move.

Finally, he let Dean go, with a check and a pledge to see him soon.

A Dazzling Anger

Walker asked the bartender at Ray's Tavern if he could use the phone, but the man said no for the second time. He rubbed the back of his neck. He thought he was on decent terms with the guy, spending money here, but to no advantage, it appeared, at this dump.

"No long distance calls," the bartender growled.

"Here's five bucks. Three minutes. That's all I need. It's important, or I wouldn't ask."

The bartender stood with arms crossed over his round gut while Walker twisted a book of matches. He came here reasonably drunk from the Lookout Bar and Grille, where he ate dinner and downed shots of tequila.

He didn't know why he kept coming back to this hick dive. He was already sick of its clientele, an unremarkable group that asked the same questions and told the same jokes as if they had forgotten the last time they said them. A fight broke out one night when one drunk was sure another farted next to him on purpose. The woman was still friendly, but only because she was guaranteed a free drink. She liked to grope him and lick his ear, but Walker wasn't interested. He was less keen on the other hags who hung here.

Tonight Walker saw a woman at the Lookout who reminded him so much of Edie he used the restaurant's pay phone to call her. His back was to the room when he dialed the numbers. His free hand was flat on the wall as if he were guarding the phone. When Edie answered, her hello struck such a tender spot he began to cry. She knew what was going on, because she said his name in a hollow whisper that snatched his voice. He hung up the phone and drove to Ray's.

Walker wanted another try. He'd let Edie know he was living at his camp, that he needed her to save him, that his heart felt sour and dark.

"I'll give you ten bucks for a three-minute call," he told the bartender.

"Keep your money. I ain't lettin' you use the phone."

The drinkers' heads swung from one man to the other.

"It's only Conwell. Not too far."

"Listen. If it's so damn important why don't you drive there?" The bartender shoved his thumb toward the door. "You know what? I'm sick of your face. Time for you to hit the road."

Walker threw a bill on the bar's top.

"Shit, here's a twenty. How about thirty bucks?"

"Asshole, you're really pissing me off." The bartender whistled sharply through his teeth and nodded at a large man who came from out back. "Get this son of a bitch outta here."

The man hustled Walker from the building and dumped him on the parking lot's dirt. He stood there with crossed arms, warning Walker what would happen if he went back. Walker got to his feet and into the front seat of his truck to consider his options, but he thought of only one. He wanted to talk with Edie. Another chance. That was all.

Then he passed out.

Walker stayed that way for hours until the bartender rapped his knuckles against a window. He snorted awake when the driver's door opened. The cab's light confused him at first, but he got angry when he recognized the man. Beyond, the bar was dark, and no other vehicles were in the lot.

"Hey, buster, you can't sleep here. Move it."

The bartender shook his fist, but Walker was no longer too drunk to defend himself. He leaped from the truck and smacked the man across the jaw. The bartender took a swing, but it fell short. Walker laughed. He got up close, punching the bartender's ribs. He felt a couple give and laughed again. This man would remember him whenever he sucked air for a while.

The bartender was his height but built softer, and no one was around to protect him. Walker punched the man's head with a hard knock then another. He was filled by such a dazzling anger it bordered on joy. It fueled his arms and fists. The man pleaded with him, but it was too late to stop, and when the bartender fell to the ground, Walker rammed the sharp toes of his cowboy boots against his head and body.

Walker couldn't make out the man in the darkness, but he heard a moan and a loud, wet gurgle until finally he was quiet.

Fighting Fair

The next day Edie glanced up from the sink behind the store's deli counter. Dean looked as if he was bringing bad news.

"Somethin' happen?"

"Gotta minute?"

She wiped her hands on a towel. She was ready to quit work anyway.

Dean checked around the store before he spoke.

"I went to see Walker yesterday at his camp. He's acting really strange, Edie, like he's given up on everything. He looks like shit. I bet he hasn't been eating much." He frowned. "He's not the man we know."

Edie stared at the floor. She thought about Walker's call last night. His sobs touched her. She pressed her lips.

"What am I supposed to do?" she asked Dean.

"Edie, just get him back here. He can stay with me. I bet he'll listen to you."

"He scares me."

"You're the only one he wants."

"What about Fred and Marie? They're his parents."

"What's the matter? Do you need to get your little girl?"

"No, no, she's away at camp."

"Edie, you know Gil would want you to do this for his brother."

"Shit, Dean, you're not fighting fair."

A Black Hole

It took Edie longer than she expected to reach the lake. She went
home first, where she met Pop, who was picking up his twenty-two
to shoot rats at the dump, and Aunt Leona, who flagged her down in
her driveway, so she could talk about missing Amber. She didn't tell
them where she was going. They wouldn't have let her.

Edie thought about Walker. He was the one who drove her to the
hospital when Amber was born. She couldn't reach her father or
Leona, and it was a wild ride, her labor coming on so hard and fast,
she yelped and writhed in the front seat of his truck. Walker made his
voice soft and steady as he tried to ease her from the pain.

After Amber was born, Walker found Edie crying in her room,
grieving for Gil. He let her sob in his arms, and then a nurse carried
Amber into the room. The nurse showed the baby to Walker.

"Mr. St. Claire, you have a beautiful, little girl," she said, placing
the baby in his arms.

"I believe she looks just like her mother," he told her.

Misguided by Dean's directions, Edie now wandered down a dirt
road until she came to a farm at its dead end. A crew of men hoisted

hay bales onto a wagon. When Pop was younger, he worked summers on a hay crew, one of the many seasonal jobs he did to support his family. It was awfully hard work, but Edie remembered how clean Pop smelled when he came home, sunburned, dusty, and his clothes stuck with hay.

She backtracked to a general store. Three police cruisers were parked in front, and when she paid for sandwiches and cold drinks for her and Walker, the woman at the register said a man was beaten to death outside his bar.

"A logger found him this morning," she told Edie. "The cops aren't talking, but I heard someone say his head was so bashed in, you could see his brains. I don't believe anything like that could happen here. Do you?"

"Wow, that's awful. Who could've done something like that?"

"The cops say somebody must've had it in for him."

The woman handed Edie her change.

"Did he have family?" she asked.

"His boy lives in Arizona. He's on his way back. Where you headed? To the lake? Be careful. They haven't caught whoever did it."

"I hope they find him soon. What an awful thing to do."

Edie sat in her car. She should go home. She should be glad Walker was leaving her alone. But she steered her car past the cruisers in front of the store.

Using the directions the cashier gave her, she got her bearings on the lakeside road, where trees hung in a thick canopy. She caught familiar glimpses of the gray lake through the forest until she found Walker's driveway. She wound the car toward his camp and parked behind his pickup truck.

Edie clutched the bag containing the food and cans of soda as she made her way toward the cabin. She listened and looked for some sign of Walker. Her steps were slow. She stopped once but kept going until she found him, sitting in a high-back chair positioned in the middle of the dock. His eyes were closed. He held a revolver and a can of beer on his lap. She thought to leave without him knowing, but Walker sputtered awake. He grabbed the gun and blinked at Edie.

"It's you, baby."

His face was unshaven, his body unwashed.

"I brought us food and something to drink. See?" Edie raised the bag then set it on the dock when he didn't respond. "How are you, Walker?"

"Never better." He hummed through his nose. "You sure look real pretty in that dress. Shit, where are my manners? Take my chair. No? Then sit on my lap." He slapped his thigh. "Shy? That's not like Edie, the queen of the Do-Si-Do. Or is it the new Edie?" He raised the beer for the last swallow and chucked the empty onto the pile near the shore. "It's okay. I don't mind. Honey, I'll take you any way you are."

The wind rose off the water, raising the hem of her skirt above her knees. Speedboats whizzed across the lake behind her.

"I'll sit on the box."

"No, no, the chair's for you."

Walker was on his feet, giving her his seat. His boot heels knocked against the dock as he paced. She sat back, gauging the tension of his hand on the gun. He grinned big for her. Why did she ever listen to Dean?

"I've been doing a lot of thinkin'. About you mostly. Sorry. Can't help it. About Gil, too." Walker held his head sideways. "Who sent you here? Never mind. It was that pest Dean. He'd make a better mother than my own dear mother. It don't matter. You came."

He resumed his march.

"Walker, how about putting that gun away?"

He laughed.

"I like guns. I like the feel of them, the way they sound when they go off. Gil never liked guns. It's why he died over there in Vietnam. It's the God's honest truth, Edie. He didn't have the fight in him." Walker waggled the gun. "If I'd gone, I'd have shot every gook I saw. I wouldn't have left a beautiful wife behind. I would've fought my way back." He shook his head. "Tell me, babe. Did you really feel anything for me? Did you give me any of the love you gave my brother?"

"Course, I did," she said quietly.

He raised his gun in triumph.

"All right." He rubbed his face with his free hand. He gave her a long, sad look. "How about you and your little girl coming to live here with me? Our own little family. Huh, what do you think?"

She didn't answer.

Walker dropped to his knees before her. He set the gun on the dock. Edie thought to kick it into the water, but she didn't think she could move fast enough. Walker touched the buttons on the front of her dress, rolling the edges between his fingers. She clamped her hands over his as if they were praying together.

"Baby, last night, I beat a bartender who wouldn't let me use the phone to call you. Can you believe it?"

"Walker, it's you?"

The corners of his mouth turned up.

"You got that right. It's always been me."

He silenced her by placing his lips on hers, giving her a kiss, half-chaste, half lustful. Her chest moved in a heavy whirl.

Walker aimed his gun at her. His darting eyes were the only part of his face that moved. She began to cry for Amber, for Pop, and Aunt Leona, who'd be left without her.

Her heart beat hard.

"Please, Walker, I'll do whatever you want. I have a little girl I love."

"Sure you do, Edie. Sure you do. Now say you love me." He cried, too. "Say it. Say it and mean it."

Edie saw the black hole at the end of the revolver, and she knew how Gil felt when his chopper rushed to the jungle floor. He wanted to live. She flew to her feet, screaming, as Walker fired. Then he put the gun in his mouth and took a second shot.

Twisted And Tragic

Edie paced the dock near Walker's body. She used her trembling hands to shield the sunlight. The shots were in her ears still, and she could see Walker's face, twisted and tragic, before he stuck the gun in his mouth.

She moaned his name.

A boat sped from the middle of the lake, and two boys yelled, but she felt too dumb to call or wave. Instead, she touched her forehead, the spot where it stung, and came away with a palm filled with blood. She tried to swipe her hand clean along her hip, but blood and something else was on her dress. She cried aloud, her breath coming from her chest in deep, hard shudders when a shirtless boy bounded onto the boards.

"We heard the shots. You screaming." He glanced at Walker and took a quick step backward. "Shit, look at that. What happened?"

"He shot himself."

"Christ, this is bad. You got a phone here? No?" He shouted to his friend. "Go call the cops. Tell 'em there's a dead guy here, and she's been hurt." The other boy talked. "What's the address here?" Edie didn't answer. "Tell 'em we'll wait on the side of the road."

Edie cried harder. Everything around her was blocked away, and she barely heard the boy's shout or the motor's roar when the boat took off. The boy who stayed, his face tanned and hairless, just a high school kid, checked her forehead while she watched Walker's blood soak into the dock's floorboards.

"He tried to shoot me."

The boy took hold of her upper arm, leading her from the dock to the road.

"Jesus, don't look at him. Come on. We're gonna meet the cops." His hand tightened. "How bad are you hurt?"

"I dunno."

The boy shook his head and pulled her forward.

Edie sniffed. Walker wanted her to die with him. It was that simple. The police were coming, and she'd have to answer their questions. Then there were Fred and Marie, Sharon, and Walker's two boys. Everything fell over her in a thick, gummy web.

Edie glanced toward the cabin, but the trees obscured the dock. The boy jumped in front, startling her.

"What's taking 'em so long?" His voice broke high. "Wait a minute. I hear 'em."

Sirens wailed in the distance, and when she shifted her eyes toward that direction, blue cruiser lights glimmered like broken glass though the forest.

"Over here." The boy waved his arms in sweeping motions to the cruiser rushing toward them. "Over here."

The cruiser braked for the boy, who stuck his head into the open window. The cop's car continued toward the camp, followed soon by two more. The boy signaled for Edie to follow him.

She wiped her hand across her face, then her dress. She wiped again. There was so much blood.

Not With Us

Edie sat in the back seat of a cruiser with the door open. The air was warm, but she wore a blanket around her shoulders while an EMT cleaned the blood from her face. Someone found a shirt and shorts in the trunk of her car. They let her use the boathouse to change, shivering all the while, as a trooper kept guard. He packed her clothes and sandals in a plastic bag for evidence, he explained, but she didn't want them anymore. They took other things from the cabin.

The EMT grew up in Conwell and knew her family. He was in Vietnam, too, a medic in the Army. His voice was warm and his hands gentle as he touched her.

"It's too bad about Walker. He was an okay guy." The EMT examined the wound on her forehead. "It appears the bullet sliced you right here. You got outta the way just in time. You're real lucky about that anyway." He wiped her skin with gauze. "You're shook up, but you're gonna be all right. Head wounds are always bloody. You should go to the hospital and get this stitched properly, or it'll leave a scar." He paused. "They finally got a hold of your father. He's on his way. He has somebody with him."

Edie nodded. Maybe Pop was bringing one of his drinking buddies. Somebody would have to drive her car back home. The cops wouldn't let her.

The local police chief, his body packed tightly in his uniform's shirt, stepped toward the cruiser. She spoke with him once already and with two state troopers, but he was back, leaning over her. The ends of his fingers made tapping noises on the cruiser's roof.

"How's she doing?" the chief asked the EMT, and then he dropped his face toward Edie. "Miss, you look a little better. Mind if I ask a few more questions? He can finish up later." The chief came forward as the EMT moved to the right. "We had another incident here in town. A man got killed, and we're figuring there might be a connection to Mr. St. Claire." He cleared his throat. "Do you have any idea what he might've been doing last night?"

"He called my home. It sounded like he was at a restaurant or a bar."

"When was that?"

"I remember it was still light out. He didn't say much."

"How'd you know it was him?"

"I know his voice. He was crying. I told you before he was upset." She paused. "He's been calling a lot."

The chief's belly rose as if a pulley rigged it. A sweat spot shaped like a delta was on the chest of his blue shirt.

"Was there anything he might have said?"

Edie saw Walker kneeling before her. He kissed her. How could she have stopped him? Could she have kicked the gun away? She raised her head.

"He said he tried to call me at another place, but a man wouldn't let him. Walker said he beat him."

The chief's eyes closed in tight creases.

"You might like to know we sent someone to tell his wife and parents."

"Am I in trouble?" she said faintly.

"Not with us you ain't."

She blinked slowly. On the dock, EMTs zipped Walker's body into a black bag. The police took photos and measured the area. They searched his camp and truck, taking whatever they needed. They knew everything about her and Walker, and the tears came again as the chief gestured with his hand, so the EMT could finish.

A Smile So Sad

Harlan drove his pickup slowly over the dirt road. Beside him, Benny Sweet chain-smoked and talked about Edie. Benny had been keyed up ever since he barged into Harlan's workshop, yelling like a madman.

"Harlan, I need your help," Benny said. "You gotta come. That fucker Walker tried to kill my Edie, then he offed himself. Shot himself in the head, the stupid bastard. She got away, but they say she's hurt. I fuckin' can't believe it."

Benny talked nonstop during the ride. He flicked the spent butt out the window.

"I've got three girls, but the other two won't have nothin' to do with me," he told Harlan. "I haven't seen them or their families for years. They're too good for their old man, shamed of me cause I run the town dump, but not my Edie. I did right raisin' her. Her mother'd be proud."

He fished in his shirt pocket for his pack.

"I never trusted Walker St. Claire. Never. His brother, Gil, was nothin' like him. An awful shame he got killed. But Walker?" Benny spat out the window before he lit another cigarette. "I'm not the kind of father to stick my nose in my daughter's business, but I should've, especially after he beat her. You saw the bruises." He winced. "Walker knew how to work her to get what he wanted. What she got out of it, I dunno."

Harlan touched a scar that ran from the ridge of his cheekbone to the jaw line on the right side of his face. The skin was dry and rough as if it were a dead thing. He squinted at Benny. He knew why. Edie was lonely.

"You're awfully quiet there, Harlan." Benny blew smoke through the corner of his mouth. "You okay?"

Harlan nodded.

Benny came to Harlan's house from the dump, so his overalls were thick with the worst kind of dirt. The town's police chief went there to tell him about Edie. Benny didn't want to take the time to change. He had to see Edie right away.

"I was just wondering why she'd come all the way out here to see Walker," Harlan said.

Benny flicked the cigarette's ash out the window.

"The chief didn't say much, just about Walker being messed up," he said. "I bet that damn Walker tricked her into comin', or maybe she came here for his parents, you know Fred and Marie, to do their dirty work. I seen her before she left. She didn't say where she's going, but she acted like she was hiding somethin'. She knew I wouldn't let her go. My sister, Leona, said the same thing when I called her."

Benny tossed the butt out the window.

"Edie tried to keep that thing with Walker from me. Ha. I'm old, but I'm not blind. There was that time he hit her real hard. She said he was sorry. She said he didn't mean to, but, shit, I knew what kinda guy he was. No fuckin' good. A wife and two kids, and foolin' around with my Edie. She deserves better. I called my sister, Leona, you know, the bossy one. She practically screamed over the phone. She wanted to come, but I knew she'd be useless driving. That's why I asked you, Harlan. Hope you don't mind."

"I'm glad to help."

Harlan continued to rub the scar. A smoky light came through the truck's windows. This was far for Edie to drive alone. The forest was thick here, and there were fewer houses than in Conwell. He hadn't seen any power lines for a while now. She could have broken down or something could have happened to her. Something did, and his throat got thick as he thought about it.

Benny slid forward in the seat, guiding Harlan toward Walker's camp. They were close, he said, as he spotted landmarks. Benny had been to the lake before to fish. He remembered the route. They came to a road on the left, and Benny pointed to its sign.

"Turn here. This is it."

The blue bar of a cruiser flashed ahead on the road. An ambulance with its siren off passed slowly on the narrow road.

"Told ya," Benny croaked.

A local cop commanding the road told Harlan where to park after they spoke about their business here. His leg was stiff and useless, so he punched it a bit to get it moving before he stepped down. Benny was already on the ground. Harlan told him to go. He'd be right there. Benny leaned against the truck's front fender.

"What I said in the truck, I'm worried for Edie. She and Amber mean more to me than anybody in the world. Anybody. I'd give my life for them." His eyes shined. "I think you like her. That's okay by me. You seem like a real decent guy. But this ain't over by a long shot. It ain't gonna be easy for her when she gets back. You don't know how hard this town can be until you make a mistake. Ask my sister, Leona, if you don't believe me." Harlan started to speak, but Benny raised his hand. "Let's just find her. I wanna make sure she's okay."

Harlan made his slow way past the line of vehicles. Benny was already with Edie. She gave Harlan a smile so sad, he felt like weeping with her.

Keeping Up

Edie stared straight ahead while Pop drove her home. Harlan was behind them in his pickup truck. She didn't speak. Neither did Pop. He kept checking her though. His mouth opened and shut. He turned the radio's knob on and off.

They passed the Stakeout Bar and Grille, where she and Walker ate.

"You hungry, honey? You want me to run in and get ya somethin' to eat?"

She shook her head.

"No, Pop."

The front of his white hair fell over his eyes. He brushed the shock aside.

She half-turned in her seat. Harlan kept up with them.

"Edie, why'd you go to Walker's camp? You could've got yourself killed."

Her eyes glassed with tears when her father's voice broke.

"I almost did, Pop." She sniffed. "It wasn't my idea. Dean asked me to. He said Walker was in a bad way, and he wanted me to talk him into coming back to his place. I almost went back, twice. I should've." Her head was down. "Pop, I kept thinking about Amber and you and Aunt Leona. I didn't want to die. Then he did that to himself. It was awful."

Jarring Pictures

Once again jarring pictures woke Edie. Walker was going to shoot her, but this time she couldn't get out of the way fast enough when he pulled the trigger. This time she died. She and Walker lay on the dock. Blood was everywhere.

Edie threw off the top sheet. It was too hot. She was staying with Leona in one of her spare bedrooms upstairs. She came here after Pop brought her home from Walker's camp, stopping at her house briefly, so she could pack.

Harlan, who had followed Pop's truck, stopped to see if she was okay.

"Yeah, I am," she told him.

"I believe I understand why you went to help him," he said. "I would've done the same for my ex-wife."

All the while she packed, the phone in her house kept ringing. She told Pop to leave it alone. She figured nothing she'd want to hear would be coming from the other end of the line. If it were somebody who mattered, they'd call Pop. No one would dare bother her at Aunt Leona's. Thank goodness, Amber was still at sleepover camp.

Edie left her bed to wander the room. She often slept here as a child, especially when her mother took sick and after she died. She and her aunt stayed up late, playing cards or watching TV. Now Amber did the same.

In the distance, thunder knocked against the hills, and lightning bleached the sky. She studied the photos on the bedroom's wall. They were all about the family, including the one taken of her and Gil at their wedding.

"You got yourself a real special one, Edie," her aunt told her then.

Harlan said he understood why she went to see Walker. Her best comfort came from her family and a near stranger. Others wouldn't be as generous. She heard enough gossip when she worked in the store. People here thrived on the misery of others: the drunks and cheaters; the wife and kid beaters; those who owed money; those who broke the law and got caught, those who didn't; the deadbeats who deserted their families; and the feeble, old people left to fend for themselves by their ungrateful children.

But this story was bigger and dirtier than any of those. The news about Walker was on the front page of the local paper, Pop told her, and Aunt Leona saw it on the TV news. Her name was in it and the bartender the cops say Walker beat to death. They even mentioned Gil. She didn't want to see or hear any of it. She hoped instead it would pass as quickly as this storm, but that was unlikely. Fred called Pop to say she couldn't work at the store anymore. She wasn't welcome to shop there either. No, this wouldn't end fast.

The thunder grew louder, and rain splashed against the house. Edie shut the bedroom windows. She went downstairs and toward the kitchen, where a light shined. Aunt Leona was at the table. Cards were spread over its top for solitaire.

"Can't sleep either?" Leona asked without looking up from her cards.

Edie took the chair across from Leona. Her aunt frowned as she studied her possibilities.

"I can't stop thinking about what happened," Edie told her.

She cried, so much crying lately. She was sick of it. Leona dropped her cards. She shook her head.

"Maybe we should bring Amber home. She might make you feel better."

"No, I don't wanna take her from camp. Let her have fun. It won't be the same when she gets back. I don't know how Fred and Marie will be."

"If that's what you want, Edie." Leona shook her finger. "Don't you worry about those two."

"It's not just them."

"People couldn't stop wagging their tongues when I married a man forty years older than me." She snorted. "The joke was on them. When Ralph kicked, I was set for life unless I did something foolish with the money. Course, that was before I ran away with his son, Tom. Now that was something real foolish."

The rain fell steadily, sending cooler air into the room.

"I'm going to the wake tomorrow. Pop said he'd take me."

"You changed your mind."

"I don't wanna see Sharon, but I owe it to Fred and Marie." She paused. "Walker did mean something to me. I hope you understand."

Leona didn't take her eyes away.

"Then count me in. I'm going, too."

Edie swiped the tears with the back of her hand."

"You sure?"

Leona patted her arm.

"You know what we always say in times like these. We Sweets stick together."

A Very Interesting Person

Edie knocked on Harlan's kitchen door, and when she didn't hear an answer she helped herself inside. The kitchen was the only room she had entered in all the years she knew Harlan's grandmother. Elmira Doyle baked bread Saturday mornings, and when she and Amber delivered her groceries, she gave them a warm loaf to take home. She was a thoughtful neighbor who sent dinner after her mother died. She remembered Amber on her birthday and Christmas.

She followed the sound of hammering to a back room. Harlan was there, his head bowed, so engrossed in the task someone could have taken his picture, and he wouldn't have known. His eyes were up when he heard her finally.

"Sorry, for just comin' in," she said. "I tried knocking, but I guess you didn't hear me."

He put down a mallet and grinned at her.

"I'm glad you did."

Her head was angled to the right.

"I just came to thank you for the other day. For bringing Pop."

"No problem. How are you?"

She shook her head.

"Not so good. I'm having a hard time sleeping. Vera from the store called Aunt Leona's this morning. She said my in-laws don't want me working there anymore." She shook her head. "I knew it already. Fred told Pop. She just wanted to rub it in. She's Sharon St. Claire's sister. Vera seemed to enjoy telling me. I expected that, too."

He stared past her briefly before he spoke.

"Edie, one night I was up late working in my shop. I went outside when I heard an owl in the woods across the road. The moon was out." He paused. "When I walked to the end of the driveway, I saw a truck parked near your house. I recognized Walker's pickup. It was pretty late. I saw him again another time when I was coming home, but he took off soon after. I should've done something more. I'm sorry."

Her eyes narrowed.

"I don't know if it would've stopped him."

Harlan shook his head.

"What are you going to do?"

"I don't have a clue. But I'm not gonna worry about it now." She looked around the room. "You've done a lot in here."

"It'll do until I fix up the barn for a workshop."

"That sounds like a big project."

"It will be. The barn needs to be cleaned and winterized, but it has a solid timber frame of hemlock, a sound metal roof, and plenty of space." He grinned. "I need to go to the lumberyard your father told me about to get an estimate for the material."

"What about this room?"

"It's too small. I need a real workshop."

Edie wandered through the tools and stacks of lumber.

"What are you building?"

He ran his hand across a tabletop.

"This is for a client in Boston. I'm using quarter-sawn oak. See the swirls here. This will be so slick when it's finished. It's a birthday present for his wife."

Walker showed her the way he attached the top to the legs, pulling the table apart, so she could see the mortise-and-tenon joints. He explained how he roughed the post-like tenons on the table saw before he chiseled them by hand.

"By hand?"

"There's no other way to get it right. It takes a while."

"How'd you learn to do this?"

He shrugged.

"I studied art in college, but I was lousy at it. I guess I'm more of a craftsman than an artist. I took a couple of classes in furniture making and began working for the teacher, then myself." He nodded. "What do you think?"

"That you're a very interesting person, Harlan Doyle." Her hands were on her hips. "I've been wondering if we might've met when we were kids. You know when your folks brought you from Florida to visit your grandparents."

"I didn't meet many people outside our family. I do remember a girl in front of your house. She had gold-colored hair and was wearing a dress. She played with a tire swing, not on it, just twirling it. Maybe it was you, or maybe I dreamed it."

"We used to have a tire swing."

She stood in front of him.

"Hmm. I probably would've been twelve. You would have been?"

"Maybe four or five. Younger than Amber I'm guessing."

"Four or five? Just a little baby."

She smiled.

"Yup, just a little baby.

Stick Together

Edie came through the front door. Her aunt was in her customary place on the couch, watching TV while she waited to go to Walker's wake. Edie went home to change and came back dressed in black. Pop waited outside in her car.

"Jesus, honey, you look like hell," Leona said, pointing to the spot beside her. "Sit here."

Edie sighed.

"Okay."

She knew it'd be only a few minutes before Pop started banging the car's horn, but Leona was in no rush. Her thin hand patted Edie's knee.

"You worried about going?"

"Yeah, I am. I don't wanna see any of them."

Leona's red hair shook as if it were on fire.

"You wait a minute, Edie. Hold your head up high. You might've made a mistake hooking up with Walker, but it wasn't your fault what he did."

"That's what Pop says. It's just not easy remembering."

Pop tooted the horn. He wanted to get this over with, too. She told Pop and Leona they didn't have to go with her to the wake. She would face the family alone, but both insisted. "We Sweets stick together." It was an old family joke, and Pop winked when he said it, too, hoping to make her smile at least. Edie gave that much to her father although it was difficult.

Pop pressed the horn again, and Leona pawed at the air impatiently.

"God Almighty, we better get going before Alban wears out that damn horn. Jesus, Edie, take my hand and help me up."

The Wake

The parking lot at the Brewster Funeral Home in Tyler was jammed with cars and pickups, as were both sides of the road, but Pop found a tight spot closer. He led the way, smoking a butt with his head down as if he were reading words off the pavement. Edie clutched Leona's arm. Leona tripped, but her aunt said to keep on, so they slowed and let Pop have his speedy pace.

Walker's crew, including Dean, stood outside the funeral home. She knew them all, friendly guys who worked hard and liked their boss even when he was a jerk. They used to come with Walker to the store for lunch or the Do-Si-Do for drinks after work. A few flirted, but she was never interested. Besides, Walker would have fired them.

Dean came unsteadily toward Edie. His eyes were heavy and glassy, and he hadn't shaved for days. A black tie hung loosely around the neck of his wrinkled, white shirt.

"Damn it, Edie. Why'd he have to go and do that? I don't fuckin' understand it. Do you?" His voice slurred. "I should never have asked you to go." He clutched Edie's arm. "Can you forgive me?"

"There's nothing to forgive, Dean."

Dean gave Edie a sloppy hug and a kiss on the cheek. He began filling her ear with the saddest stuff about Walker, her, and him.

"Remember when you gave Walker those four hand-tied flies last Christmas?" He sobbed. "He kept the box on his desk in his shop. He showed me those flies all the time. You made him so happy." He held her tighter. "Walker was messed up, but he loved you, Edie. He really did. He should've ditched everything for you years ago. Then he wouldn't have, you know, done what he did."

"Shh, shh, shh, take it easy, Dean. You can let me go now."

Dean kept his arms around Edie.

"I should've gotten him myself. I should've told his folks."

The men from Walker's crew listened and waited. Edie felt tears come.

"Dean, let me go."

Edie squirmed until finally one of the crew pulled him away.

"Get it together," one man warned Dean. "We gotta go inside."

Dean used both hands to wipe the tears from his face.

"Edie, you're like a sister to me."

He pitched forward, but one of the crew yanked him back by his shirt, tearing a seam at the shoulder. His tie fell to the pavement. He blubbered her name.

Edie backed away.

Pop hopped from foot to foot.

Leona complained, "Jesus, somebody take this guy home. He's in no shape to go to a wake."

Edie and Leona trailed Pop through the funeral home's foyer to its large, hot room. The place was packed tightly with people from town, many of them customers from the store and friends of the family. Most she knew all her life. She tried not to look at any of them.

On the far side, the polished wood of Walker's closed coffin glowed beneath a row of spotlights. A throw of white carnations covered its top. The words – OUR BELOVED SON WALKER – were written in gold on its blue ribbon. To the right, Fred and Marie, Sharon, and her family, chatted with mourners. Heads bobbed. Voices buzzed.

Edie squeezed Leona's arm.

When Gil died, Edie stood in a place of honor with his family. She was eight months pregnant with Amber. Her belly was out to there, and no one let her do a thing but cry for him. People stood in a line that stretched out the door, so they could tell her how sorry they were.

Edie took a deep breath before she moved forward with Leona. Two large fans stirred the air, but they brought no relief to the people whose foreheads glistened with sweat.

Leona fanned an envelope she found in her purse.

"This place is about ready to burn up."

"What'd you say, Aunt Leona?" Edie asked.

"Take a look."

Leona's mouth was pressed into a thin, red line, and when Edie glanced around, she understood. People stared at them. As her eyes went from one person to the next, she guessed who still liked her. She didn't see many: her teammate, Patsy, who gave a low wave across the room; friends of Pop and Aunt Leona; the old folks on her Saturday delivery route. One man, a regular who lived alone since his wife died last winter, placed his hand on her shoulder and creaked, "Bless you, Edie. I know you meant good."

Edie clutched Leona's arm. She wasn't letting go.

Walker's crew stood near the door without Dean. They appeared out of place in the somber room. One of Sharon's brothers, Buddy the cop, strolled across the carpeted floor to escort the men to the head of the line. Edie and Leona exchanged glances. Each knew what the other thought.

Leona uttered a warning beneath her breath as the funeral home director walked across the room. Moments before, he talked with Sharon and her family. His face was pious as he pressed his hands together. His breath smelled like sugary mints.

"The family was hoping for a quiet gathering this evening to remember the deceased," he spoke in a hushed tone.

Leona's face was locked in a frown.

"That's why we came," she said.

The director cleared his throat.

"We don't want to have a scene here."

"Then maybe you should leave us the hell alone," Leona snapped.

The director clamped his mouth shut and left. Now ten people separated Edie from the family. Her stomach churned.

Marie sat on a wooden chair next to Walker's sons. Fred stood beside them, blanked by his grief. Edie worked with her father-in-law for years. He was always the first one in the store, she the second, coming with Amber when she was in school and by herself during the summer. They arrived as he stood on the front porch, fetching the bundle of newspapers or doing some other chore.

He'd say, "Hey, Edie, how's my girl?" and Amber would giggle and tell Fred, "Grandpa, I'm right here." He asked the same question if Amber wasn't with her, and Edie would let Fred know what her daughter did since the last time he saw her.

Sharon hugged a well-wisher. She dabbed her eyes with a tissue and pointed toward the closed coffin. Edie touched the bandage on her forehead and thought again about what she could say to Walker's family. But as she studied their grim faces, it didn't seem possible she'd be able to speak.

Pop, back from a smoke and a nip outside, led them forward. It was their turn to greet the family. He extended his hand to each man, but only Fred gave a stiff shake.

"This is a hard time for your family," Pop said. "We came to pay our respects."

Leona spoke, too, but Edie felt too sick to hear what she said. It was her time now, and her voice trembled when she told her father-in-law, "Fred, I'm so sorry about Walker. I wish it didn't happen."

Fred held out his hands as if he was going to hug her, but instead he let them flop to his sides. He was breaking into pieces in front of her. Both sons were gone, one he loved and one he didn't understand. What was left?

She whispered near Fred's ear, "Amber loves you."

He stammered, "Oh."

Marie kept her head lowered. Edie bent to say the same thing, but her mother-in-law threw up her hands. Fred went to her, but she squawked his name, and he stood there, helpless.

"Who told you all to come?" Marie moaned.

Edie stepped back, ready to leave, but Leona shoved her toward Sharon. The woman made an anguished cry and spun toward the wall. Edie bit her lip, waiting, but Sharon kept her back to her. So instead, Edie crouched in front of Walker's twins. Shane and Randy wore white shirts with black bowties. Their eyes were dark and wet. She cried with them.

"Your daddy was a real good man, and he loved you boys so much. He was proud of you both. Don't ever forget that. I'm so sorry. I really am."

She wanted to hug Walker's sons, they were taking this so hard, but their mother hissed, "Get away from them. Those are my boys. Mine and Walker's."

Edie looked up at Sharon's hard face. So did her sons.

"I just wanna say something to the boys."

"You've done enough already. Git the hell outta here. Don't you even try going to the funeral tomorrow. I'll have you kicked out in front of all those people. You hear?" She motioned to her brothers, who hustled to her side. "I want her out now."

Edie rose.

"Believe me, you don't know how sorry I am. I'm sorry for you and your boys. I'm sorry for Fred and Marie. But mostly I'm sorry for Walker."

Neither Sharon nor her brothers spoke as Edie took a moment to stand in front of the casket. She bowed her head and placed her right hand on its top.

"Good-bye, Walker. Rest in peace," she whispered before she linked arms with Leona to follow Pop from the over-heated room.

Heat Wave

The sky was chalked a thick, gray haze when Edie left her house. She lifted the back of her hair to cool her neck and used bobby pins from her pocket to put it up.

The heat that began before Walker died didn't appear to be ending anytime soon. At night, she slept on top of the spread. Sometimes she woke and was ready to check for Walker's pickup until she realized it was no longer necessary. She let the fan that swirled the hot air in her room lull her back to sleep.

Aunt Leona said the heat was a sign they'd have a very cold winter.

"I've lived long enough to know what happens around here," she said.

Edie stepped off the porch. Pop was in back of their house, attaching a hose to the faucet. She eyed his dirty, rusty pickup and laughed.

"You're not really gonna wash that old heap of yours, are you?" she asked.

Her father gave her a pained expression as he dragged the hose along the driveway.

242

"Honey, I was hopin' I'd get this done before you saw it."

"Saw what?"

Her father's head jerked toward the house.

"Go ahead. Check it out."

Edie went to the part of the house facing the road. She held her hand to her mouth and let out a cry. The white clapboards and parts of the windows were splattered with eggs, dozens of them.

Pop stood near her.

"Li'l fuckers did it last night. Heard 'em, but by time I got on my drawers, they were peelin' outta here. Got a look at the car though. I'm sure who owns it."

"Who?"

Pop spat on the ground.

"One of those punk Crocker kids. Jim's oldest boy. I seen that car of his around town. He had his pals with him. They're probably the ones who dumped the garbage the night before." He spat again. "I cleaned it up before you saw it. I think it was pig guts. Came home and saw the cats in it. Shit."

"Gee, Pop, I didn't hear a thing."

His chin bounced.

"That's okay. I can take care of this trouble by myself just fine." He nodded toward the house. "You might want to go shut the windows on this side, so I don't make more of a mess."

Edie ran inside to lower the windows, and when she returned, Pop handed her the hose's nozzle. He marched toward the house to turn on the faucet. The hose filled slowly, and by time it spurted hard, he took it from her.

"Stand back," he said.

Edie leaned against her car. She only knew the Crocker boy from her vantage point at the store. When he was small, he was the boy who always got the candy he wanted from his mother. His father, Jim, let him sit in on the men's talk.

"I know who you're talking about," she said. "Cocky kid. He came into the store sometimes. I bet he did it on his own, but he won't get into trouble at home." She snorted. "They'll likely be proud."

"Yup, it'll be a big, fat joke for all the Crockers their boy did this," he said.

Pop jumped about the grass, muttering curses as he aimed water over the dried egg. He moved closer to the house.

"Try not to take the paint off, Pop."

He waved at her.

"I got a hold of the chief. He should be here soon. I'm not lettin' those bastards get away with this. Who knows what shit they'll pull next?"

Edie shook her head.

"What good's the chief gonna do?"

Pop twisted the nozzle all the way before he went to inspect the house. He shrugged. His overalls were soaked through in the front.

"That's the best I can get it. A couple of storms should take the rest off."

Both turned when the chief parked his cruiser behind Pop's pickup. He got out of the front seat slowly.

The man had been the town's chief for decades. The only thing that kept him from quitting was he retired from his job at the sawmill, and he didn't have anything else to do. At least, that was Pop's opinion. The chief wasn't a bad cop, just a hick-town cop not used to crime. He thought married people should work out their differences and not bother the police. The only speeders who should get ticketed were out-of-towners. The chief was also loath to make an arrest and miss a meal hauling someone to jail. He left that task to his underlings, like Buddy Crocker, who were more than willing to stay on the clock. But the chief was the most reasonable cop on the force, and Pop claimed they were related in a distant way, close enough he thought he had an in with the man.

The chief said Pop's name and hers. Her father let the nozzle fall to the ground. He wiped his palms across the back of his overalls before he shook his hand.

"Glad you could make it, chief."

Edie was silent as her father retold the story. The chief's face got grim when Pop mentioned Jim Crocker's boy, and after he was done, he said, "You sure, Benny? I mean it was nighttime."

"I tell you I recognized the car. If you don't believe me, go find a blue '71 Mustang with a busted left taillight, and you got your boy."

The chief made a humming noise deep in his throat. His head rocked. Everyone knew who drove what in Conwell.

"He's a good kid, hangs around with a decent crowd. You know kids though. Sometimes they act up, do stupid pranks like this." He made a hollow chuckle. "You were young once, Benny. Me, too."

"Suppose my granddaughter had been home when this happened? What about her? What about the stuff they dumped the other night?"

The chief studied the house's clapboards. He cleared his throat.

"Things are a bit touchy right now. People are still upset about what happened to Walker, and, eh, what led up to that situation. I'm afraid the hard feelings are gonna last a while." The chief eyed Edie. "I'd hate to make trouble for these boys. They come from good families."

Edie felt her neck and face burn. She wanted a turn, but Pop beat her to it.

"Yeah? What about this good family? You tellin' me you ain't gonna do nothin' about this?"

Edie touched Pop's arm, but he snatched it away.

"Pop, Pop, take it easy."

Her father's focus stayed on the chief.

"Hell, tonight I'm sittin' in my truck, and if they show up, I'm gonna shoot the tires off the kid's car." He pulled his chin up. "You and me have gone hunting together plenty of times. I believe you can recall what a dead shot I am."

The chief raised his hand.

"Hold on, Benny. I don't want to hear talk like this. You could get yourself in a whole lot of trouble."

"Seems to me we already are."

"Okay, okay, I'll talk to Buddy about the boy. He's his uncle. That all right?"

Edie stepped away. She could no longer listen. The chief would get his way. Buddy would tell his nephew to stay clear, but he wouldn't be serious about it, and then something else would happen. Edie thought she was safe here. She was wrong.

She shut the door hard when she went inside her house. The air felt cooked, but she left the windows closed. She went through the mail Pop piled on the kitchen table: a few bills, junk, and a postcard from Amber, but no envelope still from her in-laws although Fred promised Pop to mail her last check. Surely, they knew she needed it.

She reread her daughter's note. Amber didn't like the food at camp, but she went swimming every day. She was making presents for everyone. She missed being at home. She signed it: I LOVE YOU THE MOST, AMBER.

Edie carried the card into her daughter's bedroom as neat as she left it before she went to camp. Two baby-faced dolls passed down from Edie's mother stared unblinking on the pink chenille spread. She left the card on the bureau. Pop was right. Suppose Amber was here when this happened? She was coming home tomorrow. She knew nothing about what happened while she was gone.

Pop, her ears in town, told Edie what people were saying about her and Walker, some of it wrong, most of it harsh. One time he got so hot, he almost came to blows with someone at the dump defending her. He couldn't help himself. But she worried more about Amber and what she could hear.

Edie continued through the house. Water drops from the hose clung to the windows in the living room. Bits of egg were on the screens. She watched Pop and the chief in the driveway. The chief was talking, and whatever he said was not making her father happy. Pop's face was red. His head shook.

Edie rushed outside and down the porch steps. The chief appeared startled at her rapid arrival, but Pop kept on until she touched his arm.

"Pop, please," she said before she spoke to the chief. "It seems like you're in a pretty tough spot, you being close to the Crocker family. Buddy's an officer on your force after all." She took a breath. "I'm real worried about Amber. She's coming home from camp tomorrow. And I don't want Pop taking the law into his hands."

The chief's smooth chin jutted forward.

"You're right about that, Edie," he said.

She patted her father's arm.

"So, I'm thinking it'd be best to let the state police handle this one. Course, they'll likely press charges against the kids. That okay with you, chief? I could go now and make the call."

The chief cleared his throat.

"Uh, that won't be necessary, Edie. I'll go see the boy myself right now. I'll give him a stern warning to leave you all alone. I believe he's working at his Uncle Buddy's garage during the summer."

Pop winked at Edie. He caught on fast what she was trying to do. He rubbed the whiskers on his chin.

"Just as long as they leave this good family alone," Pop said.

"I'll see what I can do," he told her.

Edie smiled.

"Thanks, chief."

The man nodded before he walked toward his cruiser. He made a three-point turn and was gone.

"That's that," Pop said, patting her back. "You did fine, Edie. Don't know if it'll change things, but you did real fine."

Beautiful And Wild

Harlan made his slow, uneven way to the river. He had been working in his shop on the dovetail joints for a desk's drawers, but the hot, humid air drove him away from this job. The weather was supposed to break soon although that possibility seemed remote as the heat closed around him.

He grinned when he found Edie floating on her back in the deepest part of the river. He swam nearly every day, but he hadn't seen her here since Walker's death.

Edie greeted him right away.

"Hey, neighbor, looks like you had the same idea," she sang.

"Yeah, neighbor. Amber still at camp?"

"Yup. It's just you and me today."

Harlan grinned all the while he untied his sneakers and walked tender-footed to the water. He made a shallow dive toward Edie, keeping about four feet between them. She dropped into the water, so she faced him.

"How have you been?" he asked.

She pulled her mouth inward.

"All right, I suppose, but those damn Crockers won't give up. Last night, they threw eggs at the house. The other night, it was pig guts."

"Did you call the police?"

"The chief came. He wasn't going to do anything about it. You know boys will be boys." She shook her head. "I got him by threatening to call the state cops."

"The police chief wasn't going to do anything? I don't believe it. Too bad I wasn't there to help."

"Thanks, but it's not your fight, Harlan Doyle. There's one thing more you need to learn about this town: who you are and who you know matters. Right now, I'm nobody, worse actually cause I messed up bad. It's the way it is."

He thought about the police chief's reluctance to get involved in Edie and Benny's problems. Elsewhere, the chief would have had the kids brought in, but Conwell wasn't elsewhere, he realized. He was at the store the other day when he heard the woman at the counter, Vera, talk about Edie to her customers. She told Harlan, "So, what do you think of your neighbor now?" He told her, "Those were some pretty harsh words you said about my neighbor." Vera's mouth fell open.

He messed up badly, too, after his wife left him, but he, at least, had the anonymity of the city. Edie was a target here even although she didn't deserve it.

"That's unfair," he told Edie.

"You'd better get used to it if you plan to stick around, Harlan," she said.

"I was planning to."

"Glad to hear it." Edie's mouth formed a thin, crooked grin. "I do have to say, Harlan, there's something about you that's bothering me. A lot. I can't stop thinking about it."

His heart sank a bit although she smiled.

"What is it?"

"Your hair. It's still dry." She giggled. "Guess I'll have to fix it."

She dove forward, slapping the water hard, so it hit Harlan's head in sharp waves. She didn't stop, and Harlan, surprised, lunged after Edie, grabbing her bare waist. Her muscles tightened as she fought him off, splashing and laughing in a high voice. Harlan held on, feeling as if he had caught something beautiful and wild, and there, she pushed her hip against him. She smoothed her lips in a flirty smile.

"I was wondering how long it'd take you to do something like that," she said.

Harlan was so happy, he let her go, and then he wished he hadn't because he wanted to touch her. She stayed away by an arm's length, giggling. Her eyes shined above the water.

"You got me," he told her.

"Yeah, I did."

In the distance, thunder shook against the hills. Both looked in that direction.

"I think we better get back," he said.

"Uh-huh."

Harlan followed her to the river's edge, where rain fell over them in cold sheets. Some hail mixed in. Thunder came harder and closer. Edie ran ahead, but Harlan couldn't keep up. She turned and waved. He wanted to chase after her, but he couldn't.

"See you soon," she shouted.

A Real Hard Time

The next morning, Edie took a short cut along a rough dirt road to Conwell's main village, where fine old homes were clustered near the church, town hall, and school. The route toward Amber's camp was on the left, but she needed to take care of some business first, so she made a right.

The Conwell General Store was only a mile away, and she went through the front screen door before she changed her mind. She glanced around at the nearly empty store. Her timing was good.

She swept past Vera, who made an awful face, to the deli counter, where Fred handed a package to a woman. Edie held back when she recognized the preacher's wife, but Fred noticed her, and the woman did, too. A table of old-timers turned to see as well.

Edie was embarrassed standing in the aisle, so she went to the dairy case, waiting, and the preacher's wife gave her a stony stare before she left. Fred kept his head down as he put a slab of lunch-meat away. He took his time.

"How are you, Fred?"

The soft spot near his right eye twitched.

"Not so good, Edie. Marie's been real upset. She hasn't been coming to the store."

"I didn't come to make things harder. I'm on my way to get Amber from camp, and I was hoping you had my last paycheck."

Fred squeezed his brow.

"Vera was supposed to mail it to you."

"Vera." Edie spoke louder then regretted it. "Fred, I didn't get anything in the mail."

"You didn't? Strange. I asked her twice."

Edie eyed Vera, who pretended to ignore what was happening at the deli counter.

"Could you ask her again? Please."

Fred left instead for the office and returned after several minutes. He clutched an envelope.

"I found this in the desk drawer. I'm sorry. I thought she sent it."

Edie nodded as she shoved the envelope in her purse.

"I hope you both know how sorry I am about what happened to Walker. I didn't realize how bad off he was until I got there. Really."

Fred bowed his head.

"I didn't either. I failed my son."

Edie's breath came in short stutters.

"Walker wasn't an easy person to understand." She paused. "You and Marie don't want me around. That's okay. Please, don't punish Amber for anything I did."

Fred wiped a tear. Edie knew Marie ran that family. She was the one who tried to talk Gil out of marrying her. Edie and her family weren't good enough. Marie didn't seem to mind Sharon, whose father was a truck driver, marrying Walker, but then again, she didn't pay much attention to what her other son did.

"I'll talk with Marie, but I don't know if she'll listen," he said. "Truth is she's taking it real hard right now, real hard."

Edie understood her mother-in-law was drinking and crying in her room. She did the same after Gil died. Amber's birth helped pull her from her grief.

"Amber loves you so much. She'll want to see you both when she gets back. Like before."

Fred's head was down.

"I understand."

"Please, don't forget. Bye, Fred."

Edie was ready to leave. Nosy Vera watched her exchange with Fred from her spot in the store. Her face was twisted as if she tasted something bitter. Edie's plan was to walk by her as if she weren't there. She spun back when Fred called her name.

"What are you going to do for work?"

She shrugged.

"I'll figure out something. Don't you worry about me and Amber."

Minutes later, Edie groaned when she drove by the town commons. The spots in front of the crosses for Gil and the other soldiers were untended and weedy. The wreath her in-laws placed there Memorial Day leaned against the boulder, its flowers brittle and dry. Marie was the one who took care of this spot, coming once or twice a week with jugs of water. She often brought Amber.

Edie stopped her car on the edge of the road. She knelt on the ground, pulling the grass and weeds around the geraniums her mother-in-law planted. She broke off the dead blossoms. The plants lasted until September, when Marie brought mums, one for each cross. In the spring, tulips and daffodils bloomed. Marie said the other families would be offended if she only took care of her son's cross.

She removed the ribbon with Gil's name and stuck it in the pocket of her dress. She was trying to take apart the wreath when the wrecker from the Conwell Garage pulled behind her car. Buddy Crocker dropped from the driver's seat, and his fat face frowned as he strutted toward her. She decided to stow the whole thing in the trunk of her car and deal with it later.

Buddy stood at attention a few feet away. He wore his blue mechanic's uniform.

"What are you doing, Edie?"

She froze.

"I'm cleaning up. I'm taking this dried-up wreath outta here." The flower petals crumbled onto her dress. "Seems Marie didn't get a chance to do it."

"She tell you to do this? I seriously doubt it."

Buddy circled her car. He clicked his tongue as he poked a finger through a rusty spot in the fender.

"You know, Edie, I keep wondering what happened between you and Walker at the lake that day." He focused one eye on her. "My gut says you're leaving somethin' out. Somethin' important. Huh? Am I right?"

Edie's hand closed on the dead carnations. She didn't speak.

"You've made a lot of trouble for my family. My sister. Those boys of hers are gonna grow up without a daddy. My brother, Jim's upset. It's gotten them all worked up, even Jim's boy. He was crazy about his uncle. Maybe you should've thought of that before." He shook a finger at her. "Anyway, I'm planning to see about reopening this case. Right now, I'm wondering if you had anything to do with the bartender's death. Maybe Walker wasn't alone."

Her lips quivered.

"I had nothing to do with that poor man's death. I was home that night. I tried to help Walker, but I couldn't."

"Is that your story?" He crossed his arms. "By the way, the chief told me all about you threatening to call the state cops on my nephew."

"Your nephew shouldn't have done what he did, and he shouldn't have lied about it either," Edie said. "All the chief had to do was search his car. The boy still had the egg cartons in the back seat. The chief told my Pop afterward."

Edie wanted to run to her car and drive away, but she worried what Buddy could do to stop her. A trooper from the state police told her they were done with their investigation into Walker's case. The trooper said it was a tragedy. She was lucky to be spared.

She looked away when Harlan's pickup slowed and parked along the road. She nearly cried when he hobbled toward her.

"Edie, what's going on? Did your car break down?" Harlan stood near Buddy. "My name's Harlan Doyle. I live next door to Edie. Is there a problem here?"

Buddy kept his arms crossed. His bullet-eyes were stuck on Harlan.

"I know who you are. Edie and I were just having a talk. Private stuff. I don't believe it concerns you."

"If it involves Edie, it does. She's my friend and neighbor."

Edie was surprised at the edge to Harlan's voice.

"I was only checking on things," Buddy told him.

"Checking?"

"Yeah, it's part of my job."

"At the garage?"

"No, no, no. I'm on the police department. A sergeant. I was just checking."

Harlan nodded.

"You said that. Edie has to get her daughter from camp. You wouldn't want her to be late and make her little girl worried, would you? Let me bring Edie to her car, and if you want, we can talk some more." Harlan's eyes dropped to Edie. His voice softened. "What's this you have? I can take it to the dump for you. Just leave it there. You need to get going."

Harlan walked her to the car.

"Thanks," she told him.

A Sad Story

Edie tried not to cry when she swooped Amber into her arms.

"Let me down, Ma, so I can show you stuff."

"Okay, okay, I just missed you so much," Edie said.

Amber squinted up at her mother.

"Where's Aunt Leona? Is she in the car?"

"No, no, she didn't come. I wanted to see you by myself." She touched her daughter's hair. "Where are we going first?"

Amber clutched her mother's hand. She guided her to the dining hall, set off the ground on piers and screened. Picnic tables were arranged in rows inside.

"That's where I sit with my friends." She pointed to a table. "The food's not like you make. But we had ice cream every night for supper."

"Every night, really?"

Her in-laws paid for Amber to go to camp. They didn't want her to be without. They did the same for field trips, winter coats, and the extras she needed. Edie wondered if they would continue to be so generous, given what happened.

"I'll take you to the waterfront," Amber said.

They followed a path through tall pines to the shoreline of the lake. Canoes were turned upside down on the beach.

"This is a real nice spot," Edie said.

Amber stood on her toes and pointed toward a wooden raft off shore.

"I can swim all the way there without stopping." She spun, bright-eyed toward her mother. "Wait till you see what I made you, Poppy, and Aunt Leona. Grandma and Grandpa, too. Can we stop at their house on our way back? Or will they still be at the store?"

Edie studied Amber. She weighed what she could say to her daughter. How much would a seven-year-old understand? She gestured toward a bench set in deep shade.

"Let's go there, sweetie. I have some things to tell you."

"But I want to show you the boathouse."

"Maybe later. It's important. Something happened while you were at camp. I want you to hear it from me. It's a sad, sad story about your Uncle Walker."

Back At The Do

An old coot sat hunched over his shot glass at the Do-Si-Do. The man was one of Pop's drinking buddies, and he gave Edie a toothless grin when she said hello.

Edie took a stool nearby. She checked the bar behind her. The rest of the drinkers, a middle-aged couple and guys off early from work, were scattered about the large room. One of the men put money in the jukebox, and Pop's pal growled when jangling music blared from the speakers.

It was late Friday afternoon, so the place would get busy soon with drinkers celebrating the end of their workweek and couples out for dinner. A sign said a band would be playing at nine. Edie used to be a Friday night regular, up for drinking, dancing, and a few laughs after dropping Amber at Aunt Leona's. Walker would be here with his workers, and he'd send her coded signals or punch in her favorite tunes on the juke. Sometimes they danced, keeping it all respectable.

The last time she came here was after she quit the team. She and her aunt toasted each other.

She sighed. A lot has happened since.

Edie heard the familiar voices of Walker's crew. She stared straight ahead, hoping they wouldn't notice her. She wasn't planning to stick around much longer. She just wanted a drink to calm herself after another failed job hunt. It was her third day at it, and she was mulling her bad luck when the Do's owner, Mike, came from the kitchen.

"Well, well, well, look who's here. Gee, honey, I haven't seen you in a real long time. Must be months. How you been?" He winked as he reached inside the beer cooler. "Here. This one's on me."

"Thanks, Mike, I appreciate it."

Edie glanced over her shoulder when loud laughter erupted behind her. One of Walker's crew, George, held his bottle of beer aloft in a salute. Her fingers fluttered in a weak wave.

"Don't mind those guys," Mike said. "They're just horsing around."

Mike bent over the counter, so his head was close to Edie's.

"Listen Edie. That thing with Walker was a fuckin' tragedy. It's the only way to put it. I still can't believe he killed that guy." He grimaced. "I thought I knew the man. I mean he came in here all the time. He was of my best customers. But, honey, he brought it on himself. Anyone who says different is a fuckin' liar."

Edie nodded.

"Thanks."

"Did you go to his funeral?"

"No, I was at the wake."

"I forgot. I heard about what happened there. It's a good thing you didn't go to the funeral. It was a fuckin' circus." His head swayed back and forth. "The way the preacher talked you would've thought Walker was a saint. The preacher went on and on about what a great husband and father he supposedly was. How his parents were so damn proud of him. It wasn't the Walker I knew."

Edie winced. One of Pop's pals, who went to the funeral, told him all about it. The preacher said Walker was led by a temptation he couldn't resist. He was a decent man, a family man. Pop got so caught up in the story a vein on his forehead bulged. She ordered him to stop. She was going to ask the bartender to do the same.

She told him, "I heard about the funeral. You're right. I'm glad I didn't go."

"Sorry, Edie, I didn't mean to upset you."

"I know you didn't. It's okay. I just don't wanna talk about Walker."

He reached for his pack of smokes beneath the counter.

"Tell me what brings you here today."

"I'm hunting for a job."

Edie pulled a paper from her purse. She had written every business in Conwell and the towns around she thought would hire people. She crossed out the places she went. She went today to a hardware store, a school bus company, and gravel yard. Not one had an opening, or so they said. She went to a propane business in Butterfield, which advertised in the paper for an office manager. She thought she had a shot, given her experience at the store, but the owner told her he'd never hire her because he was distant kin to the St. Claires. He wasn't even nice about it. She hurried from the place, embarrassed for not remembering.

"You try Nelson's Potato Farm? Harvest's gonna start soon. R.J.'s always desperate for pickers."

"I didn't bother. His wife is Marie's niece."

"Shit, I forgot. Jesus, I dunno if there's anybody in town not related to somebody. Well, not the newcomers."

The local possibilities were dwindling. Tomorrow she'd try a sawmill and a job waiting tables at a joint in Tyler. The bartender read her list.

"Edie, I wish I had a job to offer you. It's too bad you didn't come in a coupla days sooner. I just hired a girl." He swiped the bar with a wet rag. "Maybe she won't last. I pay minimum wage, but you can make a lot on tips, especially on the weekends. I'll keep you in mind if she doesn't work out."

Edie nodded. She didn't want to be serving drunks she knew, but it was a job nonetheless. The money she got from the government for Gil wasn't enough.

Most ads in the paper were for jobs in the city, working in stores or offices, and she worried about leaving her girl alone so much. Since Amber came home from camp, she tried hard to find things for her daughter to do. They played poker with Leona and visited Pop at the dump. She took her shopping and to eat at the breakfast place in Tyler. They swam at the river, sometimes meeting up with Harlan if it was late in the afternoon. Amber showed him how well she swam. Soon she would be back in school.

Amber kept asking about her grandparents and why they hadn't seen her. They must know she's back from camp. Edie said her grandparents needed time.

"I called Grandma today. I let it ring and ring and ring, but she didn't answer. I called the store, and they said she wasn't there. Maybe she's sick. I should go see her," Amber told Edie yesterday when she brought her home from Leona's.

Mike wiped the bar with a rag.

Edie gave him a smile.

"Thanks for the beer," she told him.

"Leaving so soon?"

"Leona's watching Amber."

She slid off her stool and walked toward the door. She stopped when someone tugged her arm and swung her around as if they were dancing. It was George, from Walker's crew.

"Where you goin' in such a rush, Edie? Got time enough to talk with Mike, but not us, eh? Sit down and have a drink with us."

"Not tonight. My little girl's waiting." She tried to snatch her arm away, but George held his grip. "Hey, let go."

"I will when you sit down with us."

Edie could tell he was in a drinker's good mood. Nothing would deter him, so she took the empty chair beside George, who signaled the waitress for another round. George worked for Walker almost as long as Dean. In his forties, his hair, which hung to his shoulders, was dark with some gray mixed in. He was tight and lean from work, and many women would say he was handsome. Walker always trusted Dean because they grew up together. George was another story. He used to say George wanted whatever he had.

The other men at the table stretched back in their chairs, laughing at each other's jokes. One guy made a wise crack to the waitress carrying longneck bottles in both hands, and they all howled when she told them she heard better and dirtier at another table.

George looked directly at Edie. She took a sip. She hadn't eaten since this morning, and she was getting a buzz from the beer. She should have been home an hour ago. Her aunt might be worried. She checked the payphone near the men's toilet, but someone used it. She would make this fast.

"Where's Dean?"

George frowned.

"Dean? You didn't hear? He got shit-canned. Think old Dean brought back way too many bad memories for Sharon. She's running the business. She wanted to put her brother-in-law in charge, but the guy doesn't know shit about building." He pointed to his chest. "I'm foreman now. How about that?"

She smiled uneasily.

"That's good, George. Walker said you were one of the best. Do you ever see Dean?"

"He comes in here. Doesn't say too much. Looks like he's hitting the sauce pretty hard." His fingers slapped the table. "Let's not talk about Dean. He's a real sorry pain in the ass. We're here for a good time. Right, boys?"

The men at the table were a chorus of low remarks and laughter. Edie set down her bottle, thanking George for the beer. She smiled when she stood.

"Nice seeing you guys."

George leaned back, coaxing her to stay, but she said no.

Outside, Edie swore when she realized the front left tire of her car was flat. She didn't remember it going soft on her drive, and besides the tires were new used ones Pop put on this spring. She opened the trunk and swore again. The spare was missing. She vaguely remembered it leaning against the porch steps. Pop must have taken it out when he rummaged in the trunk for a toolbox. She slammed the lid and marched toward the Do.

Edie kept her back to the men's room door as she dialed Pop's number, letting it ring and ring, but he didn't answer. When she called Leona, her aunt told her everything was fine on her end.

"I'm stuck at the Do. My car's got a flat, and the spare's at home," she shouted over the barroom's noise.

Edie felt a tap on her shoulder.

George said in her ear, "I'll give you a lift home."

"No, no, it's okay. I'll wait for Pop."

"Don't be silly. It's no trouble at all. It'll only take me a few minutes to drop you. If you want, we can bring back the spare and change the tire. Go ahead. Tell your aunt."

He stood beside her, waiting, so Edie told Leona she had a ride. She followed George to his table, where he informed the rest of the crew what he was doing. He downed the last of his beer and placed his hand on the small of her back. He chuckled when she said "Hey!" and bucked forward. People stared, but she kept going. George was right behind her.

"Truck's over here." He went for her arm, but she dodged him. "Jesus, what's the rush?"

Edie climbed into the truck, and George put it in gear, lowering the volume on the radio while some cowboy singer crooned about cheating love.

"Wanna smoke? No? Mind if I do? Okay, darlin'." He rested his elbow in the open window of his door. "Rotten luck about your flat tire." He shook his head. "Have you noticed the weather's beginning to change? You sure can feel it at night. Where'd summer go? Pretty soon I'll be tuning up my snowmobile." He blew the smoke out the window. "You're looking good, Edie. Real good."

George grinned at her. He grew up in Tyler, but moved to Conwell after he married young, then divorced a few years later. Walker told her George had a child with a cousin, who he didn't claim, except for the court-ordered support checks. The woman, who had kids by two other men, thought it was all right. George at least paid.

Neither spoke for a while. George fiddled with the radio, so the station came in clearer. He kept giving her little looks. She hugged herself tightly and stayed close to the door.

"I bet it's been rough for you lately, Edie. I've heard things. People can be so cruel." He sweetened the tone of his voice. "I always had a hunch about you and Walker. I saw the way he was when you were around." He grinned. "It all makes sense Walker leaving work early. Dean covering for him all the time. Walker may have fooled his wife, but a man knows when another man has a thing for a woman."

Edie exhaled deeply when they got to the top of Doyle Road. George made the turn, but he stopped the truck on the shoulder. He shifted in his seat. A corner of his mouth curled upward.

"I'd like to get to know you better, Edie. We could spend some time alone together. Get what I mean, sugar?" His hand slipped beneath the hem of her dress. He rubbed her thigh. "We could have a lot of fun, you and me. I could make you forget all about this trouble you got yourself in."

He laughed when she shoved his hand away.

"What in the hell are you doing? Get your hands off me."

"It's okay, baby. Take it easy."

She went for the door. But he was on top of her, kissing her and trying to get back under her skirt. The man was all muscle, so much heavier than her. His whiskers burned as he tried to kiss her. His hands tugged at her panties.

"Shit, George, let me go."

Edie fought hard, slapping and pushing him away. He laughed as if it were a game.

"I like a woman who puts up a fight. Was it this way with you and Walker?"

George took one hand away to work at his belt buckle. Edie reached for the door's handle, and George lunged for her when he realized what she was doing. But she had the door open. She dropped to the ground.

Her purse knocked against her hip as she ran. She didn't dare glance back.

His Awkward Way

Harlan loosened the last bolt on the flat tire while Edie held the flashlight. He needed a break from being on his knees, but he stayed in this position after he set the tire on the ground. He poked a fingertip through a hole in the tire's wall.

"Did you hit something on the way here?"

"No. Why?"

He reached for the spare.

"Tell me again where you went."

She shrugged.

"I drove around trying to find work before I came here for a beer. My car seemed perfectly fine."

Harlan eyed the bar's full lot.

"How long were you parked here?"

"Maybe an hour, maybe more."

Edie called him from her aunt's house, out of breath, upset, more than warranted, he felt, for a flat tire. She couldn't reach her father. She said she didn't have anyone else to call. Harlan saw the looks between Edie and her aunt when he came to get her. Something else happened.

He shook his head.

"Edie, this wasn't an accident. See? My guess is somebody stuck something sharp in here. Maybe a knife." He touched the hole again. "Think anybody in the Do could've seen what happened? We could ask around."

"Do we have to? It could've been anybody who knows my car, somebody who doesn't like me. That could be a lot of people these days. I'll just be more careful where I park."

"Edie, you can't let anybody get away with this. We should call the cops."

"Again? Who'll come? The old chief? He's probably sleeping in front of his TV. Buddy Crocker? No, Harlan. I'm mad, but I don't wanna make a big deal about this. It'll just give people another reason to talk about me. It'll make things worse. Believe me."

Harlan glanced toward the bar, its windows lit by neon beer signs. Music poured through the door each time it opened.

"Okay, have it your way about the cops. Why don't you head on back to Amber when I'm done here."

Harlan waited until the taillights of Edie's car were out of sight before he went inside the Do. Most people concentrated on drinking and carousing. He wasn't interested in any of that. One of Walker's hired men gave Edie a ride home, and as the crew fooled around with a waitress and some of the other women, he guessed the man forced himself on Edie. It was likely Harlan couldn't do anything about the flat tire, but this he would handle for her.

As the crew erupted in laughter over a joke, one man watched Harlan make his clumsy way through the tightly packed tables. Harlan remembered him from the men who worked on his roof. His name was George.

Harlan's brow tightened.

"Someone here give Edie a ride tonight?"

The others, finishing up their good moment, sized him up. George held his stare.

"I did," he spoke at last.

"George, right? Just wanted to thank you for bringing Edie home." Harlan kept his voice friendly. "If there's a next time, I'd like to be the one to do it. All right?"

The man's teeth showed when he grinned.

"Sure enough, pal. I'll keep it in mind."

"Glad to hear it. Enjoy your night. See you guys around."

Harlan was about to leave when George spoke loudly to the man beside him.

"That guy better watch his step with Edie. You should've seen her in my truck. She was all over me. I couldn't believe it. I bet the horny bitch'll get it on with just about anybody."

Harlan spun around. He shoved a chair out of his way. George still laughed, but he stopped when Harlan seized the front of his t-shirt with two hands. He dragged the man across the table, sending bottles and glasses to the floor. George tried to pull back, but Harlan held him close enough that he saw the fillings on the man's back teeth.

"If I were you, I'd watch what you say about Edie."

Harlan gave the man a shove, so he fell butt-hard onto his chair. George scrambled to his feet, but one of the crew pulled him back.

"Get that asshole outta here," George yelled.

Harlan didn't see any friendly faces in the crowd circling the table. He figured he was in trouble. At the least, he'd get thrown out, or he'd have to fight George, but it was too late to back down.

A hand patted his back, and Edie's friend, Dean, was saying, "Harlan, take it easy. Old George ain't worth it."

"Fuck off, you drunk," George hollered at Dean.

"Gee, George, you really hurt my feelings just then. Tell me somethin' I don't know." Dean laughed, and a few of the people standing near the table joined him. He patted Harlan's back.

"Hey, pal, time for you to hit the road. I'll take it from here." His voice was drunken-sloppy.

"When you see Edie, tell the girl I love her. Don't you forget."

Harlan nodded as George sputtered curses.

"Thanks," he told Dean before he made his awkward way toward the door.

People stared. He didn't care. He was used to it by now.

No Ambulance

Edie knocked on Pop's door, and then she and Amber were inside calling for him. Her father's end of the house was dark although his truck was parked outside. Pop never went to bed this early on a Friday night.

"Pop, you lucky stiff, you got outta helping me fix a flat. Where the heck were you?"

"Edie, thank God, you're home."

Pop squinted from the sudden light when she switched on a lamp. Her father lay on his leather recliner. His head rested beside the tape covering the bullet hole.

"What are you doing in the dark?" Edie stepped forward. "Pop, you don't look so hot. Why are you holding your arm like that? You bang it or something?"

"If you wanna know, I feel like crap. I need ya to take me to the hospital."

Edie knelt before her father.

"Hospital? What's wrong?"

"I think a heart attack's comin' on. Remember Duke at the road crew? I seen it with him. I seen it a coupla other times. I know what happens." His breath came in short rifts. His words were halting. "You better drive me now, Edie."

She went for the phone.

"No, no, I'll call the ambulance. The firefighters will be here first to help you."

Pop shook his head.

"I ain't takin' no ambulance to the hospital. Maybe nobody'll show up. Even if they do, I'll be a goner by then."

He winced as he pushed the chair's lever.

"Pop, you're being a stubborn old man."

"Just get me in your car and drive me there. Fast."

Edie glanced at Amber. Her girl sucked the tip of her thumb. Her eyes were wide.

"Amber, could you get the door, honey? Then hop in the back seat of the car," she said. "Okay, okay. Come with me, Pop. Hold on. That's right."

Slowly, Edie and Pop made their way to the car. Pop leaned heavily as they took the steps. He grunted when he fell onto the front seat.

"Is Poppy all right?" Amber asked.

Edie saw her daughter's frightened face when she ran the car in reverse.

"I think so. I'm gonna stop at Aunt Leona's. I want you to run inside and stay with her. Explain what happened. Tell her I'll call her when I know what's goin' on."

Along the way to the hospital, Edie kept checking her father, who hadn't spoken a word since he whispered, "Bye, sweetie," to Amber. His eyes were closed. Edie pushed the car beyond the speed limit. She knew the road well, where it curved, dipped, and climbed. No traffic was in the way. She figured they had fifteen minutes more to reach the hospital, maybe ten if there weren't any cops when they got to the city. The hospital was just over the line.

She pressed the gas pedal harder.

"How are you doin', Pop?" Edie asked.

Pop's eyes blinked open.

"Same," and after a while, "I got some things to tell you, Edie."

"Shh, shh, not now."

"Yeah, now. In the big barn, I hid a metal strongbox under one of the floorboards. It's to the right and next to that tall bureau I got off old lady Stowe. Look for the board with no nails." He made a stuttering breath. "You'll find my will inside the box."

"Pop."

He ignored her.

"You'll find my will inside the box," he repeated. "I got that drunk lawyer who comes to the Legion to draw it up for me. I'm leavin' the house and land to you. There's cash inside, too. It's for you and Amber. I'm givin' each of your sisters one buck, so make sure you pay 'em."

"Why are you telling me this?"

"Cause this is as close to dyin' I got so far, and I want you to know that stuff. Edie, you've been a damn good daughter to me. I couldn't ask for more."

"Oh, Pop."

"One last thing." His voice slimmed to a whisper. "Tomorrow's Saturday. It's dump day. It's gotta get open."

"Don't you worry. I'll take care of it," Edie said. "Pop, we're almost there. See the lights? There's the hospital. Hang in there."

"I'm tryin' honey. I'm really tryin'."

Minutes later, when they reached the emergency room entrance, Edie bounded from the car and through the door.

"Help, it's my father," she yelled. "He's having a heart attack."

Buy the Farm

Hours later, Edie waited at the payphone for her aunt to pick up her end of the line.

"Aunt Leona, it's me. I'm at the hospital still. Did I wake you?"

"Nah, I was waiting for your call. How's that brother of mine doing? Did he buy the farm?" Leona exhaled into the phone's receiver. "Don't mind me, Edie. If Alban kicked I would've heard it in your voice already."

Edie turned from the payphone toward a woman being wheeled down the hall on a gurney.

"Pop had a heart attack." She sighed. "You're right. He's gonna be okay, but he'll be here for a while. He's resting in his room."

Leona cackled.

"That man's so stubborn he'd fight off dying," she said. "Stay as long as you need, Edie. Amber's asleep upstairs. Tell Alban I may come and see him. Hospitals give me the creeps, but he is my only brother."

"I'll call if there's a change." She reached into her pocket for coins and a paper with the number Pop gave her. "Could you keep Amber tomorrow? I'm gonna work the dump for Pop."

"What? No niece of mine is going to work at the town dump. You call up those selectmen and tell them they can find somebody else or shut the damn place down."

"Pop asked me, and I said yes. He's afraid of losing his job."

"Jesus Christ, Edie, who else would want it?"

"I said the same thing, but he wouldn't hear of it. I'm gonna go now and check on Pop before I head home. It's been a real long day."

"You do that, honey. I'll see you tomorrow."

Edie hung up the phone. She thought briefly of the day behind her, not finding a job, the flat, and the trouble with George. Her father was in the hospital, and she didn't know for how long. She shook it all off and dialed the number on the paper.

At The Dump

Edie pushed open the metal gates guarding the dump before she
parked her car beside the attendant's shack. She knew Pop's Saturday
routine was to arrive earlier than the first customers and check the
place over. It appeared Pop had moved the piles around Wednesday.
The smell of rot wasn't so bad.

She unlocked the shack. The place was a mess, filled with stuff Pop
thought was too good to throw out but hadn't brought home. She'd
straighten it out later. She dropped her lunch bag and a thermos of
coffee on the desk Pop somehow fit inside. Or maybe he built the
shack around it. Pop has been working the dump so long it could have
happened that way.

She caught herself in a dusty mirror propped in the corner. She wore
jeans and a flannel shirt over her t-shirt. None of it was new.

"You're doin' this for Pop," she told herself.

The dump had been here as long as people in town needed a place
to get rid of their garbage instead of burying it in their back yards. It
was on the western side of town in the middle of the woods and not
far from the Do-Si-Do, which was a convenient stopping place for the

dump's customers, and after it closed, Pop. But Edie wasn't planning to go to the Do after what happened last night with George.

Pop told her there was talk the state will make the town shut down the dump and bury it with dirt. The town might have to buy a compactor, which would squeeze the garbage inside a big metal box before it was hauled away to a dump run by the state. It wouldn't put Pop out of a job though. Somebody has to be in charge, he told her. Somebody has to push the machine's button. He winked at Amber.

"I'll let you do it sometime, sweetie," he had said.

"Okay, Poppy," Amber said.

A car's wheels crushed gravel on the dump's approach. Edie got her work gloves and headed out the door. She recognized her father-in-law's car as it backed toward the pile. Fred didn't usually come first thing to the dump, she recalled from her years working at the store. He went in the afternoon and made a quick stop at the Do. Marie didn't catch on, but Edie knew by the smell of booze, something hard, on his breath. She kept it their secret.

Of course, Fred heard about Pop. News about the town came first to the store.

Edie waved and walked toward the trunk, filled with flattened boxes from stocking the store's shelves. She untied the rope holding the trunk's lid to the bumper and began carrying the cardboard to the pile. Her father-in-law came toward her.

"Edie, how's Benny doing?"

"Pop's gonna be laid up for a while, but he's okay. I'll tell him you asked when I see him tonight."

Edie threw the cardboard onto the freshest pile of garbage and went for more. Fred stood beside her. His brown eyes blinked.

"Edie, why are you doing this?"

She tipped her head.

"I'm holding it for Pop. The selectmen said it was okay. They were in a bind if the dump didn't open today. I said I'd stick around until Pop's okay to work."

"You haven't found another job?"

"No." She filled her arms with cardboard. "It's not like I haven't tried. A lot."

Fred ran his fingers over his bald head.

"I'm sorry about all of this, Edie."

"Me, too."

"How's my Amber?"

Edie felt something rise. She understood why she couldn't work at the store. Amber not seeing her grandparents was something else.

She cocked one eye.

"Amber? She's asks about you and Marie a lot. I try to explain, but she doesn't understand. She's just a kid."

Fred's mouth opened then shut.

Edie shook her head.

"Let me get the rest of this stuff, so you can get back to the store." She nodded toward the dump road. "I've got more customers anyway."

"Sure, Edie."

The day ticked on with a steady flow of customers. Edie was outside the shack to greet each one. She babied the newcomers, toting their garbage although it confused some of the older men. Many hadn't heard about Pop. She wasn't surprised since they weren't part of the locals network. One of the selectmen, a friendly guy who at least was no relation to the St. Claires or Crockers, stopped by the dump.

"You shouldn't drive the dozer if you don't know what you're doing," he told her. "We can get one of the guys from the highway crew."

"That's not necessary. I've done it lots of times for Pop."

"Really?"

Then there were the locals. Just like at Walker's wake she sized up who would feel what fast. She did what she had to do. She ignored their smirks and remarks. Pop must have put up with a lot because of her and Walker. No wonder he had a heart attack.

She leaned against the shack's doorjamb, draining the last of the lukewarm coffee in the thermos. It was fifteen minutes to closing. She eyed an end table someone was throwing out and five window screens with wooden frames. Pop would be proud she was bringing them home.

Through the trees she saw a blue truck, and then as it passed through the gate, the man's face in the windshield. Sharon St. Claire's brother, Jim, was at the wheel. He worked on the highway crew. His boy was the one who threw pig guts and eggs at her house. Jim put the truck in reverse and backed it with such force it appeared the pickup would ram the pile of garbage, but it stopped at its edge. He left the door ajar before he marched toward the rear.

Edie watched.

"You need any help?"

Jim dropped the tailgate. An orange cat with a bullet hole in its head lay on the pickup's bed.

Edie swallowed hard.

"Uh, Jim, you can't leave that here."

He glared.

"Who says?"

"We don't take dead animals at the dump. Town rule."

"You do today."

Jim grasped the cat's back legs and flung the animal hard, so its body landed high on the pile of garbage. With a satisfied grunt, he was back in his truck. Jim spat through the open window, not close to Edie, but in her direction before he drove away slower than he came.

Edie sat on the shack's stoop. She eyed the dead cat. There was no way she could climb the pile of garbage to give it the burial Jim should have done. She wondered what the cat did to deserve being shot. Knowing the Crockers, it was probably nothing. Maybe Jim killed the animal just for her benefit. That family was cruel enough.

"Stupid Crockers," she said.

Edie didn't have time to feel sorry for the animal or herself. She had to run the dozer. She'd take care of the cat that way. Amber was waiting at Aunt Leona's to see Pop. Her aunt called early this morning to say she might come, too.

Edie swore when she heard a truck's engine. This would definitely be her last customer. Maybe Jim was coming back. If so, what else would he do? She wished she had a phone in the shack.

She smiled when she saw Harlan's pickup. He beeped the horn in a friendly way.

Edie went to the driver's side.

"You're lucky," she told him. "I was just ready to shut the gate."

"That so? I actually didn't bring anything to throw away. I came to see if you needed any help."

"I gotta run the dozer and close things up." She nodded toward the shack. "See those wooden screens and that little table? I was gonna bring them back. There's a pie safe in the shack, too."

He eased himself to the ground.

"Those look like good finds. I can put them in the back of my pick-up." He studied her. "How'd it go today?"

"As best to be expected. Those that like me, still do. The others hate my guts. I'd say they were the majority." She shrugged. "The newcomers don't know the difference."

Harlan gestured toward the top of the pile.

"Is that a dead cat up there?"

"Uh-huh, one of the Crockers brought it by. Guess he was making a point."

His head shook.

"Edie, I'm sorry."

"I'm more sorry for the cat." She pulled her gloves from the back pocket of her jeans. "I better get to work."

Harlan limped toward the shack for the screens.

"Why don't you do what you need to get done," he said. "I've got this. Besides, I've never seen a woman run a dozer before."

Smiling, she decided this was the best moment of her day.

"Stand back, Harlan Doyle, and enjoy the show."

Heebie-Jeebies

Edie led Aunt Leona and Amber to Pop's hospital room.

"This place gives me the heebie-jeebies." Leona gripped Edie's arm. "If I get real sick, promise me, Edie, you won't bring me here."

Edie slowed her steps.

"You want me to bring you someplace else?"

"Nah, just let me go."

"Aunt Leona, suppose you're only a little sick, and you ain't gonna die?"

Leona's bony hand wrapped tighter.

"If I'm only a little sick, I'll get better on my own," she said.

"I don't know who's stubborner, you or Pop."

"You might say we have a contest going although I do believe Alban is a little bit ahead this week." She snorted. "Do your sisters know?"

"I left messages. Maybe they'll call back."

"Those two," Leona said.

Edie glanced over her shoulder. Amber walked a few feet behind.

"Stay closer," she told her daughter. "If anyone asks how old you are, you say you're eight. Okay?"

Leona snorted again.

"You can tell 'em you're small for your age like your Ma."

Edie pointed.

"That's his room."

Pop grinned when he saw them.

"My favorite girls," he said. "Nice to see you too, Leona."

Edie slid a chair beside the bed. She nodded to her aunt, who lowered herself onto its seat. Amber moved behind her.

"Alban, don't make me sorry I came all this way to see you." Leona frowned. "When are they letting you out?"

"Not soon enough. Damn noisy place. I can't get enough sleep. Someone's always pokin' and flashin' a light at me."

Edie studied her father. He looked tired but not from the lack of sleep.

"You see the doctor today?" she asked.

Pop waved.

"That quack says I gotta stay here for a while. Then I gotta take it easy at home. I asked him how I'm supposed to work at the dump if I gotta take it easy. He says I won't for a while." He paused. "You call your sisters?"

"I did. They send their love."

Pop snorted.

"Likely story."

"Honestly, you don't look half bad for someone who almost kicked," Leona told him. "Glad you decided to stick around, Alban."

Pop made a whistling laugh.

"Me, too," he said, and then his eyes were on Amber. "Come here, sweetie. I won't bite."

Amber stepped closer.

"Hi, Poppy." She handed him a folded paper. "It's a card. I made it for you. That's you in your chair. See? You're watching TV."

Pop studied the card.

"That's me all right. Why don't you put it on that table for me?"

A nurse, all rustles in her white uniform, came into the room.

"How are you doing, Mr. Sweet?"

"Sweet as ever," he joked.

The nurse laughed.

"I see you have company. Is this your granddaughter?"

Amber raised her hand.

"I'm eight and small for my age like my Ma," she said.

"I can see that." The nurse laughed again. "I'm going to check on your neighbor."

Pop shook his head.

"You do that, honey. Poor bastard worked in a sawmill. His lungs are filled with sawdust." He waited until the nurse passed. "How'd it go today at the dump?"

"It went okay," Edie said.

Pop's eyes narrowed to slits.

"Nobody gave ya a hard time?"

Edie thought of Jim Crocker and the dead cat then let them go.

"I said it was okay." She paused. "Pop, I was thinking I could do your job for you until you get better. You know, as your substitute."

Leona's red head shook.

"What the hell?"

"I know what you're thinking, Aunt Leona. It's dirty work, but it's only open two days, and one of them's a half-day. Besides, Pop wants to keep his job, and I can't find anyone to hire me around here."

The features on Leona's face sharpened.

"Sons of a bitches," she swore.

"You got that right." Pop lifted his head a couple of inches from his pillow. "You sure you wanna, honey?"

"Pop, I've been there enough times to know what to do. I already told one of the selectman, the really nice one, I'll take over for now."

His head fell back onto his pillow.

"I ain't doubting you can do the job." He fingered a tear. "Don't you forget you gotta be extra nice to the newcomers. They give big tips at Christmas when you help 'em with their trash. Carry their bags and tell 'em hick stuff like what bird is making that racket in the trees and talk about the weather. They like that kinda shit."

"Yeah, Pop."

Pop winced.

"It might not be so easy with the locals, I'm afraid. You know because of what's goin' on in town over… "

Edie didn't let him finish. She gave a warning eye to her aunt. The doctor said Pop shouldn't get excited.

"Eh, don't you worry about me. I can handle myself. I was a Sweet before I was a St. Claire. We're tougher. Besides, I can always bring Aunt Leona with me. She'd take care of the troublemakers."

"I'd like to see any of them try," Leona said.

Her father winked.

"If you gets a little thirsty, there's a bottle or two stashed in the shack," he said.

Edie rolled her eyes.

"I'll remember," she said.

Pop chuckled.

"By the way, you three ain't my only visitors today. Guess who else came?"

"One of your pals?" Edie said.

"Nah, it was our neighbor."

"Harlan? He didn't tell me he saw you when he came by the dump."

"He was just being neighborly. Asked me if I needed anything. Edie, I told him to keep an eye on you and Amber. He says he plans to."

Leona's head turned upward. She made a tittering laugh.

"You should see your face, Edie. I didn't know it could get so red."

"Aunt Leona, you're being silly."

"Ha, am I?"

The Ring

Dean swung open the door to his singlewide.

"What are you doin' here?" he asked Edie.

"Hello, yourself."

"Edie, you don't wanna come inside. The place is a pigsty."

"Dean, take a look at me. I'm filthy, so I'll feel right at home." She brushed dirt from the front of her flannel shirt. "I'm running the dump for Pop until he's back on his feet. He had a heart attack."

"A heart attack? Christ, I hadn't heard. Then I don't get around much anymore." He shook his head. "How's your old man doin'?"

"Better. He's outta the hospital anyway. I don't know how that's gonna work. The doc says no smoking. Pop says fat chance he'll give it up. He made me stop at a store on the way home from the hospital. I hated buying them for him, but he threatened to get them himself. What a stubborn old cuss."

Dean winced.

"You workin' at the dump for him? Jesus, Edie."

She gave a half-shrug.

"It's okay."

"That bad, eh?"

"I don't mind the garbage as much as some of the people. I think the Crockers and their pals come to the dump more just to see me. Gives those sick bastards some kinda joy. But, hell, today's Wednesday. It's only a half-day. I only got to see half of 'em. Ask me Saturday when all of 'em come." Edie didn't budge from Dean's door. "You gonna let me in, or do I have to talk with you out here?"

"All right, all right, but I warned you," he said.

The place was a sty, as Dean described. Trash was everywhere. The place stunk of something dying. She lifted a foot over a pile of dirty clothes.

"You weren't lying," she told him.

"Let me clear a space at the kitchen table," he said. "We can talk over there."

Dean shoved dirty dishes to one side of the table. He left a half-filled bottle of Southern Comfort in the empty spot.

"Wanna drink?"

"No, thanks."

Dean reached for the Comfort, but yanked his hand back as if the bottle might sting him. Instead, he stretched backward for a pack of smokes on the kitchen counter.

"Maybe later, eh?" He made jerky laughs in the back of his throat. "Why you here?"

"I heard about you getting kicked off Walker's crew," she said. "I should've come a lot sooner, but I've been busy with Pop and Amber. Sorry."

Dean tilted his head, blowing smoke upward in a strong, steady stream. He pulled the bottle toward himself.

"What are you sorry about?" Dean said. "You didn't do anything to me. The way I see it, we both got screwed when Walker offed himself. Stupid Sharon went around saying I should've asked her to go up there. Yeah, right. She would've stopped him." His voice was hoarse. "Shit, Edie, I didn't know he was so fucked up."

She closed her eyes for a moment. She and Dean had known each other since they were babies. They hung in the same crowd through school, and he was a pallbearer for Gil. She had enough to worry about these days without taking care of Dean, too. She studied the man as he drank from the bottle. Dean tipped it toward her, but she waved it away.

"A lot of things are messed up." Her voice cracked. "At least half the town hates me. Maybe more. My little girl never sees her grandparents. I can't even shop in their store. Jesus, how long did I work there? When Gil died, everybody treated me like I never did anything wrong. With Walker, it's like that's all I've ever done."

Dean's gaze hung somewhere over the table as if he was watching her words tumble in the smoky air. Suddenly, he sat upright. His fingers folded tightly around the bottle.

"You know what I say? Fuck 'em. Fuck Walker, fuck Sharon, and fuck fuckin' George. That asshole wanted to be foreman all along. And while you're at it, fuck the whole damn town. I've had it."

"What are you gonna do?"

Dean brought the bottle to his mouth. He drank again.

"I'll find work. Don't you worry. I'm not lettin' those bastards get to me. I can take care of myself." He raised his eyebrows. "And you can see what an excellent job I'm doin'."

She stared at the bottle then Dean.

"Very funny."

Dean stubbed his cigarette into an ashtray filled with butts and roaches. He got to his feet and picked his way through a pile of boxes and duffle bags in the corner. He had his back to her, and when he sat down again, he dropped a small box covered in black velvet on the table.

"Go ahead. It's for you."

She opened the lid and gasped when she saw the ring inside. Its diamond was as large as the ones Marie wore.

"What's this for?"

He tapped the diamond.

"Walker bought it for you. He showed it to me a coupla times."

She slid the box toward Dean.

"I don't want it."

"I'm not givin' this ring to that bitch. She never loved Walker, and he sure as hell didn't love her." His head shook. "I don't blame him. Did ya know she tricked him into marrying her? She told him she was knocked up, but she wasn't. He didn't find out until after she threw him out. Walker was so pissed. He felt like he wasted his life. It's all he talked about. Sharon got her brother, Buddy, after him. It drove him over, I tell ya."

"Poor Walker."

Dean held the box, snapping the lid over and over.

"Poor Walker, all right. It really fucked things for him. He could've had a happy life. He could've had a beautiful wife who loved him. I'm talking about you, Edie."

Edie cast her eyes downward. Once again, the old sadness filled her. Dean was getting it wrong, but she didn't want to tell him. She recognized the old sadness in him, too.

"I didn't know any of this," she said.

"Nobody did." He cleared the back of his throat. "I told Sharon at the funeral Walker had stuff here. Her brother, Buddy, came for the guns and cash. He told me to throw the rest out. That's the stuff in the corner. He didn't bother going through it. He didn't give a shit." He slid the box toward Edie. "Sell the ring. I know how much it cost. You could take the money and move someplace else. You could get out of this shit-hole town. People here ain't gonna give you any peace, Edie. You could find it somewhere else. Walker owed it to you. He really did."

Edie gazed at the ring, thinking about what Walker wanted from her and what Dean said. She pressed her finger on the top, so the box shut with a quick, tight shot.

"No, I can't take it. Do what you want with it." She rose. "I gotta go, Dean. Amber's with Pop. Call me once in a while, why don't you?"

Dean tore at the bottle's label.

"You seein' that guy?"

"What guy?"

"The one who lives next door to you, Harlan Doyle."

"Harlan? We're just neighbors."

"Neighbors? That's all?" Dean's head moved as if it were keeping a beat. "Did you know he almost fought with George at the Do after you left that time?" He made a hooting laugh. "You look surprised. He didn't say anything? Now that tells me a lot about him."

"What happened?"

"Your neighbor had George practically by the throat when he made some smart ass comment about you."

Her mouth hung open.

"He took on George?"

"Your neighbor didn't seem the type to put up a fight. I'll give him credit though. He didn't back down." Dean made a satisfied grin. "I saw the whole thing. Man, he caught that asshole off guard. Pulled him up by the shirt. George wanted to tear his head off. Good thing I stepped in, or Harlan would've gotten the shit kicked outta him."

Edie clicked her tongue.

"He really took on George?"

Dean chuckled as he brought the bottle to his mouth.

"He sure did."

Close To His Heart

Pop's chest moved beneath his flannel shirt in slow, shallow lifts. Edie stubbed a smoldering butt into the ashtray on the chair's arm. She frowned at the untouched grilled cheese sandwich and the bowl of tomato soup from the can.

Amber sat close to the TV with the volume on low. She held a finger to her lips.

"Shh, shh, shh, Poppy's real tired."

"Uh-huh. I see you made him food. That was very thoughtful of you."

"He didn't eat."

"Don't worry. He will later. How long's he been sleeping?"

"Only a little while."

Edie glanced around her father's place, neater after she washed and put away his clothes. He let her clear out the stacks of yellowed newspapers and magazines, but now, he had insisted, they were in one of his shacks out back with the rest of his junk.

"Why don't you get your backpack? I'm gonna tell Poppy we're going." Edie gently shook her father's shoulder until his blue eyes broke open. "Thanks, Pop. I'm taking Amber home. You didn't eat your food. You feeling okay?"

Pop gave her a sleepy smile.

"I'm fine, honey," he mumbled.

"You sure, Pop?" Edie tapped her father's shoulder. She spoke to him so gently he could have been her child. "You taking it easy? Did you have anything for lunch? No? Maybe that's why you feel so crummy, Pop." She sniffed and lowered her voice. "Aw, you've been drinking already? Gee, Pop, you know what the doctor said."

He shook his finger.

"Edie, you're sounding just like a certain redheaded sister of mine. Real bossy-like. I'll be glad when she goes back to Florida this winter. She comes over and tells me what to do. Or she calls me on that damn phone. I feel like rippin' it outta the wall. If you wanna know, I'm feelin' fine considering, and I'd appreciate it if you all stop treatin' me like I'm touched in the head."

"No, Pop, I'm treating you like a stubborn, old fool who won't take care of himself." She crossed her arms. "Don't forget we're seeing the doctor next week. He's gonna ask you about the smoking and drinking."

Pop spat a yellow wad of phlegm into a raggedy bandana.

"That quack? I'm not lettin' him tell me what to do. When I kick, I'm gonna have a big, fat smile, a cigarette in one hand, and a bottle in the other. That's the way to go, eh? You can put me in the ground just like that."

"Pop, stop talking like that."

Benny's face crinkled.

"How's things at the dump? Rats gettin' thick again?"

"Nah, I went in early to move stuff around." Edie studied her father closely. "Maybe it's time you retired. Running the dump's a lot of work."

"And do what? You might as well take me out in the back yard and bury me with Leona's mutt."

"Pop, you could do lots of things. Go fishing. Hang out with your friends. You could sell the stuff you have in the barn. It'd help with your Social Security."

"That's what Harlan said the last time he was here. Says he knows people who might be interested. Him, too. He could fix up stuff and sell 'em. That's not such a bad idea. But quit the dump? I just need some help now and then when I get back."

Edie sat on the arm of Pop's recliner. Her father was getting too old to be toting people's trash and dragging home their discards. She thought of him venturing out in his snowmobile suit from the attendant's shack during the winter. Snow clung to his woolen cap and ice crystals formed on his whiskers. She brought up the subject before, but this was the first time he gave in a little.

"You think about it some more. Maybe you could spend some time in Florida with Leona. I hear the trailer park she stays at is really nice. Lots of widowed ladies live there. You'd like that."

Amber stood beside her grandfather's chair. She handed her mother a large envelope. Her school photo showed through its cellophane. Amber had a good smile in the picture, not too silly or forced, so she was the girl Edie wanted her to be. She'd have a family who loved her. She'd have friends and get good grades, so she went to college. She would only live in Conwell if she wanted.

In the past, her mother-in-law paid for the most expensive package, so she could have her pick of the photos. Marie always took the eight-by-ten for the engraved silver frame she had in her living room. She hung it next to several pictures taken of Gil: when he was a boy; at his high school graduation; with Edie on their wedding day; and in his uniform before he left for Vietnam. Marie always made a fuss about Amber's new photo. She gushed about how much Amber had changed before she slipped the previous year's picture from the frame into an album. It was "our girl" this and "our girl" that, and Amber loved every minute of it.

"Here, Poppy, this is for you."

Amber gave her grandfather a photo to tack on his bedroom wall with the others of her, plus one for his wallet. She already cut them to size.

Pop pulled the wallet from his back pocket.

"I'm gonna keep this right next to my heart, sweetie pie."

Amber giggled.

"Poppy, that's not near your heart."

"It's close enough." He nodded. "You tell your Ma about school?"

Amber peeked at Pop.

"No."

"Go ahead," he said, but the girl stayed silent. "Never mind. Kids were sayin' things on the bus. About you. She was crying when she got off."

Edie frowned.

"Is Shirl still your driver? She didn't say anything to those brats? Don't you worry, Amber. I'll make sure it doesn't happen again."

Amber's face was raised, her expression trusting.

"Okay, Ma," she said.

A truck pulled in the driveway, and Edie recognized Harlan's uneven step on the porch. He was saying through the screen door, "Mind if I come in?" before Amber opened it.

"Hello there," Harlan said to Amber. "Thanks for getting the door for me."

"You're welcome, Harlan," she said.

Pop sat up.

"If it isn't my best customer. What can I do for you today?"

Harlan chuckled.

"I was wondering if you might have a desk and chair to sell me. I need a file cabinet, too, three drawers if you have one. They're for my office."

Benny scratched his chin, trying to recall what he had in the barn and shacks out back. He snapped his fingers.

"I believe so. I kinda remember a roll-top desk with a nice wooden swivel chair. It used to belong to a doctor in town. Maybe a file cabinet, too. If I still got 'em, I'll give you my best price."

"It sounds like we have ourselves a deal." Harlan glanced at the envelope in Edie's hand. "Say, what do you have there? It's picture of Amber. So cute."

Amber pointed toward the envelope.

"Would you like one? I cut them already." She turned. "You can give him one of the small ones, Ma."

Harlan nodded.

"I sure would. Thank you."

Edie inhaled Harlan's clean scent of cut wood as he tucked the photo into the breast pocket of his t-shirt. She smiled when she bent to kiss her father's cheek.

"I gotta go now. If you need me, I'm next door. Do you mind?"

Her father waved his hand.

"Go ahead, honey. I wanna rest a bit." He swung his head around, whistling happily at Amber when he found her. "Thanks for the grub and pictures."

Edie stepped onto the porch toward her part of the house. Amber let the screen door shut softly behind her. Harlan was still there.

"Is your father okay?"

"I don't know. He's not gonna stop smoking and drinking. And he needs to stop working at the dump. I think all the talk in town about me didn't help." Her head was down, and then she looked directly at Harlan. "By the way, I visited my friend, Dean, today. I hadn't seen him since the wake. I wanted to know how he's making out."

"How is he?"

"Not so good. He's been drinking heavy." She smiled as she tipped her head to one side. "He did tell me an interesting story about you and George getting into a fight at the Do."

Harlan grinned shyly.

"I wouldn't exactly call it a fight, Edie. I dragged him across the table and let him flop back on his chair." He shrugged. "He was drunk.

It wasn't too hard."

She shook her head.

"He could've hurt you really bad, Harlan."

He snorted.

"Edie, my body might be messed up, but I can stand up for myself or people I care about. You should know that about me."

"You're different than George and the others. You talk things over."

He shook his head.

"I tried that approach. It didn't work with George."

She smiled. He was telling her something she already knew.

"Nice of you to keep buying stuff from Pop. Maybe soon we can have that barn and his shacks empty if you keep it up."

Harlan grinned.

"It's not all I came here for." He paused. "I wanted to ask you to dinner Saturday night. I'd take you out, but I can't think of anywhere close that's good to go. I'll do the cooking. Don't be so surprised, Edie. I'm a great cook. I did most of it when I was married."

Edie smiled.

"I've never had a man cook for me, except Pop," she said. "Let me ask my aunt if Amber can stay with her. I bet she won't mind. She can cheat at cards and feed Amber all the ice cream she wants." She smiled again. "When should I come over?"

Slow Dance

Edie brought two beers to Harlan's kitchen table. Dinner was over. Harlan made spaghetti with homemade sauce and garlic bread that Edie liked. The dishes were in the sink. Harlan said he'd wash them later, not to worry.

The only light on in his house was the one over the table. The radio's volume was lowered, so they could talk, and Harlan hummed to the tune playing on the country station. Edie handed him a cold bottle.

"Your favorite music," she teased.

He chuckled.

"I believe it's growing on me, at least the old-timey stuff. Have a seat. I want to show you something."

As Edie watched, Harlan went to the hutch for a roll of papers, which he spread over the tabletop.

"These are the plans I drew up for my new shop. This here is where the workbenches and machinery will go in the barn's first floor. See how I'll partition one corner for an office?"

She shook her head, amused. Harlan used quick, light strokes to draw a woman writing at a desk.

She pointed.

"Who's that?"

"My secretary. I'll need to hire someone when I get this business going. Know anyone who might be interested?"

"I'd ask around, but nobody's speaking to me these days." Edie took a closer look. Her head bounced up. She smiled at Harlan. "Hey, she looks like me."

"I did a pretty good likeness, don't you think?" He studied her. "You might want to consider the job. It'd only be part-time at first."

Edie sighed.

"I'm not sure if I have what it takes."

"You'd be good with customers. It's the most important require- ment." His hands flattened the paper's curl. "You could help me with some of the small stuff in the shop, too, like hand-sanding."

"I'm working at the dump for a few weeks more. Either Pop will be well enough to take back the job, or he won't, and I'll quit, and they'll have to find somebody else to run that place. I'm not staying any longer than I have to."

"Something happen today?"

Edie frowned.

"Nothing I can't handle. Some people sure like giving me a hard time. Today a newcomer took me aside to say one of the Crocker cousins was being awfully rude. He told me I should complain to the selectmen. I told him thank you, but it wouldn't help."

"Isn't there somebody else you could tell?"

She smiled.

"I believe I just did." She shook a finger. "But I don't want you doing anything about it this time."

Harlan chuckled.

"Rescuing you has become my specialty, Edie. Anyway, I should be ready for you in about a month. Why don't you think it over?"

She kept smiling.

"I will."

Edie set the paper down and picked up another. This one had a sketch of the barn's exterior. It was painted a smart red. A sign above the double-doors said: HARLAN DOYLE FINE WOODWORK-ING. The sign's background was a creamy yellow, its lettering black. Her fingers fluttered over the drawing. It was perfect.

A new song came from the station, a fast-mover about a man hell-bent on fun. It was a favorite of the dancers and some of the bands that played at the Do. She hadn't heard it in a while.

She smiled at him over the paper.

"Do you remember, Harlan, the time at the Do when I asked if you ever dance?"

He grinned back.

"I believe I told you I used to, but with this bum leg I probably could only manage a slow one."

She peered up at Harlan.

"Let me know when you wanna try. The offer still holds."

He couldn't stop grinning.

"I just might."

"Please, do."

Harlan grinned still, watching her intently. Edie picked up a draw-ing of the hayloft.

"The loft will be a dry spot to store lumber," he said. "I'll have to build stairs because I couldn't manage a ladder. I'll likely get to it this winter when I can find some help."

She turned toward the radio as a song exploded with violins, and Patsy Cline began singing "Crazy" in her you-got-me voice. She was a woman who couldn't stop loving a man. Edie tipped her head and murmured. Patsy got the woman's feelings just right.

Edie lifted her eyes as the legs on Harlan's chair scraped against the floor. He stood in front of her. He held out both hands.

"Edie, I believe this might be that slow song we've been waiting for."

Giggling, she got to her feet and in his arms.

"I believe you're right."

Harlan danced awkwardly at first. He couldn't seem to find the beat.

Edie whispered, "Take your time, Harlan. This song was made for slow moving."

He relaxed. His feet made small rocking steps across the floor as she followed his lead. She and Harlan made one spin, and then another over the linoleum, so cool beneath her bare feet. She laughed when Harlan dipped her backward and used his strong arms to draw her toward him. He laughed, too, as he made his steps longer. She was tight inside his arms when they twirled again. He slowed. Edie rested her head in a comfortable place against his chest.

He murmured, "This is nice."

"Yes, it is."

The song ended, and the announcer introduced the next. He was taking requests, and this tune was going out to a couple celebrating an anniversary. Harlan stopped dancing, but he didn't release Edie. His heart beat steadily in her ear. She looked up.

"What are you thinking about, Harlan?"

"I'm thinking about you and me."

"You and me."

His face had taken on the shy expression he wore the first time she met him. He lived in his tent and sat on the porch because everything he had was soaked from the rain. His head was cocked to one side when she introduced herself as his neighbor. Pop, who met him first, told her some about him. Now she knew more.

Their lips touched, and then their tongues, and she felt they were tumbling into some hot, wet place as they kept at it. He guided her backwards to his bedroom, where they kissed until they were breathless.

The Caring Side

Edie used a fingertip to trace a scar along Harlan's leg. He took her in, enjoying her touch, she could see. She wanted to make him feel as good as she now felt. The rough tracks where the doctor sewed him together extended from his pelvis to the calf of his bad leg. He cast his eyes dreamily toward her.

"I'm quite a mess, huh?" he said.

She shushed him.

"To tell you the truth, I've seen worse."

"Worse?"

"A man from Gil's unit came to visit me. He got hurt a few days before Gil's chopper went down, so he wasn't on board when it crashed. He was in a VA hospital for a real long time. A few months after he got out, he came to see me. He showed up at my apartment above the general store. I hadn't moved in with Pop yet."

She held a hand to Harlan's cheek.

"His name was Dave. He was from New Hampshire, a real country boy like my Gil. They were close buddies," she said. "He gave me a picture someone took of Gil in front of their chopper. Amber has it

299

framed in her room. He told me everything he could remember about him, and I let him hold Amber. She was just a baby. We read aloud all the letters Gil sent me from Vietnam, and we cried."

She sighed.

"I let him sleep with me. When I saw his naked body, I could see how much he'd been hurt. I kissed every scar, thinking he could be Gil coming home to me this way. I wouldn't have cared. I missed him so much."

She stretched beside Harlan.

"Everybody came to see Dave. They wanted to hear his stories about Gil and Vietnam. My in-laws did, too. Walker took him to the Do. He ended up staying five days, and then he went back to his mother's in New Hampshire."

Harlan pulled the sheet over Edie's trembling body.

"What happened to him?"

"I don't know. I sent him Christmas cards with pictures of me and Amber for a couple of years, but I didn't hear any more from him. I think it was too hard for both of us. I really hope he found someone who loves him. I hope he's okay."

Harlan rose on one elbow.

"Do you think you could love someone like you did Gil?"

Edie reached to pat his cheek.

"I want to. I really do." She paused. "I suppose you're wondering why I got involved with his brother, Walker."

"I'd be lying if I said I didn't."

She turned, so she faced Harlan.

"I knew a different side of Walker, the caring side." She sighed. "He was the one who helped me the most after Gil died. He stayed after everyone left the day I found out. He lay down beside me in my bed. He said he'd wait until I fell asleep, but he stayed longer."

She stopped.

"Go on."

"I woke up in the middle of the night, and Walker was still there.

He fell asleep, too. His hand was on my belly, and I felt Amber moving." She closed her eyes briefly. "For a moment, I thought he was Gil. I wanted him to be. It was easy. They looked so much alike, only a year apart, that people who didn't know better thought they were twins." She sighed again. "He kissed me. It wasn't a sexy kind of kiss but a soft kiss. We cried for Gil. We both loved him so. The next morning when I woke up, Walker was gone. I never forgot."

Each Song

Harlan stood in the doorway to his kitchen. Just out of the shower, he was shirtless, barefoot, and wearing clean jeans.

Edie's back was to him as she used a spatula to flip fried eggs from a cast iron skillet onto a plate. She hummed along with the tune playing on the country station she liked so much. She kept telling Harlan to listen to the words. Each song told a story about what people loved. Sometimes they lost and got it back. Sometimes they never did. Those were the saddest.

Edie sang along with the chorus. Her voice was louder now, high like her laughter. Her hips shook. The sun showed through the fabric of her dress as if it were x-raying her. He could see her nipples, the small bulge of her belly, her thighs, and backside when she spread her legs apart. Harlan felt thick and lustful again.

He wanted to surprise her, twirl her in his arms, but when he came toward her, she heard his clumsy footfall and turned. His mouth loosened into a smile. Could he be any happier? He didn't know.

"Just in time," she said.

He followed her to the table, where she set down his plate.

"This is great. Aren't you going to join me?" He reached for her hand. "Stay with me, Edie. I'll make you happy all day long."

Edie laughed. She peeked at the wall clock.

"Yeah? Now that's awfully tempting, but I promised Amber I'd take her shopping in the city for new shoes. That girl keeps on growing." She brought her hands to his face. She kissed him. "I'll take you up on your offer real soon."

Not So Old

Leona glanced up from the folded newspaper on the kitchen table. She was working the crossword puzzle. A pen was in her hand. She said only sissies used pencil.

"I recognize that smile." She cackled. "I'm betting Harlan showed you a swell time if you get what I mean."

"Aunt Leona."

"Don't Aunt Leona me. I'm not so old I don't remember what it's like for a man to make you feel good in bed." Her red hair shook as she cackled again. "Don't mind me. I've been rooting for the guy ever since he moved here."

Edie rolled her eyes.

"Where's Amber?"

"She's out back, bouncing that darn ball of hers. Hear it? Bump, bump, bump."

Through the window, she watched Amber throw a pink ball upward. The ball hammered the roof, and her girl danced around the grass as she waited for it to drop. Edie knocked at the window, and Amber smiled when she held the ball aloft.

"She's been at it for a while. I'll say this for the girl: She can keep herself occupied." Leona put her pen down. "By the way, I've been thinking I might not go to Florida this year."

"But you like it there. It's nice and warm in the winter. The trailer park where you stay has lots of men."

Leona shook her head.

"I don't know if I'm up for making the trip. I'm not a spring chicken anymore."

"What do you mean?"

She frowned.

"It means I'm getting old, Edie. I need to be around family who can watch out for me."

Edie made a teasing smile.

"You mean Pop?"

"Nah, not Alban. You know what I'm saying, Edie. I'm not planning on seizing up any time soon, but if I need somebody to help me, I'd rather it be you than a perfect stranger. Don't worry. I'm not going to be a burden to you." She paused. "Besides, I want to see how this thing works out between you and Harlan. It's been years since I've been to a wedding."

"Aunt Leona, I dunno if it'll go that way."

Her aunt shook a finger.

"Shucks, Edie, don't you disappoint me now."

An IOU

Dean stuck his head through the barn door, giving a "Hey, there" to Harlan as he stepped inside. Harlan flipped the switch on the table saw when he recognized Edie's friend. From her say, the man was having a rough time, but as Dean walked through the barn, he was clearly a man on the go. His skin was pale and greasy, but his hair was cut, and he was clean-shaven. His clothes appeared new.

"Is Edie here by any chance? I went by her place, but no one's home." He gave the barn the once-over. "Whoa, you've fixing this old barn up nice. Great place for a shop."

Harlan, too, was pleased with his progress. Raw pine boards were nailed over the insulation. Cinderblocks were stacked to build a chimney for the woodstove he bought from Benny. Today he was doing the trim around the new windows, nothing fancy, just picture frame.

Harlan dropped the stubby pencil he used to mark boards and offered his hand. Dean's was shaky although it gave a pleasant grip.

"What brings you here?" Harlan asked.

"I have somethin' for Edie. I stopped by her aunt's and father's, but nobody's home. Mind if I leave it with you?"

"No, not at all. I can drop it off later. She's at the dump. It's Wednesday. She went in early."

Dean did a nervous shuffle.

"The dump. How's that workin' out for her?"

"You know Edie. It isn't easy, but she doesn't complain unless I ask. It's just temporary anyway. Benny's raring to go, but the doctor says no just yet. At least, he can drive now. He's probably down at the dump checking on her."

"That's Edie alright, making the best of a situation. She probably told you we grew up together. We've been through a lot."

"Yes, she told me, at least some."

Dean reached into his canvas vest, fumbling as he pulled out a thick, white envelope.

"I'm on my way to Maine. I don't wanna go, but my cousin's got a job for me, and there's nothin' here." His brow rose and fell. "Except for Edie, and we're kinda in the same boat. I got my place up for sale. I even managed to get out of that little jam at court. Amazing what a city lawyer can do."

"Edie will be awfully disappointed if she doesn't get a chance to see you off."

Dean smiled forlornly.

"It's better this way." He thrust the envelope toward Harlan. "This is for her. She'll know where it's from. Tell her I kept half." He snorted. "Don't worry. It's nothin' crooked. I'll let her tell you about it. For now, it's just an IOU from an old friend."

Harlan took the envelope stuffed with bills.

"You don't want to give this to her yourself?"

"Nah, she wouldn't take it. But I bet she can use it. I told Edie she and her little girl should get out the hell of this shit-hole town."

"I hope not."

"Ha."

Dean made a smile Harlan recognized. Here was a man willing to break from everything familiar to save himself. Nothing was working out for him in Conwell. Harlan clutched the thick envelope.

"If you change your mind, stop by the dump."

Dean shrugged.

"Shoot, I better get goin'. I got my dogs in the truck." He held out his hand. "I really hope it works out for you here."

Miss Ya

Edie walked with Pop while he did a full inspection of the dump. He nodded as he went from the shack to the piles.

"You've been doing a fine job here," he told her. "Good work with the dozer. You're keepin' the stink down."

"Thanks, Pop."

"You even cleaned up the shack. It's nice enough now for lace curtains." He chuckled at his joke. "Funny though, I can't find the bottles I stashed there. You been drinkin' on the job?"

"Nah, I dumped them out."

"You did what?"

"You heard what the doctor said about the hard stuff."

"Shoot, Edie, I was lookin' forward to a sip while I watched you work."

"Too bad, Pop."

Both turned as a pickup drove fast through the gate. The man at the wheel gave the horn a series of loud honks.

"Somebody's in a helluva rush," Pop said. "Hey, that's Dean's truck. See all that stuff in the back. His dogs, too. Looks like he and his mutts are packed up to go somewhere."

"Sure does. I'm gonna see what he wants."

Edie walked toward Dean, who leaned out the window of his truck and said, "Howdy." He gave a wave to her father. "Benny, nice to see ya alive."

"Yeah, I tricked the devil one more time."

Dean's dogs whimpered to get near Edie, but he ordered them back in the bed.

"What are you doin'? You goin' somewhere?" she asked.

"Leo's got work for me in Maine." He tried to smile big for her, but he kept wiping tears with the cuff of his flannel shirt. "Shit, this is why I didn't wanna see you, Edie. Here I go, a big baby all over again. What's the matter with me?"

Edie pecked his smooth cheek.

"Nothing's wrong with you, Dean, and I would've been real mad if you left without saying good-bye. Real mad."

"Aw, Edie, I'm gonna miss ya like hell."

Felt Richer

Harlan pressed the bills into Benny Sweet's hand for the washing machine sitting on the ground behind his pickup. The old man mopped his brow with a white handkerchief stained brown as he shoved the money into his pants pocket. There was no way he could ask Benny to help him. Harlan managed to wrestle the washer from the barn and got this far with a handcart Benny had. He figured with a great deal of effort he could pull or push the washer up the planks leaned against the pickup's tailgate.

He turned when he heard Edie's car. Amber was with her. Edie greeted Harlan then focused her attention quickly on her father.

"Pop, you weren't gonna help Harlan, were you?"

"I wouldn't let him," Harlan said.

Edie patted her father's shoulder. She studied Harlan and the washer.

"You don't look so good, Pop. I bet you didn't have anything to eat today."

"Edie, knock it off, will ya?"

"Come on, Harlan. I'll give you a hand."

"You, Edie?" her father said. "You're such a delicate thing."

"I'm not so delicate. I toughened up at the dump."

Her father snorted.

"That's my girl."

Harlan smiled. The ornery so-and-so moved his mouth. The flesh around his eyes was loose. Edie had him bound in her love. Harlan admired their closeness, the rough, warm ways they cared for each other. Benny Sweet might be an old drunk who ran the dump, but he had family who treated him better than most could boast. Harlan felt richer to be even a small part of it.

Edie gestured for Amber.

"Take Poppy inside, and make him a sandwich and get him something to drink, but no beer. Come on, Pop, go with her."

"No beer? You gotta be kiddin' me."

"Lean on me, Poppy," Amber said, carrying the same note of concern Harlan heard in her mother's voice.

Benny held onto his granddaughter's arm, appearing more tired and older than when Harlan saw him a half-hour ago. Edie watched them go into the house, and then she announced to Harlan, "I'm ready. I see you've got the planks in place. Why don't you use the handcart? You pull it backwards, and I'll push from the front."

"You sure, Edie?"

"I don't see any other way. Do you?"

"No, I don't."

They worked the washer onto the truck. Harlan peered over the machine.

"I have something for you at the house. I should've brought it, but I didn't expect to see you. I thought I could get this by myself."

"What is it?"

"You'll just have to wait a short ride to find out."

Harlan drove the pickup slowly over the dirt road, its surface much smoother than when he first moved here.

Edie nibbled a fingernail.

"Something going on?" he asked.

She shook her head.

"I went to Amber's school today. Kids have been pickin' on her, you know, about Walker and me. And me workin' at the dump. It's mostly the Crocker kids. Those folks breed like rabbits. The ones I mind are the big kids on the bus. They like making her cry."

"How'd it work out?"

"Not the way I wanted. They didn't seem as concerned as me. I might just have to take care of this myself."

Harlan backed the truck to his house. His plan was to run the plank from the tailgate to the porch. He thought they could manage it easily.

Edie jumped on the truck's bed, yelping when she realized the handcart belonged to the Conwell Highway Department. She pointed at the lettering.

"My old man just won't learn," she said when Harlan chuckled. "We'll be lucky to get plowed at all this winter."

They worked together, bringing the washer into the kitchen where Harlan's grandmother kept hers. He said he'd hook it up later. He planned to string clothesline in the back. Eventually, he'd get a dryer.

"Can you stay awhile?" he asked.

"Yeah. Let me call home first and make sure Pop's all right."

Harlan leaned against the washer as he listened to Edie quiz Amber about her father's health over the kitchen phone. Edie stood barefoot on the linoleum floor, and smiling, she spun around while she listened to Amber. His heart made an identical turn.

"I told Amber I'll be home soon. What's the surprise?"

He smiled. She hadn't forgotten what he said.

"Just a sec."

"Guess who I saw today?" she said. "Dean. He was heading out of town. He came by the dump to say bye, he and his hounds."

"He did go after all." Harlan walked to the hutch and got the white envelope. He handed it to Edie. "Dean was here earlier. He left this for you."

She touched the edges of the bills, all hundreds.

"That's a lotta money," she said.

"Where'd it come from?"

She sighed.

"I went to see Dean a ways back after work. He showed me a ring Walker was gonna give me. You should've seen how big the diamond was." Her breath whistled through her lips. "Dean told me to take the ring. He said to sell it. I told him I didn't want anything to do with it." She sighed. "It looks like Dean took care of it himself."

"He said he kept half."

"Half." She did a quick count of the bills. "He shouldn't have done this. It's too much."

"He really wanted you to have it, Edie. He said it was an IOU."

"How silly. He doesn't owe me a thing. I wouldn't have taken the ring from Walker. I understood what he wanted, and I couldn't give it to him."

She was silent for several minutes as Harlan traced the scar along his right cheek, moving the end of his finger up and down about an inch. She gazed into his eyes.

"What do you think I should do with it?" she asked.

"Does Sharon need it?"

Edie shook her head.

"Nah, I heard from Pop she has a new car already. She's keeping the business going. Walker took care of her and the boys. He did that much for them at least."

"If you want my advice, I believe you should keep it. You'll find something worthwhile to do with it." His voice was tender. "Dean said you should use it to leave town."

"He did, did he?" Edie fingered the edges of the bills. "Ha, I wasn't planning to leave, Harlan. This is where I live."

The Big Picture

Edie pushed the gates of the dump closed and fixed the padlock. She walked to her car. The bushes in the swampy areas near the dump and the oldest trees along the roadsides had already changed color, but the rest of the woods would remain green for a week or so. Then the hills would fill out red, orange, and yellow, except where the tall pines grew.

Harlan's folks were coming soon to see their son, to check his progress with the house, and, he said, to meet her and Amber. The last part got her saying, "Suppose they don't like me?" Harlan told her not to worry. He was certain they would.

She tossed her work gloves and thermos on the floor. She pulled off her sweatshirt and reached for a sweater in the back. She changed from her boots to sneakers. She brushed the dirt from her jeans as best she could.

Edie picked up the flat envelope on the seat that held Amber's large school photo, plus two wallet-sized ones and a note from her daughter. It said: "DEAR GRANDMA, I MISS YOU AND GRANDPA TOO MUCH. I'VE BEEN VERY, VERY GOOD. DON'T BE SO

SAD ANYMORE. PLEASE SEE ME SOON. LOVE, AMBER."

She reread her daughter's note and slid it inside the envelope. She used the cracked mirror on the visor to clean the smudges from her face and to neaten her hair. She poked the key into the ignition.

"Let's get this over with," she told herself.

Stage Road was the shortest route back to the center of Conwell and the one with the best view although not the smoothest ride. She decided to take it. The road began a steep rise through a thick curtain of forest. Her car strained a bit near the top of the hill, where it was washed out, but the tires recovered their grip, and the road flattened at an apple orchard.

Behind the rows of trees, the land stretched, dipped, and rose into the Berkshires to the west. She braked and stuck her head out the open window. A red-tailed hawk cruised above, its shadow sailing across the hood of the car as it rode the air currents.

Edie drove on, passing a buttoned-up farmhouse, and behind it a barn with a plank holding its wide doors shut. A for-sale sign was nailed to a tree in the front yard. Edie dragged out an "Oh." The couple, really nice folks, had been on her delivery route, too. The woman died a few years ago. The man tried to keep the orchard going, but he got too sick and forgetful. He's probably living in a home in the city.

The couple had five kids, but none were around anymore. They didn't want this kind of life, she supposed. Growing apples was a hard way to make a living. A late frost in spring, when the trees were in bloom, meant the end of the crop. There were lots of other problems: Bugs, diseases, finding reliable workers. The old man used to tell her all about it when she and Amber visited Saturday mornings.

She took her gaze from the sign. When it sells, the kids will get money. The orchard will likely be broken into building lots for rich newcomers. The trees would be cut down. Apples wouldn't grow here anymore. She sighed. The old man would be hurt to see it this way.

The town always seems so peaceful up here. It's what people driving through Conwell always said when they came into the store. They all wished they could move here. Harlan said he didn't understand why his father ever left Conwell to live in Florida. She told him she knew why. He fell in love. He wanted to make his wife happy by being closer to her family.

Edie's mind up was made up about what she would do today. She passed the town highway garage and seeing Jim Crocker's truck parked in the yard, she stopped. The highway crew didn't usually work Saturdays, but the front door was open, and she heard the sound of metal against metal. This would be easier than going to the man's house.

She went inside the garage.

Jim Crocker was hunched over a truck's engine. His head swung upward when he heard her call. He glared when he realized who she was.

"You got some nerve comin' here."

She stood on the other side of the truck, using it as a shield.

"I hate to say it, Jim, but your teenage boys keep picking on my little girl. They give her a hard time on the bus and make her cry. Amber's only seven, and your boys are teenagers."

She watched his fingers play on the grip of a wrench.

"What am I supposed to do about it?"

"You're the dad. You can tell 'em to leave Amber alone."

"You know, Edie, it'd be good for everyone if you and your girl just moved the hell outta town. Take your old man and that crazy aunt of yours with you while you're at it."

The toe of her right foot tapped the concrete floor.

"You all blame me for Walker's death. I own up to my part but not all of it." She raised her chin. "Just so you know, I'm not going anywhere. This is my home. The same goes for my family. You can forget about us leaving town." Her voice was louder than when she started. "What kind of a father are you anyway, thinking it's okay your boys do stuff like that?"

Jim Crocker puffed up his chest.

"A pretty damn good one. And I don't appreciate you threatening to call the state cops on my oldest."

"Jim, you and your family won't ever like me. I get it. But my little girl has nothin' to do with this." She read his face, trying to gauge whether her words made any change in the man. "I believe you have a daughter a year younger than Amber. Sandy. I've seen her. She's real cute. Amber likes her. They play together at recess." Her eyes locked on the man. "Tell me, Jim. How'd you like it if some teenage boys made her cry for something you did? I believe you'd be having this same conversation with their parents." She paused. "Your family's fight is with me and not my little girl."

Jim Crocker fingered the lid of his grease-stained cap as if he was going to tip it although she knew he wouldn't.

"I'll talk to my boys tonight. They'll leave her alone. You have my word." He worked his mouth. "You're right about one thing though. I'll never like you. None of us will."

"Fair enough, Jim."

Edie spun around and left the garage.

"Okay, Edie, that's one down," she told herself outside.

She drove straight to her in-laws'.

Marie was home, and so was Fred, Edie discovered, when he answered the door inside the screened-in breezeway that connected their house and garage. Fred blinked before speaking.

"Edie, is everything okay? Amber?"

"She's fine, Fred. Is Marie home? I have something for her."

Fred stared at the envelope in her hand.

"I'll get her."

Edie heard her in-laws talk in the kitchen. Marie asked what she wanted, and Fred told her to go see. When she finally appeared in the doorway, Marie squeezed herself tightly with her arms as if she were in danger of falling apart.

Her mother-in-law was thinner. She had let her hair go white, no longer a brassy yellow, and she wore it short and straight. Edie detected liquor on her mother-in-law's breath, something sweet, port or sherry, but the drink didn't soften Marie as she stood guard at the kitchen door.

Edie sighed. She spent countless times in their home, a grand Colonial filled with fine furniture and antiques passed down through their families. The house never went long without fresh paint. The lawn and gardens were always tended.

Marie stiffened.

"What do you want, Edie?"

"Here. This is for you from Amber."

Edie handed Marie the envelope.

"You didn't." Her voice collapsed as she lifted the flap and peeked inside. "She's growing so fast."

Edie stood straighter.

"Yes, she is. There's something else in there from her. A letter."

Marie made a nervous cough as she reached inside. Her head was up after she finished reading.

"Tell Amber thanks."

"No, Marie, you should do it yourself. She can't understand why you haven't seen her. Neither can I. You used to spend so much time with her." Edie wedged her hand against her hip. "The other day Amber asked me what would have happened to her if I had died with Walker. I told her you and Fred would have taken care of her, brought her up. You know what she said? 'Maybe they don't love me anymore.' It broke my heart listening to her."

Marie brought her fingers to her mouth.

"Oh, no."

"Amber's your granddaughter, for God's sake. She's Gil's daughter. Don't punish her for what Walker and me did."

"Walker. Please, don't."

Marie wiped at her eyes.

"I didn't come here, Marie, to upset you. I came here for Amber. She misses you so much."

Fred stood in the kitchen door. His hand clutched the jamb, but Marie didn't pay any attention.

"Tell me the truth, Edie. Did you love my son?" she asked.

"Gil? Of course, I did, with all my heart. You knew that."

"No, no. I meant Walker."

Edie let her lungs fill and empty slowly.

"I did. It just wasn't the same."

Marie nodded. Fred cleared his throat.

"My son was so unhappy. I see it now." Marie's voice drained to a whisper. "I'm afraid I didn't help at all. I didn't listen. Neither did Fred or her. At least you... I really wish you could've done something to stop him. But then there's that trouble with the man from the bar. My poor boy."

Edie struggled to stop her tears.

"Don't blame yourselves," she said. "Walker could be hard on the people who loved him."

Her mother-in-law pulled a handkerchief from the pocket of her skirt.

"How are you doing? Are you making out okay? Does Amber need anything? New clothes? Money?"

Edie shook her head.

"She doesn't need anything like that, but thanks for asking."

"I'm sorry. I can't have you working at the store." Marie touched her throat. "I just can't."

"It's all right. I've been filling in for Pop."

"The dump. I heard."

"I'm almost done. Pop will be back to work soon. I have a shot at another job. There's something else I gotta tell you." She paused because Marie appeared interested. "Before Dean went to Maine, he left an envelope filled with money. He sold a diamond ring Walker was going to give me. I didn't know about it until after." Her head dipped briefly. "It's a lot of money."

Marie glanced back at Fred. He nodded.

"Keep it, Edie." Her voice cracked. "I believe it's what my sons would want. You meant so much to the both of them."

Edie nodded.

"Thank you for saying that," she said. "Look. I gotta get home."

Edie took one step off the stoop. She stopped when Marie called. Fred moved beside her.

"Take care, Edie," Marie said. "Tell Amber we'll see her soon."

"That'd be good, really good, Marie."

She glanced back when she reached her car. Marie gave a wave before she went inside the house.

Edie smiled. Harlan, she knew, was waiting to hear how everything worked out. They talked it over last night. Today he and Amber were hanging a swing he made for the large maple in her front yard. Maybe they were already done. If so, Harlan would be sitting on the porch, watching Amber play. He'd ask Edie if she had a hard day, and she would tell him yes, but now everything was just fine.

The End